Praise for *Selecte*

"Brilliant, beautiful, and tender are the words that come to mind at the end of reading Michael Glenn's remarkable book, Selected Stories. The arc of the book spans 60 years of Glenn's writing beginning with a few startling avant-garde stories around mostly difficult and not necessarily likeable people and then blossoms into a wonder-full collection of stories about a wide variety of people all struggling to find some measure of love, peace, and safety within themselves and their relationships. He captures the poignancy and tensions of their journeys with deep insight and profound empathy. Nothing is a 'must read' these days, but Michael Glenn's treasure of a book is not to be missed."

— David Treadway, Ph.D
Nationally known therapist and author of *Dead Reckoning* and *Treating Couples Well: A Practical Guide to Collaborative Couple Therapy*

"With Michael Glenn's Selected Stories, we are in the hands of a master dedicated to wrapping us in stories that at first may seem distant to our lived experience, but are disturbingly intimate and familiar. To read him is to take the gloves off and be face to face with characters and story, as in a John Cassavetes' hand-held camera view of life. We are in the kitchen, the streets, the bedrooms and doctors' offices where words and gestures land or don't. It's a trip into a less-tech world where people actually talk to one another, or if not, to themselves as in 'The Room,' a hermetic tale of a writer encased in memory whose wistful prompts reveal a part-lived life. In 'Jackie,' a young doctor is gripped by the reality of his patient's condition. In the openness of 'The Seventies,' a couple inches toward the lip of a volcano of their own creation, as they confuse freedom to have sex with whoever they want with the freedom that comes from loving another.

Many of Glenn's characters are hobbled by class, habit, ignorance, prejudice, too little or too much education or vision. Nobody gets a free ride here. It's a place of few illusions—illusions are expensive and there's little to go around. And if one should rise out from one's past, as in 'A Meeting,' there's a former schoolteacher to remind you of where you've come from. To readers accustomed to minimalist prose, you will be rewarded by the opposite: a chance to luxuriate in descriptions lengthy and precise that will make you wonder how it was you left that rich palette for a slimmer one."

— Kendall Dudley
Writer, artist, teacher, career/retirement designer at kendalldudley.com

Praise for *Selected Stories* (cont'd)

"Beautifully crafted and consistently thought-provoking, these stories quickly draw us into urgent moments in ordinary—and some not so ordinary—people's lives. From a young doctor caring for a terminally ill child, to a grown man's surprising encounter with his second-grade teacher, to a daughter of immigrants faced with an impossible choice, this collection is always fascinating. Sometimes bleak, sometimes funny, Glenn writes with great insight into the hidden workings of the human mind."

— Elizabeth Ammons Ph.D
Harriet H. Fay Professor of Literature Emerita, Tufts University

"In these astute short stories, Michael Glenn combines his medical background with a love of the written word to cleverly delve into the mystery and puzzle of human motive, human emotion. He's a talented writer. This is very good material that reminds me of Beckett and Carver, with the same taste for minimalism and the idea that when nothing happens, everything happens. Which is absolutely true, of course. He does that style well, not forgetting tension and puzzlement. There are style reminders also at times of Orwell and Winston Smith. A sort of Ministry of Fear tone, emotionally flat and ominous at the same time."

— John J. Ronan
Poet, playwright, movie producer, and journalist, NEA Fellow, former Poet Laureate of Gloucester, Professor Emeritus at North Shore Community College, Danvers, MA, author of *Marrowbone Lane* and *Taking the Train of Singularity South from Midtown*

"An extraordinary collection of sharply observed tales—sometimes frightening, often deeply moving, and always with an unsparing eye for hard truths. These stories will burrow under your skin and resonate in your heart, long after you've turned the final page."

— Diane (Didi) Stewart
Associate Professor (Voice Department), Berklee College of Music, composer, writer, performer, two-time winner of the Boston Music Award for best female vocalist, known for her bands, Didi Stewart and the Amplifiers and Girls' Night Out

"Michael Glenn's Selected Stories shines in transparent style and solid images, and his themes uncoil from speakers whose lives center, precariously, on fixations remembered. Unlike the opacities of, say, John Updike, Glenn's lucid style reveals uninterpretable Dinge an sich to one's senses. Here, liminal speakers unfold themselves as they reveal the persistence of earlier memories, often centered on an idealized figure as in the closing stories 'Davidoff,' 'Piano Lesson,' and 'Bree.' Well before this final move to closure, the stories have widened to imagistic collegiate sketches ('The Visitor'), time-capsules of threatened and edgy idealism ('The Seventies'), and eidetic memories ('Flamingoes,' 'Making Friends,' 'Donna and the Doctor').

In Selected Stories, life shambles out. It's a burgeoning sculpture of transience. Still, its armature—what centers life itself—holds firm. Here, as in medieval times, love moves the sun and all the other stars."

— A. McA. (Mac) Miller, Ph.D
Emeritus Professor of Literature at New College, Florida, longtime editor of *New CollAge* magazine and author of *Overdrive: Selected Poems*, LTC USAR AA RET

"I first met Michael Glenn sixty years ago as a fellow recipient of a stipend from the International Fellows program at Columbia University. Before long, he showed me some fiction he had written at the time, including a long story that I recommended he offer to The Hudson Review, which published it in 1965–66 and I reprinted it in The Young American Writers (1967). As I became a fulltime artist/writer, Michael became a physician fulfilling his military obligation in North Dakota. While there he founded and edited The Radical Therapist (1970–72), by far the most radical psychiatric magazine of its time (and perhaps ever). When we reconnected, alive in our 80s, I was glad to see that he had continued writing fiction and collecting them here in a book with work spanning six decades. The classic for me is 'The Room,' which seems to me more deeply felt and stylistically distinctive. Others might differ."

— Richard Kostelanetz
Independent artist and writer, author of *The End of Intelligent Writing: Literary Politics in America*

SELECTED
STORIES

—

MICHAEL
GLENN

GRAY DOVE PRESS

Books by Michael L. Glenn

FICTION

Trouble on the Hill and Other Stories

NON-FICTION

Repression or Revolution? Therapy in the United States Today
(with Richard Kunnes)

Voices from the Asylum (editor)

The Radical Therapist
(with Jerome Agel and The Radical Therapist Collective)

Rough Times (with Jerome Agel and The Rough Times Staff)

On Diagnosis: A Systemic Approach

Collaborative Health Care: A Family-Oriented Model

Couples: Exploring and Understanding the Cycles of Intimate Relationships
(with Barry Dym)

TRANSLATION

Renovation of the Moon (*Renovación de la Luna,* by Emma Romeu)

Now That Life's Given Me a Minute
(*Ahora Que Me Deja un Minuto la Vida,* by Emma Romeu)

"Rondacq" was originally published in the *Nassau Literary Magazine,* Vol. CXVII, No. 2, (Ides Issue, 1959).
"The Room" is reprinted by permission from *The Hudson Review,* Vol XVIII, No. 4 (Winter 1965-66). Copyright © 1965 by The Hudson Review, Inc.
"The Schedule" was originally published in *The Antioch Review,* Vol. XXVI, No. 4 (Winter 1966-67)
"Making Friends" was originally published as "Moving" in *Trouble on the Hill and Other Stories,* by Michael Glenn (Chicago: Liberator Press, 1979).

ISBN: 978-1-953253-02-6

 GRAY DOVE PRESS
www.graydovepress.com
Editor: Patricia Crotty
Cover Design: Dylan Jhirad

To my family

Contents

Introduction 1

Rondacq *(1958)* 7

The Visitor *(1959)* 11

Jackie *(1988)* 23

The Room *(1964)* 41

Dimes *(1963)* 61

Flamingoes *(1968)* 79

On Being On *(1968)* 95

The Schedule *(1966)* 103

The Seventies *(1986)* 113

Making Friends *(1979)* 131

Selfish? I Don't Think So *(1979)* 151

A Meeting *(1986)* 157

Donna and the Doctor *(1988)* 169

Rooms *(1988)* 185

Early Autumn *(1989)* 191

Davidoff *(1989)* 207

The Oldest in the Family *(1990)* 225

Piano Lesson *(2012)* 233

Bree *(2012)* 243

Introduction

Writing was my earliest ambition, and it has always been close to my core. As a third grader, I composed stories about "Little Tree" and his friends in the forest. When my teacher, Miss Lake, invited me to share them with the class, I did ... and was delighted when my classmates loved them! Such was my first experience with the joys of writing and the pleasure of being read. From then on, writing remained a constant interest, a leitmotif that impelled me to produce a variety of stories, plays, poems, novels, and non-fiction over the years.

Except for a short time during my college and post-graduate years, though, writing was virtually never my main focus. There was always some other, more important, duty to pursue. Whether it was medical school, psychiatric training, the Air Force, family life, political organizing, or my medical practice ... there was always "something else" to put first. And yet, I continued to write.

This collection includes stories I've written over more than sixty years, and in different styles. When I told my old friend, author and critic Richard Kostelanetz[1], that I was putting this book together, he suggested I offer the reader a "frame" to contextualize the work. I hope this Introduction will do that.

The first two stories in this collection date back to my last year at Princeton in 1958-59. Four of the following six stories

1 In 1962, I was in medical school, and Kostelanetz and I were both part of Columbia University's International Fellows Program. We became friends. He read my work and encouraged me to submit part of my novel *The Room* to *The Hudson Review*. The excerpt was accepted and would appear as "The Room" in the Winter of 1965-66 issue. Kostelanetz later republished it in his anthology, *The Young American Writers* (Funk & Wagnalls, NY, 1967). It appears here as "The Room."

display a rather bleak, internal, obsessional tone and often focus on the world of objects. I know this style echoes Samuel Beckett, whose novels were filled with internal monologues. Beckett had a big impact on me, and I discussed his work, among others, in my senior thesis "On the Fictional Confession."

I was also influenced by the French writers Michel Butor and Alain Robbe-Grillet, whose work I encountered during my Junior Year in France (1957-58). Butor, with whom I had a brief correspondence, was a leading exponent of what French critics called the *nouveau roman*. His novels didn't follow the traditional approach to chronology or plot, and the narrator was often suspect. Robbe-Grillet's style has been called "a theory of pure surface [in which] methodical, geometric, and often repetitive descriptions of objects replace (though often reveal) the psychology and interiority of the character."[2] This orientation influenced me deeply during those early years, especially in my novel-length manuscripts *The Room* and *The Square of Little Joseph*.

At the same time, I also explored less-experimental fiction. For example, the first novel I attempted, *Precious the Time* (loosely inspired by my experiences in France), took a more conventional form. Later, during psychiatry residency, I wrote another less "objectivist" manuscript about a young man's infatuation with a woman, called *The Journals of Leo Ish*.

Two critical decisions about writing shaped my life. The first came in 1960, while I was in graduate school in Comparative Literature. I didn't fancy the prospect of being an academic and imagined writing full-time instead. But I wasn't sure I was "good enough." A director in Atlanta, Frank Wittow, whom I'd worked with in summer stock after graduating high school—and who'd put on one of my one-act plays while I was in college—invited me to Atlanta to be playwright-in-residence at his Academy Theater. He said I needed to work with an actual troupe to develop as a playwright. But I didn't want to be back in Atlanta and turned him down.

---

2 Referenced in Wikipedia as being from Rachel Donadio's February 24, 2008 piece in the New York Times, "He Was Nouveau When It Was New."

Not understanding that most writers need an apprenticeship, and unsure of my talent, I decided to go to medical school. That choice promised greater security and had the added advantage of fulfilling my dad's unmet ambition of being a doctor. I took a year of pre-med classes, married my first wife, Sara (Snow)—she left Bennington to join me—and we left Boston for New York in 1961.

The second decision came as I was finishing medical school. When *The Hudson Review* accepted *The Room*, I felt validated as a writer, but again wondered whether to continue my career—this time, becoming a psychiatrist—or abandon it to write full-time. Uncertain, I continued with my training, but resolved to write in whatever time I could find.

When my story came out, Julie Fallowfield, from the literary agency Otis and McIntosh, contacted me and offered to be my agent. She served as such for several years, diligently trying to market what I wrote, but I didn't help her: I wrote irregularly, avoided feedback, and was loathe to rewrite. In retrospect, I was suffering from the Romantic "genius theory," that works of art simply "appear" from the pen of the gifted few.

Psychiatry residency segued into two years in the Air Force, and I moved in other directions: anti-war activism and political organizing. Plus, I now had a family. During my Air Force years, friends from the USAF base at Minot and I founded a journal called "The Radical Therapist." This was a time when similar radical publications were appearing in many major professions. The journal found an audience. When I left the service, Sara and I moved to Somerville with our two children, Jason and Ezra, and we brought "The RT" with us. My life then changed quickly: I met Susan (Jhirad). Sara and I separated. I left the collective that was putting out the journal.[3] And I moved into Susan's commune in Cambridge. Together, she and I then got involved in radical

3 The new Somerville collective had become dominated by people who were critical of all professionals and "elites" (like therapists). They changed the name of the journal to "Rough Times" and focused it around political issues and concerns of groups like the Mental Patients Liberation Front. All the therapists left, myself included.

politics and workplace organizing.

A few years later, we married and had a daughter, Catherine. With Susan's son Raj, we now had a "blended family" with four children. During all this time, I had been writing very little. From then on, my life could be divided into decades: a decade of political organizing, another as a family physician in Everett, and a decade and a half as a psychiatrist and therapist in Cambridge.

My experience as a factory worker and organizer (1972-1980) inspired me to compose stories about working-class life, some of which appeared in *Trouble on the Hill*, published by Paul Elitzik (Liberator Press, 1979). I wrote these stories in a simple narrative style.

While I was working as a family doctor in Everett (1980-1989), both Susan and I took classes with the Cambridge writing teacher Mameve Medwed. Susan was writing screenplays as well as stories and a novel, and I had begun writing stories about the conflicts inherent in relationships, especially the medical encounter. Several of the stories in this book originated in Mameve's classes, both at the Cambridge Center for Adult Education and at her house. Eventually, my experiences in Everett generated a lengthy manuscript called *Confessions of a Family Doctor.*

In all of this, I still felt the influence of the "objectivist" perspective, looking in from the outside unless I was writing in the first person; and I described hospital and family practice themes in a fairly flat way. The doctors in these stories were rarely heroes. I also remember reading a lot of Raymond Carver in those days and admiring the pithiness of his minimalist approach.

By 1990, working as a therapist again, I was still writing—non-fiction, an autobiography, stories, and several screenplays. After I retired in 2003, I had spells of intense, revived interest in short fiction, this time from the viewpoint of "looking back." This is evident in the last five stories in this collection, though I'm sure you can still hear my old preoccupations in them.

I hope this collection brings the reader an appreciation of the different themes I've pursued, as well as the perspectives I've taken to explore them. I'm honored to share these stories with you now.

Rondacq

Why anyone should dislike me, I cannot imagine, and yet I am sure that Rondacq does. Again today, as I accidentally met him on my way to my rooms, he behaved in that certain manner which could only be a sign of distaste, or—what is worse—contempt. It was really quite simple. I saw him coming in advance and prepared to smile, while he, whether he saw me or not, steadfastly looked at the ground before him. When we were about ten feet apart I called out "Rondacq! Hello!" and he muttered the same back at me, still staring at the ground. Not to be thwarted I asked cheerfully, "How are you?" To this he worked his lips rapidly into a grimace, paused for a split second, and then squeezed out between his tightened lips, "Not bad," and we passed each other.

Of course I may be reprimanded for not having stopped him nor engaged him in conversation; but, in all seriousness, what were we to discuss? Besides these infrequent meetings in the street, I almost never see him anymore, and have no idea of his problems or activities, except insofar as everyone knows about them. Once, a few months ago, it is true, he and I had lunch together; and once again we even sat down to sup together on salad, oysters, and spaghetti; but he seems to have forgotten these times.

This really should not bother me at all, I know, no one has to tell me. It just may be that I cannot understand his persistent coldness. Rondacq is a great man, and great men should be allowed their whims. Nevertheless, we should at least be civil to each other, and if we are not, then he is to blame, and not I. If I am not a great man, at least I pride myself on being civil. This is why Rondacq's behavior irritates me. In a sense he is upsetting my entire mode of life.

About two years ago this man and I were in fact friendly. We used to read poetry aloud to each other and revel in the fact that each of us shared the other's tastes, a curious fact for revel, but everybody seems to rejoice in finding those who share their tastes, and we were no exception.

Rondacq would flash his tiny eyes at me in ecstasy over certain passages of Lautréamont, and we would take turns reading speeches from the works of Wilde, Huysmans, or Hesse. He would entertain me at his rooms frequently, where, amidst strange bits of art collected from his many travels, we would sit, music playing softly in the background like the hypnotic melodies of the Pan-god, and sip fine red claret as we discussed some aesthetic or literary point of interest to us both. The aversion we both shared to the professional *littérateurs*, to the facile critics, and to the stereotypical masses, spoon-fed by the same few magazines, would crackle as we tore into the current successes and amused ourselves with the exercise of wit, aptly applied to the unimpeachable gods of the day.

Why it was that Rondacq, who even at this time was admired by almost all those people he scorned, had chosen me for a friend, me whom he had met while walking by the river, was incomprehensible then, and still is now. I can only suppose that he recognized in me many of the features which he himself possessed when he had been my age. At first I was suspicious of him, but at the end of a few weeks I knew that these fears were groundless. And thus had we spent much time together over a period of about three months until I had to go abroad for a year. Rondacq, who was planning to go himself a few months later, urged me to write him, and I could hardly have wished to refuse. His friends abroad and the doors they could open to me were countless.

Yet, when I found myself abroad, I did not write immediately. In my search for an identity I was determined to create my life, rather than be shaped by it myself. I refused to visit the friends of friends, thinking that I would make my own acquaintances, or none at all. Thus I neglected the opportunities that I had, and spent the greater part of the year chasing vague forms across the magic continent, and grasping none of these ideals within my hands.

My year was lost in wine and reverie, and my elaborate plans were paralyzed from too much self-awareness. By the time I finally realized my position, and struggled to rise above it, it was too late. When I tried to write Rondacq I could not, being unable to explain my long silence. And so Rondacq came to Paris and to Rome, and I did not see him. I saw his name registered in Vienna ten days before my arrival, but our paths never crossed; and I was much too prideful to reach out to him. Looking back on the experience, it is perhaps true that I was wiser after all in relying upon myself. Still, I shall never cease to wonder if this process of self-development might not have been accelerated by my having been with those I eventually met from the start, and by moving about in those enviable circles into which Rondacq's name would have been my letter of introduction.

Upon my return to the States, I plunged into my work, oblivious of anything else about me. Only after my manuscript was finished, and redone with the adornments of my small bug-like pencil marks, had I time to emerge once more onto the American scene. My book caught on sufficiently for people to remember my name, and I was able to breathe more easily for a while. Yet through all this Rondacq never once called, nor sent a note.

It must have been two months ago that I ran into him at a small café where we used to lunch together. I asked him if he would join me, and he very courteously accepted. There seemed to be no trace of spitefulness in him. I apologized profusely for not having written him, but he laughed my apologies away. For the rest of the meal we tried to talk about old times and about our trips abroad, but there was no life in what we said. We parted agreeing to call each other in the future.

Except for a dinner party at which we met again, one of

those bizarre *artiste* parties that the American elite attempt to make conform with their notions of "life over there," I saw Rondacq only as I did today, for brief moments. The same short conversation has always been repeated, as has his aloof attitude. It bothers me that two people once so close can find nothing to say to one another. It is almost a sad situation, for Rondacq was, in effect, the one responsible for my wishing to go abroad and the one who had encouraged me to pursue my plans for a book. Yet, without a doubt, he dislikes me now.

Perhaps he is envious of my success, although I doubt it. Perhaps he was only meditating on some profound matter when I passed and did not realize that it was I who said hello, but I doubt that too. The only explanation must be that he despises me, scorns me now for my past negligence. And yet if I could I would go to him and apologize: if it only did not involve humiliation.

No. Clearly it is better that he does dislike me; for then I can cease to worry about him and his friendship. After all, I have my own friends now, and my own future. What does it matter that some old friend has chosen to let our acquaintance fall, when the hopes I entertain today are so promising?

Yet still, I cannot help being disturbed at the careless way he addressed me, as if I were a rodent beneath his feet. What did he mean by his compressed mouth, or by his eyes rooted to the ground? And why was there an element of pity in his voice?

The Visitor

Barrett walked like a mechanical toy: his arms flailing in a rotary motion, forearms parallel to the ground; his legs churning as if connected to the mainspring of a clock; and his head bobbing up and down, looking alternately down at the ground and straight ahead. Frequently, still moving, he snapped his head up, as if gasping for breath, and stared intently all around before lowering it again. Everyone on campus knew him by this walk, and anyone who had seen him once could spot him again.

One cool March night, Barrett was churning towards his friend Vane's room. It had been a warmish day, as if spring were finally at hand; and some students had even placed wooden sun chairs on the lawn, where they still rested like gaunt night creatures. But the air had turned chilly again. Winter had not left.

The campus was quiet except for some occasional shouts. Dorm windows glowed yellow with the light of study. The trees were scrawny, their outlines stark against the sky. Barrett was smoking fitfully, jamming the cigarette to his mouth when his right arm flailed to the proper position, taking a drag, then exhaling in a thick cloud.

He was walking alone. Most other students couldn't keep up with him, and those that could usually found themselves forced off the walkway, because Barrett relentlessly veered towards any companion. Whenever he walked with someone, his feet moved to the side: there was nothing he could do about it.

But Barrett was not walking alone tonight because of this. Truth was, he'd been studying late in his room, and he was angry.

He'd heard that Vane had hosted a small party that afternoon and hadn't invited him. All of Vane's arty friends had gotten together to hang out, drink some beers, and enjoy the changing weather ... all without him. The party had to be over now, and Barrett knew that Vane would be in his room, trying to salvage a couple of hours' study.

He could see Vane's window on the second floor on the corner of the dorm ahead. Its light was on. Barrett moved faster, climbing over a green chain to his left, the grass spongy beneath his feet, and then reaching another walkway that led to the dorm. Lowering his head, he moved to the door, took another drag of his cigarette, then opened it. There was a short hallway, then a flight of steps. When he reached the landing, he opened the door with his shoulder and strode down the hall. He stopped and knocked at the last door.

"Yeah?"

"It's Barrett."

"Come on in."

Vane was at his desk, at his typewriter, a book to his side, its place held open by an ashtray. He was a slim, sandy-haired youth with glasses. He looked up. "Hi, Barrett."

Barrett moved quickly into the room and walked over to Vane's bookcase. He ran his thumb over the spines of the books.

"Looking for something?" Vane said. "Maybe I can help." He closed his book, inserting a pencil as a marker and swiveled to face Barrett. "What are you looking for?"

Barrett turned. "That Dostoevsky we read last month." His hand darted towards the shelf like a snake's tongue, then came back with a book. "This one. Mind if I look through it?"

"Go ahead." Vane yawned. "I'm almost ready for bed. It's been a long day. But if you want to hang out a few minutes that's fine."

"I want to look up a passage."

"You want a drink? There's beer in the frig."

Barrett grinned. "Sure." He took out a beer, then sat on the sofa.

Vane pulled his window shade down. He turned his thermostat up. "Too cold to sleep without heat tonight," he said. While Barrett was leafing through the book, Vane took his toothbrush and soap out of a drawer, plucked his towel off the sofa, and walked to the door with the towel over his shoulder like a prizefighter.

"I'll be right back," he said. "Just want to wash up."

"Take your time," Barrett said. He waited until Vane had left, then stood up and walked around the room, peering at Vane's desk, ruffling through the papers. He put his cigarette out in Vane's ashtray. Then he sat down again and opened the book he'd taken from the shelf. A smile spread over his sallow features. The ceiling light overhead highlighted his high cheekbones and made his eyes shine like tiny olives.

Vane's room was not like his own. There wasn't any rug, and Vane didn't have much furniture. Vane's sofa was old and ratty, its red cover torn, and some of the stuffing was coming out. But, by contrast, Vane's bookcase was huge. Books of different sizes and colors were crammed into its shelves and on top of one another, and there were heaps of white and yellow papers on the lower shelf, some clipped together, some in manila folders or torn boxes.

In the corner, a guitar leaned against a charcoal nude portrait. Other charcoal portraits were taped to the walls and over the mantelpiece: amateurish and distorted. Vane had been taking a class in sketching.

Vane came back, threw his towel on the sofa and returned his toothbrush and soap to the drawer. Barrett stared at him. "Was that the book you wanted?" Vane said.

"Yes." Barrett put the book face-down on the sofa and leaned forward, his hands on his knees. "You know, Vane," he said. "Your room's a mess. But then I guess all artists live like that."

Vane shrugged and smiled, his face like a dried fig.

Barrett slapped his knees. He got up and stood awkwardly in the center of the room, looking around, with his hands on his hips. A large gawky cardboard skeleton dangled from the top of the doorway separating Vane's living room from his sleeping cubby and cast a shadow there. Barrett studied it, then waved his hand at the drawings. "I guess you're learning," he said.

"Just starting," Vane said. "You should try it."

"Not me," Barrett said. "I don't have the talent. But you do. I think you do." He paused. "But what's with the artsy candles?"

There was a black candle on either side of the drawing over the mantelpiece. "Nothing," Vane said. "I just like the look. If you think it's phony, go think it. I don't care."

"Did D.H. Lawrence say something about candles? Or Rilke? Who have you been reading now? Christ, Vane! Candles!" Barrett laughed harshly, his scrawny neck thrust back.

"Sorry you don't like the drawings," Vane said churlishly.

"Oh, I like the drawings," Barrett said. "I just want to know why you artists have to dress everything up …"

"I don't think you'd understand," Vane said.

"I like the drawing. I just don't understand …"

Vane looked at him wearily. "It's late, Barrett," he said. "What do you want?"

"I've read Freud, too," Barrett said. He walked about the room, staring intently at each of the sketches in turn, then sat down on the sofa again. He picked up the Dostoevsky book and looked at Vane.

"What?" Van said. "I've got to get to bed."

Barrett leaned back, the sofa sinking under his weight. His lips twitched, and he lit a cigarette. Vane went to his desk, rearranged his papers, and turned off his desk lamp. He looked at Barrett again. "Time to hit the sack."

Blowing smoke, Barrett walked to the bookcase and put the book back. He stood in the center of the room, the bare yellow light shining directly over his head. "Where'd you get the models for those sketches?"

"The art class, of course."

Barrett laughed in a mocking voice. "Oh, I thought maybe

you got a girlfriend hidden somewhere."

Vane shook his head. "You think if I had a girlfriend I'd have her pictures all over my room for you to gawk at?"

"The face reminded me of Ellie somehow. You know? The eyes?"

"Everything seems to remind you of Ellie, if I remember," Vane said.

"I got a note from her."

"Ellie?"

"Yep. I'd completely confused her by sending her roses after telling her to go to hell." He guffawed. "She didn't know what to think."

"I thought she was a nice girl," Vane said. "Why'd you tell her to go to hell?"

"I don't know. She got on my nerves, I guess. Another one who likes to pretend she's an artist."

"I liked her."

"Still. Ellie. I think I've got her wondering. What should I do next?"

"Do what you want, Barrett. It's late."

"I'd ask her out again, except for one thing." Vane was silent. Barrett guffawed again. "Tell you the truth, I don't think she likes me." He took a drag of his cigarette and exhaled. "And I thought I was in love ..."

"Well," Vane said, yawning. "I'm sure you'll figure it out. Look, Barrett, I hate to run you out, but I've got to hit the sack." He took a step towards the door. "Thanks for stopping by."

Barrett followed him. When they got to the door, he paused an instant, looking like he'd just remembered something.

"Good night," Vane sighed. "See you in the morning."

"Wait a minute," Barrett said. "Can I have another beer?"

"What the hell? Take one for the road, but I'm going to sleep."

Barrett took another beer from the frig and opened it. Then

he sat on the sofa again and stretched his legs out so that one foot brushed against a pile of books on the floor.

"Hey. Careful," Vane said.

Barrett drew on his cigarette again. Smoke curled around the ceiling light. He smiled, then took a long swig from his beer and belched.

"So you can take the rest home," Vane said, taking a step towards his cubby. "Good night, Barrett. I'm going to bed."

Barrett kept smiling, but he didn't move. He held his cigarette delicately between two fingers. Vane went into his bedroom cubby. He slipped off his shoes, then removed his socks. Then he pulled his shirt over his head, leaving his T-shirt on, and took off his pants.

"Okay, Barrett," he said. "Evening's over. See you in the morning." He gestured towards the door.

Barrett did not move.

"Come on, Barrett," Vane said. "Stop playing games. I'm tired, and I've got an early class tomorrow."

"So go to sleep. I won't hurt you."

"I want you to go. Please."

"I'm not ready to go yet."

"Barrett. Come on. Get out of here."

Barrett sucked on his cigarette and blew out a flume of smoke. "Why don't you throw me out," he said.

"Because you're bigger and stronger than I am," Vane said. "Now come on and stop the comedy."

"I'm not ready to go," Barrett said. "It's a long walk back."

Vane took a deep breath. He looked at Barrett, then at the door, then at Barrett again. "I want you to leave," he said. "I'm going to bed."

Barrett cocked his head. He began humming. Then he stood up and walked to the window. He put his cigarette out in the ashtray and quickly lit another one, tossing the match on the floor.

"You're staying?" Vane said.

Barrett didn't respond. He flicked a cigarette ash on the floor. Vane stepped forward and kicked it. "Going to bed?" Barrett said.

"I want you to leave," Vane said. "Why are you acting this way?"

Barrett moved over to the bookcase and started thumbing through the books again, his cigarette jammed in his mouth.

"Barrett. What's going on?"

"Nothing."

"Dammit, Barrett!" Vane shouted. "Go home!"

"Make me," Barrett said.

"What?"

"Make me. Throw me out," Barrett said, grinning.

"Civilized people don't do that ..."

"Oh, no?" Vane didn't answer. "If you want me to go you'll have to throw me out." Barrett sat down on the sofa, his arms crossed.

"What are you trying to do?" Vane said.

"I thought you had it figured out," Barrett said. "You're the smart one, aren't you. The so-cool guy." He was grinning broadly, his close-cropped hair tight against his skull. He dropped his cigarette on the floor and ground it out with his heel.

Vane paused. "I don't know what you're trying to do, but if I've got to throw you out, then I will." He moved over to the sofa and grabbed Barrett's arm. Barrett didn't budge. Vane grunted and pulled but could not move him. He braced his feet, put both arms on Barrett's arm and yanked with all his strength.

"Can't do it, can you?"

"Shut up, damn it. Shut up!" Vane said, stamping on the floor. He was breathing heavily now. "Normal people *leave* when you ask them to go," he said. "What do you want me to do? Attack you with a knife?"

"Go ahead," Barrett said. "Try."

Vane pulled again. This time, Barrett's shirt tore. "Now look what you've done," Barrett said. "That was one of my favorites."

"Too bad." Vane said. He let go of Barrett's shirt but kicked at his shin. Barrett slid away. Vane followed him, raising his fists as if to punch him. Barrett, laughing, grabbed Vane's hands and twisted his wrists against each other.

"Ow!" Vane cried. "Ow!"

"Mister Tough Guy."

"Dammit, Barrett. Let go."

Barrett released Vane's wrists and strode around the room in a circle.

"Get the fuck out of here!" Vane yelled.

"Sorry, but no."

"I'll call the campus cops."

"Be my guest."

"Barrett," Vane said. "Why are you acting like this?"

"You know," Barrett said.

Vane stood still for a minute, still breathing hard. Then he turned towards his bedroom. "All right," he said, his voice trembling. "All right, Barrett. If you want to play stupid little games, okay. Go ahead. Stay here. I don't care. I'm going to sleep." He turned off the overhead light and lay down in bed. Barrett lit another cigarette and sat on the sofa, the cigarette tip glowing brightly, casting an orange glimmer on his face. Tobacco smoke drifted into the bedroom. Vane was lying in his bed. A small table stood beside the bed, with a candle and book of paper matches, and a pencil and pad of paper.

"Do you often have nightmares?" Barrett said from the other room in an eerie low voice.

"Shut up," said Vane, turning his face to the wall. "Good night, Barrett."

Barrett was still for a moment. Then he got up from the sofa and sat in the desk chair. He spun it around a few times, then leaned back. The chair creaked. Then Barrett dropped his cigarette on the floor and ground it out. "You're guilty, Vane," he said, in his eerie voice.

"Barrett."

"Guilty, Vane. Guilty."

Vane leaped off his bed, ran into the living room, and turned on the light. "Barrett," he shouted. "Goddamn it, Barrett, don't play psychological games with me. I don't have the time. I don't have the patience. I have a goddamn class tomorrow, so can you just shut up."

"Guilty," Barrett said.

"Damn it, Barrett. Get out."

"Make me," Barrett said.

Vane grabbed his pants from the bedroom floor and put them on. He moved quickly to the front door, opened it and ran down the hall. Then he went down the stairway and into the first-floor hallway. He knocked on the second door.

"What?"

"It's Vane, Marc. Let me in."

A tousle-haired young man opened the door. "I'm half asleep. What is it?"

"Barrett's in my room and he won't leave."

"What do you want me to do?"

"Help me get him out?"

Marc paused. "I don't know. Why won't he leave?"

"He just won't."

Marc demurred. "I don't know. I'm not really up for that."

Vane stood still for a moment, breathing heavily. "Fine," he said. "Forget it." He stepped back.

"Sorry," Marc said. "Really sorry …" He closed the door.

Vane sighed. He took a step towards the stairs, then hesitated. He turned and, stretching both arms out against the wall, leaned against it with all his strength. He held the position for several minutes. Gradually his breathing slowed down.

Finally, he straightened up, turned, and went back up the stairs, then down the hall to his room. "Barrett," he called. "I'm coming in." There was no answer. "Barrett?" Still no response.

Vane opened the door. The room was empty. "Barrett?" he called again.

He walked slowly into his room and looked around. Barrett was gone. He went into his cubby and undressed again. Then he lay down.

It was impossible to sleep. His heart was still beating quickly, and his mind was racing. He reached out for the book of matches and lit his candle. Its flame cast flickering shadows over the rooms. The cardboard skeleton hanging between the rooms seemed to dance. The portraits seemed alive.

Vane stared at the candle. Its flame was ocher at the top, blue at the bottom. It flickered upwards like a searching finger, bending right, then left, lurching, then falling, as if it had a mind of its own. Vane looked at it for a long time. Then, with a sudden breath, he blew it out. In the last glimmer of light, he caught a glimpse of one of his portraits in the other room. Its expression seemed mocking. Then he closed his eyes and fell asleep....

He awoke suddenly, with a jerky movement. His watch said he'd only been asleep for ten minutes. He could still smell the candle's odor. It was very still.

"Barrett," he called softly. "Barrett?" There was no answer.

Vane tossed onto his other side, facing the wall, away from the living room. He tried to focus on things which usually calmed him: the ocean, animals, clouds, his sketches, but none of these worked. Slowly, he drifted in and out of sleep, sleeping, then waking after a few minutes, the word "guilty" still resounding in his head.

It was as if Barrett were still there, invisible, with his cigarette.

At about four in the morning, Vane called out several times, but there was no answer. Sleeping, he had frightening visions: evil creatures marching in a phalanx, knives cutting flesh, a sense of his face dissolving. And then, finally, he slept deeply.

It grew light around six. Vane woke and turned to face the other room. He wasn't sure how long he'd been asleep. His eyes were puffy, his face pale. He felt drained.

Barrett was gone. No one was on the sofa. The books that had been in stacks were scattered on the floor. Several cigarette butts lay stamped out on the rug. The window was halfway open.

Vane crawled out of bed. The dawn's first rays reached the windowpane and shades, seeping into the room and suffusing it in a faint red glow. For a while Vane sat on his sofa, staring dully at the ceiling. Then he got his soap, his towel, and his toothbrush and went to the bathroom to take a shower. The day had begun.

Jackie

1.

September. Luke Shands, a third-year medical student, stands in the Nine-East nurses' station, looking out. The ward has sixteen beds, eight on either side of a broad corridor, and his new patient Jackie Serrano is at the far end, asleep, an oxygen mask over her face, intravenous fluids running into each arm. She's come in the previous night, coughing and severely short of breath.

Her chart says she's seventeen, but she's already been hospitalized many times over the past several years. Her pediatrician diagnosed cystic fibrosis when she was five. The disease didn't affect her badly until she was thirteen, but over the past four years her condition has worsened.

Luke walks to her bed. She's lying still, breathing deeply: a frail, gaunt girl with long brown hair and hollow cheeks. The chart says she weighs ninety-one pounds. He touches her shoulder. "Miss Serrano? Jackie?" She stirs, wakes up, coughs. "What? What do you want?" Her voice is weak, husky.

"I'm Luke Shands. A medical student. I'm supposed to examine you?" He says it like a question.

"Could you come back later? I'm real tired now." She coughs again.

He stands beside her, hearing the rattle of her breathing. "Sure. I'll come back later."

Later that morning, the patient next to Jackie begins to moan. The nurse calls Luke and the intern. When Luke arrives,

23

the woman's face is purple, and she's struggling to breathe. While Luke and the intern are examining her, Jackie starts crying. Luke goes over to calm her down, but she is shaking all over. The intern pulls the curtain between the two beds shut and tells Luke to stay with the girl. In the meantime, the nurse has called a code. It's clear to Luke that the woman in the next bed is fighting for her life. He sits with Jackie, talking to her quietly, but she remains distraught. He strokes her hand and tells her to breathe slowly. There's a lot of activity behind the curtain—urgent, agitated voices; carts rolling back and forth; people running in and out; the "thwack" of a defibrillator. Sitting up, Jackie presses her thin arms against her chest and rocks back and forth, panic on her face.

Thirty minutes go by. The noises stop. The carts rattle away. The staff leaves. The patient has died. The intern pulls the curtains open again. The area is clear, the bed empty, the body gone.

Jackie is still trembling. She pulls her blankets over her head and moans. "No more. No more."

"What is it?" Luke says. "Are you afraid?"

"No more, no more." She won't say anything else.

After another half hour, Jackie finally calms down. She falls asleep with an odd smile on her face. Luke, feeling worn out, can leave.

When he returns the following morning, Jackie seems strangely calm, but she refuses to talk about what happened. Even so, Luke feels they've been through an important experience together.

Over the next few days, he spends more time with Jackie, talking with her about her family, her sickness, her other doctors. She grows stronger; her infection improves. He meets her family and learns that she lives in the Bronx with her parents, an eleven-year-old sister, Bianca, and an older brother. Her father is Italian by birth and works as a pressman in a rubber factory. Her mother is from Belgium and works part-time in a bakery. An older sister has already died of cystic fibrosis, and Bianca has the disease, too.

Luke asks the attending physician if he could continue seeing Jackie after she goes home. He says he's gotten to know her and wants to follow her course. The attending says no: it would be too depressing, and Luke probably won't have time to keep it up. But Luke argues. He says it would be good for Jackie to have some continuity of care, and he feels they've formed a relationship. This last point makes the attending relent, and he says that Luke can schedule out-patient visits with Jackie every two weeks. He'll find him an office and arrange for Jackie to have travel vouchers so she can travel back and forth by cab.

2.

Late October. The office is a small cubicle on the fourth floor of the hospital, usually used for psychiatric patients. It's painted robin's egg blue and contains a desk, three plastic chairs, and a small bookcase. A window at one end overlooks the river.

Luke leans forward. Jackie is sitting catty-corner from him in a yellow blouse and a dark blue skirt, her ankles tucked primly beneath her. "So, how's school going for you?"

"Not so good."

"Are you missing many classes?"

"I missed a few days. But mostly, I'm going."

"How do the other kids treat you? Do you have any friends?"

"Friends? Not really." She shakes her head. "I used to know some of the girls pretty well, but they mostly stay away now. They feel sorry for me, I think, and they try to be nice. But when I start coughing they get disgusted and act like they want to be somewhere else."

"That must be tough …"

"So I don't have any close friends really. The closest ones are people I've met in the hospital. Like Essie. Dolores. People like me. The kids in my neighborhood are just kids. They don't understand …"

3.

Luke lives in a three-room apartment six blocks from the Medical Center. His wife Karen works as a secretary downtown and takes classes toward a history degree at the School of General Studies three nights a week. They've been married four years.

"Are you going to do the shopping this week?" Karen says.

"Didn't I say I would?"

"Yes. So that's why I'm asking."

"If I said I would, then I will."

"Fine." A pause: "When?"

"Damn it, Karen. When I get a chance."

"Luke, that's not good enough. I have to know *when*, because I have to plan the meals. In case you've forgotten, we're having your friends over for dinner Friday. Will the shopping be done by then?"

"Don't I always shop by Friday?"

"Usually."

"Then I'll shop by Friday. Put everything on a list, and I'll get it."

"You don't have to snap at me."

"Sorry."

"*Are* you?"

"Yes, Karen, but I'm sick of arguing. I've got to sleep. I've got to study. And now I've also got to do the shopping."

"I've got to study, too. If something's important, you make time for it."

"I've just got work to do."

"And so do I. Do you ever think about that? Mine's just as important as yours and I've got exams next week." He looks away, tightening his lips. "Luke, what's bothering you?"

"Nothing. There's just a lot of pressure on me now."

"You keep everything to yourself. We don't talk like we used to."

"I know. But, Karen, there are just some things you wouldn't understand."

"Like what? Try me" He looks away. "Do you want to tell me about it?"

He looks at her, then away again. "No. Not now."

4.

January. "Is she pretty?" Jackie asks.

"Who?"

"Your wife." She blushes. "I just wondered. Well, is she?"

"I guess so. Sure."

She reflects. "How long have you been married?"

"Hey, whose sessions are these anyway?"

"Is it wrong to ask?"

"No. Of course not."

"Just curious." She brushes a damp lock of hair away from her forehead and looks at him sideways. "Can't help it."

"I met Karen about five years ago when we were still in college. We went out, fell in love, got married."

"Is she going to be a doctor, too?"

"I don't think so. She's finishing up her college degree now. After that, we'll see."

"Are you happy?"

"Sure."

She hesitates. "I think my folks were happy, before us kids came." She takes a breath and coughs. "They met in Europe, right after the war. My Mom's got pictures. But now they're always fighting." Another breath. "I think it's our fault." She plays with her fingers.

"If it's any consolation," Luke says, "my wife and I fight sometimes, too."

"Oh, Doctor Luke," she says, shifting to face him. "That's awful."

5.

March. "You look tired," Luke says.

"I am. I've lost three pounds in three weeks, and I'm scared. I had to miss school. I couldn't even climb the stairs."

"Can't they rearrange your schedule? Put all your classes on the main floor?"

"They say they can't."

He leans back in his chair. "Are you taking more medicine?"

"Yes. And oxygen most of the time. I've got a big tank in the bedroom, which upsets Bianca a lot. She sleeps in the same room, and all that equipment scares her."

"And your Mom?"

"Of course, she's worried. She'll start talking and forget what she's saying, and she says the same things over again."

"I can imagine that's upsetting."

"She also gets very angry."

"But things must be hard for her."

"Her!" Jackie's eyes widen. "What about *me?* How do you think it is for me?"

"I know it must be hard …"

"You know! What do you know?" She coughs fitfully. "Nobody knows what I've been going through!"

"I'm sorry. I didn't mean …"

"But that's how it came out. That's what people always say. 'I know it must be hard.'" She pauses, suddenly stricken. "Oh, Doctor Luke, why can't I be nicer about this? Why can't I be like the saints? I hate what I'm becoming."

Luke has wanted to talk to her for a long time about what happened in the hospital. "I think a lot of this started when that woman next to you died," he says. "Am I right?"

She glances at him anxiously. "I don't want you to think I'm a bad person."

"Please. I'd like to know."

"Well … If you want to know the truth," She takes a breath.

"I've been thinking about dying for four or five years. Even about killing myself. I thought about taking pills, jumping off a roof or a bridge, or even using a razor blade … but being Catholic and all, I knew it wasn't right."

"But why would you ever think about something like that?"

"Don't you understand? Because I'm such a burden. To my mom, who's already lost one child. To my dad, who works so hard to pay the bills. I couldn't *stand* it if I was them. So I just started to think, 'Look, if I'm going to die, then let me go sooner, not later. And let me go when *I* want to go and not have to wait for it and suffer.'"

"Did you ever tell anyone how you were feeling?"

"No. Except for when I talked to God." She sees him smile and frowns. "I'm serious, Doctor Luke. Maybe you're not religious. but you shouldn't smile at me if I am."

"Sorry."

"I've been talking to God ever since I was thirteen. If it's wrong to kill myself, like the Church says, then I had to know what I was living for. But until that day the woman died, I didn't know for sure."

He nods. "What happened that day?"

She takes a deep breath. "When they brought me to the hospital that time, I wasn't sure if I was going to live or die. I thought the doctors would come by the next morning and tell me my fate, and I went to bed really scared. But when you all came the next day, nobody said anything. You just thumped my chest, listened to me breathe. I thought you were all holding out on me. Later that day, when you came by, I was trying to rest, but my mind was jumping. And then the woman next to me suddenly got real sick. I know I heard someone say the word 'die' several times. That's when I started shaking. The word kept ringing in my head …"

"That was a horrible thing to go through. All that noise and rushing around …"

"When that woman died, I couldn't stand it. I wanted to

know what it meant. I was asking God to tell me why it was happening."

"I remember you looked like you were in another world."

"I was. I knew that woman was going to die. I remember, it had started to rain outside, and I knew it. I knew it the minute before she died. That's why I broke down and started crying."

"You were rocking back and forth …"

"Everybody thought I was upset because the woman had died, but that wasn't it at all. It was because I had to get an answer." She pauses and looks at him intently. "And then I understood that God chooses who He wants and when He wants them, and it's not up to us to judge. I knew I had to face life no matter what. I was crying because I'd wanted to know that for so long, and now at last I did. I even tried to tell that to the woman's husband when he came by afterwards, how God lets us know things through other people. But he was so upset, he didn't understand." She finishes, trembling, and turns to look out the window.

Luke is quiet. Then: "It amazes me," he says.

"What?"

"How sensitive you are to the death of people you don't even know, to the suffering of strangers."

"But they're not strangers to me."

"I know. I wish I had your depth of feeling."

"But you do, don't you?" she says, looking at him quizzically.

He hesitates. "To tell the truth, I don't know. I wall myself off a lot. Don't open up."

"But you've opened up to me. Haven't you?"

"You're different, Jackie."

"Am I?" She smiles. "I like that. I know doctors have to keep a piece of themselves apart. They can't get involved with their patients. But we patients are different. We can get involved with one another, because we're the same. And we need each other."

"I'm not sure who needs who," Luke says.

She starts to answer but begins coughing and has to clutch

for a Kleenex, her hand waving to show she still has more to say. Her sputum is thick and dark green. "Does it matter?" she says when she's caught her breath.

6.

May. It's raining. Luke hears Jackie coming down the hall. He knows her by her cough. She stops, then knocks. When he opens, she's wrapped in her tan raincoat, coughing uncontrollably. "I'm worse." She tries to smile, but it fades fast. "It's raining hard, too."

"I know. If you're really sick …"

"I wanted to come. My Dad said I could come if I took the taxi, so I did."

"I don't want you to get worse."

She bites her lip. "I wanted to tell you something, but I can't now."

"What?"

She shakes her head, then turns away. Her nostrils are pinched, her lips thin, blue-tinged. Her complexion is pallid and waxy, with a sprinkling of acne about the nose and cheeks. Her hair is wet from the rain and lies pasted against her temples. Her neck is bent as if her head is too heavy. She is wearing a simple black skirt and a light lavender sweater over a checkered blouse. Her figure is sparse, with its small breasts and spindly little hips. Her chest is bowed, and when she speaks her voice resonates like a cello.

"We've been talking like this for eight months," he says.

She turns towards him, now resolute. "All right. I'll tell you. This is what I wanted to say." She takes a deep breath and begins. "I had a dream and it scared me."

"Tell me."

"I'm lying in a bed right outside my school. And I'm real tired, like when I've had to walk around a lot. Some kids are there, and they're pointing at me, making fun of me, and I can't get up. Then my parents are there. My mom's upset, running back and forth, like she wants me to rest, but then she doesn't want me to rest. She's so upset, she gets my father mad, and the two of them start fighting and forget about me, and I drift deep into the bed like you drift into a cloud or a field of flowers or the ocean or something. It's amazing, but I'm feeling really comfortable. But then I realize I'm all alone, everyone is gone, and I don't want to be alone. And then everything gets dark. I hear this music, like from a horror movie, like an organ. It's like being in church, but it isn't. It's like a … a funeral. And then the bed is a hospital bed, and I'm in the iron lung. It's pumping and pumping away, but instead of getting more air, I'm choking, I'm smothering, and I know I'm dying. And now the iron lung is really a coffin, a coffin in church. And everyone's standing around it. My mom. My dad, Billy, Bianca, you, the kids from school. Only I'm dead. I'm dead and it's my funeral." And Jackie begins to cry.

Luke looks down, then back at her. He shakes his head. "I don't know what to say, Jackie," he says, his voice breaking. "What do you want me to say?"

"When they put me in the iron lung it'll be the end, won't it?"

"You can't say. It might just mean a tougher time for a while … but a time you could get better from."

"If you were there, you'd tell me, wouldn't you. You'd tell me what was happening."

"Of course."

"The worst part of the dream was being alone." She pauses, coughs.

"You want to know if I'll stick with you."

"Yes. Will you?"

7.

Early October. "Jackie, are you up to taking a short walk today?" Luke says.

"I can try."

"I just have to get out of here," he says. "It's been one of those days. And it's nice out."

"If we walk very slowly."

They leave the room and walk down the corridor, then take the elevator down to the main floor. It's sunny, with a clear sky and a light fickle wind. "You want to go to the park?"

She takes his arm, and they walk towards the park by the river. The trees are changing colors. Red and yellow leaves cling to the branches, shivering. When the breeze blows, they cut loose in twos and threes and spin earthwards, joining the piles already there which make swishing sounds underfoot. Jackie's face is pale, and she is coughing. "Doctor Luke, I have to sit down."

He leads her to a park bench, its green paint peeling, wood chipped. "Maybe this was a bad idea."

"No. I wanted to go out." She coughs again, then makes a face. "I don't ever get to go out anymore. I miss it."

They sit side by side looking at the trees, at the hills where children chase one another, at the paths, at the playground. Young mothers stroll along the sidewalks with their prams and strollers, talking together. Teenage boys play football, shouting and cursing. A young woman sits alone on a tall rock, reading a book. Beyond the trees the river, thick and slow moving, lies like a dark jellied trough, small boats pushing against its current like wind-up toys, spray and spume splashing against their prows.

"It's nice here," Jackie says. "People seem happy."

"And you?"

"I'm thinking of all the things I'll never have. Boyfriends. A family."

"Jackie, have you ever gone on a date?"

She looks away. "No. Out with a couple of kids, yes. But never on a date."

"Did you ever like anyone?"

"I guess." She coughs. "But there's no point to me feeling that way about anyone."

"Why? Shouldn't you feel what you can?"

"Doctor Luke, let's be honest. There's no way I can have a boyfriend. I'm sick. I'm always coughing." Her eyes shine.

"It doesn't seem right for you to have to miss so much."

"That's the story of my life."

He is silent.

She pauses, picks up a small twig from the ground and snaps it into bits with her fingers. "I mean, how could I let myself get serious about anyone?" She throws the pieces of twig away and brushes her skirt.

Luke is silent. He's looking at her hands, noticing how thin her fingers are. He watches her pick up some pebbles and toss them, one after another, onto the grass.

"Doctor Luke, can you imagine me getting involved with some man? Me? Can you imagine anyone kissing me, who's coughing all the time?" She coughs sardonically. "Can you see somebody making out with me in a mist-tent?"

Luke swallows. It's growing cooler, getting late. "But I'm sure you think about it, Jackie. Most adolescents do."

"All the time. But I couldn't stand some guy being nice because he felt sorry for me." She looks away.

"There must be some part of you that wants that experience."

"I guess." She's quiet, then begins coughing deeply, gasping.

"Jackie … Are you choking?"

She shakes her head, then reaches for some Kleenex.

"We'd better get back."

8.

"Do you get any time off for Thanksgiving?" Karen says.

"Yes. And I'm off New Year's. But I'm on all Christmas weekend. That's just how the schedule works out."

"I'd like us to have a little time together. Relax a bit, go somewhere, dinner and a movie. We haven't had much time to ourselves since July."

"I know. But it can't be helped. We're both working, studying …"

They're having dinner at the green card-table in the corner

of the room that's also their study. Luke has bought a bottle of chianti to go with Karen's spaghetti, and it's already two-thirds gone. "Steve and Sal are expecting," Luke says.

"So?"

"So nothing."

"I don't want a baby now, Luke. I'll be getting my degree next year. My job's going well. We need the money."

"I'm not saying we should. Just that they are."

"That's not all you're saying."

"Yes, it is."

"It isn't. And what's Sal going to do?"

"Steve says she'll work until the eighth month. Her boss loves her. He'll take her back whenever she wants."

"She won't go back to work," Karen says. "Not Sal. She'll be a mother for years. After the first one, there'll be a second. You'll see."

He nods, picking at small bits of sauce on his plate. "It's just that a lot of them are starting families now."

She drains her wine, then dabs her lips with a paper napkin. "I'm not ready to start a family now, honey. Really."

"Christ, Karen," he says. "When *will* you be ready?"

Her face blanches, and she looks shocked. He shakes his head, stammering; then moves towards her. "Karen, honey. I'm sorry. I didn't mean that."

9.

The first week in November, Jackie's cough gets worse. She stops going to school and stays in bed on oxygen and heavy doses of antibiotics. She misses two sessions with Luke; then, before he's grasped what's happening, she's in the hospital. He's rotating through a neurology elective and tries to see her when he can, but the neurology team is very demanding.

She grows weaker. After two weeks, she's still in the hospital. On December 18th she goes into an iron lung machine which can do the work of breathing for her, pulling her chest out and drawing oxygen into her lungs.

Luke asks the residents about her chances. "What can you expect?" one says. "She's already lived longer than most."

Luke visits her the Saturday before Christmas. He's bought a fake pearl necklace and wrapped it in holiday paper. When he enters the room, she seems to be sleeping. Her face is wet with perspiration, her eyes closed. The machine is sucking away, registering two liters of oxygen per minute, its sides pulling in and out, hissing and clicking, sighing, sucking, wheezing.

"Jackie," Luke says.

She opens her eyes. "Doctor Luke."

He holds the present behind his back. "How are you?"

She waits for the machine to pause. "Not good."

The IV is running. Oxygen is streaming into the ventilator mask from a plug on the wall. Jackie's head protrudes from the machine's metal core. Her eyes, sunk in purple circles, have a frightened, trapped look. "It's bad this time."

He leans against the metal respirator. "I brought you a present."

"That's nice of you." She coughs. "Unwrap it. For me." He does. "It's lovely." Her eyes grow moist. "Thank you."

"Just hope you're feeling better," he stammers.

The room is quiet but for the noise of the respirator, clucking and thumping, clicking, whooshing. "Doctor Luke."

"What?"

"Tell me … the truth."

"What?" His heart is beating fast.

"I want to know. Is this the end? Am I … ?"

"Dying?"

She nods.

He shakes his head, panic-stricken. "Jackie, how can I know? What can I say?"

"Doctor Luke." Her thin fingers tighten on his. "Please."

There's a lump in his throat. "It doesn't look good. I know that." She's crying. "But, Jackie, no one can predict the future. You know that." His heart is pounding, and he is dizzy. "What about your religion? I know it's helped you."

She closes her eyes and turns away. "I always knew what the machine meant."

"Jackie, you don't know. You just don't," he says, squeezing her hand.

"Don't be afraid for me," she says.

His stomach heaves. He looks desperately towards the doorway, wanting to leave. Jackie's mother appears like a miracle, red-eyed and bent. "Mrs. Serrano," he says, letting go of Jackie's hand. "Come in. Please. I was just going."

"Are we going downtown?" Karen says.

"Whatever you want."

"We said we'd go today, and I'd like to." He works his lips, saying nothing. "What are you undecided about? You know we've still got shopping to do. I don't want to do it all by myself."

He takes a deep breath. "It's just, there are lots of things at the hospital. Some of the patients are very sick."

"That's part of being a doctor, isn't it, Luke? Learning to live with it. Don't they say you shouldn't bring your work home?" She draws closer and rubs his arm. "Come on. Let's be friends. We can have a good time, buy some presents, maybe even stop off for some Greek food."

He looks at her green eyes, broad nose, sandy hair, and timid smile. Her smile has grown more timid in the past few months, he realizes. He's made her less sure of herself, he can sense it. "All right. We could even take in a movie in the Village."

"That would be lovely." She presses closer. "Just because there's things to work out doesn't mean I don't love you." They begin walking to the door. "You're not angry, are you?"

"No. Let's go. Really. I need a break."

They go out into the street. The winter wind whips about

them, chilling their faces. Luke feels the cold in his nostrils. They pull their coats about them; he takes her arm, and they walk to the subway.

They have a long wait for the train, but it finally comes, and they head downtown. The subway rocks back and forth like a cradle. Lulled, Luke stares at the soot and newspapers flying about. On the long stretch between 125th and 59th Streets the wheels click and clack against the rails, and the passengers' chatter blurs together. He watches his reflection in the window. Karen jostles him. "What are you thinking about?"

He turns. "One of my patients. Jackie. I told you about her."

"The girl with cystic fibrosis."

"Yes."

"What about her?"

"She's going downhill. Fast."

"She was the one you've spent so much time with." He nods. "That's too bad." He doesn't respond. "But there are other people who can take care of her, aren't there?"

"I guess."

"I mean, do you want to be there?"

He shakes his head. "I don't know. It scares me, and I feel like I'm letting her down."

"Oh, Luke." She takes his arm, leaning her head against his shoulder. The train careens into the 59th Street station, its wheels shrieking sharply.

They climb the stairs to the street and spend several hours walking from shop to shop. Karen buys the gifts she wanted. They eat dinner at a small Greek restaurant, then see a movie in the Village. When they get home it's late, and the apartment is dark. On an impulse, Luke calls the floor to see how Jackie's doing. The nurse says she's dead.

He puts the phone down, shaking. Karen asks what's wrong, and he tells her, then asks her to wait in the apartment, and he goes out. He climbs up to the roof of his building and stands there, his heart pounding, his eyes damp, looking at the sky, the stars, the bridge, the river beyond, and the brilliant towers of the Medical Center which rise majestically just a few blocks up the street. And he knows he's the biggest coward that ever lived.

The Room

I.

I am sitting at my desk. The window is to my right. Through
it I can see the street and the apartment house across the street.
When my shades are up I can see the top floor of the building,
but when they are half-down as they are now, I can only see the
bottom two stories and half of the third one. I haven't yet met
any of the people across the street. I haven't yet been out of my
room, not since I entered it, not since I paid the old lady her
rent for a month in advance and moved in with my groceries.
One large rectangle of glass forms the lower half of the window,
but the upper half, the half covered by the torn yellow shade, is
composed of six smaller rectangles of dirty glass. There is a crack
in the very top frame, to the right. But since the shades are halfway down I can't see the crack now. And it is just as good that
way. I'm sure I would feel a draft on my neck from the crack if I
could see it, but now that I cannot see it, I am sure that there is
no draft in the room.

It is cold. It is almost December. When I came here with
my groceries, the landlady made a joke about Thanksgiving, and
I laughed. But I had no turkey. I don't celebrate holidays. Every
day is like the one before it to me. But that is beside the point.
What matters is that it is cold. Perhaps there is no heat. If the
old landlady thinks I shall put up with no heat during the coldest
months of the year, she is wrong. When I see her I shall speak
to her, I shall tell her that it is cold in my room, I shall not laugh

41

at her jokes unless she promises to warm my room. I must make a note of that. But, of course, she will probably say that the heat is already on and that it must be a crack in one of my windows that is causing my room to be cold. What will I say to her then? What could I answer without affirming that, indeed, there is a crack in the uppermost right pane of the window, the one which is covered by shades now. I had best not mention it at all. If I ask her to fix the window she will become angry. She will stalk about my room waving her arms around. I do not want that. I shall say nothing to her, then. I shall pretend I do not see her if she comes. I shall lock the door. But all this is beside the point. I was talking about the room.

My bed is on my left. It is unmade, as usual. My small stack of clothing is on the floor behind me. My books are on the bed, and some are on the floor beside it in a nice pile. My apartment has only two rooms, or rather only two sections to its one room. My desk, bed, books, window and clothing are here. The toilet and sink are in the other part, and the mirror which I bought myself from the five-and-dime store when I came is over the sink. My stove and small ice-box are there too.

That doesn't seem to say it right. When I say stove, I can see it by craning my neck. It is my stove. In the ten days I have been here, I have grown to know it. My stove, with its four burners, round black holes, covered over with a circle of grimy metal on which I lay my coffee pot and frying pan, the circle resembling a star, a starfish whose innards are missing, but which I put over the flame anyway, because I need something on which to rest my coffee pot. But there is more to the stove than that. I am forgetting the pilot flame, burning blue like an eternal light. Last night, or the night before, I'm not sure, I watched it from my desk chair for an hour, the blue flame, wavering slightly in the draft that must have come through the crack in the window. And then there are the stove's great white sides, there is the oven door, its dull handle spattered with the grease from something I cooked above it. There are the black legs, short and squat, on which the stove rests like some heavy bird. There are the knobs that control everything, little white knobs for turning the gas on and off, which I played with at first for a while, pretending they were teats until the smell of gas made me sick. One can't forget the knobs. And then there is the kettle on the stove, which I brought from the other house, the one I lived at before I came here, a lightweight kettle with a piercing whistle, it holds exactly five and a third cups of water, it is always polished, it is round. The kettle is not like the knobs, though. The knobs are uneven and hard, but the kettle is somewhat plump. The kettle is my friend. I can't say the same for the knobs. Yes, that is what I mean when I say stove. Four feet high, heavy, cube-shaped. It looks like a dwarf beside my ice-box. The ice-box and the stove looking like my Mutt and Jeff, my food and sustenance, quiet servants, masters, it doesn't matter which, how can a stove matter, it's always a stove, even if it's a friendly one.

Where was I? Oh yes, the room, the stove, the desk, the window, next door. Next door they are singing. They have been singing for ten days, ever since I got here. I banged on the walls, but it was no use. They must think it's amusing. It must give them pleasure, like it gave Murray pleasure when he sang his old songs, I can still hear him singing his old songs, the songs next door make me remember, I've been remembering a lot lately, things come back, all the things I had forgotten, all the things I wanted to forget, all the things I couldn't forget, like Murray's song, like the dog, whose dog, Murray's dog, was it Murray's dog, I don't know whose dog it was, what dog, I can't start remembering the dog now, not the dog, nor the hole, the small black hole, small and oily, I can remember it now, but I should forget it, I can't be sure about that anyway, it's best to forget it, I can't forget it now, not the hole nor the dog nor the song nor the face.

I'm not to blame for any of it. I wouldn't hurt anyone, not even the old landlady, not even the people next door. If they get angry I'm sorry, but it isn't my fault, none of this is my fault, not the dog, not anything, I'm not to blame, and if I remember it's not my fault either, I can't help that.

The glass was sweating as much as he was. He took a deep breath, wiped his forehead with his sleeve, looked at the table. But the beads of sweat on his glass stayed. He didn't wipe them off. One of them began to trickle down the glass, leaving a clear stripe as it rolled, moving down, around the curve of the glass, around the bulge, and then, more quickly once it passed the bulge, rolling to the base, stopping, a pearl of water at the thick base of the glass, then, weakly, making contact with the wooden table, soaking into the grain, disappearing except to leave a dark spot, like a stain, and all the time he was looking right there, right at the base of the glass, watching the drop disappear, and not saying a word all the time.

I have to stop thinking of that. It wasn't my fault. Later, I can talk about it later. But now I have to think of other things, like the room, like the noises, like myself. For instance, I am growing bald. I can put my hand to my head, and pull out a few strands whenever I wish. At a comparatively young age, I am growing bald. My nose is running too. I think I must have caught a cold from the draft in this room. And I have a pimple on my chest which, in the past day or two, has been growing. It doesn't itch, doesn't hurt, but I can feel it. I know it will grow bigger, and when it grows big enough I shall squeeze it, pop the head between my fingers. That will amuse me. Purgation, I shall call it. Then I shall wash my hands.

I am losing the skein. The song reminded me of something, of someone. Not Murray, because I have resolved to forget about Murray for a while, but about someone else, about *her*, yes, about her. It's strange. It's strange for one to treasure one image above all others, and to feel sorrow over it. But I feel it deeply. I can see her image, I can remember her story, I can see her face. Ah, Valla, woman of my youth, love.

I must control myself. If I'm going to think about her I must use discretion. Too many sentimentalists are running around as it is. My passion was not like that. Valla, what would you say if you could see me now? Would you laugh, or sing? I think you would. Then it is just as well that I left you, that you left me, that it ended between us, all because of, because of what, of a black circle, of a small circle, of a laugh perhaps. Valla, shall I tell about it now or not? Shall I think about it?

First I'll raise the shades, so I can look out while I think, so I can see the people walking around. Valla, would you like it here in this room?

It was at least ten years ago, maybe more, I'm not sure. Time doesn't matter that much anyway when it's behind you. I was young at the time. I was lonely, too. My father had remarried after my mother's death, and I felt I was no longer welcome at the house. Besides, I had finished college, and I wanted to be out in the world on my own. For almost two years I had lived by myself in an apartment like this one, off a main street in a rather large town. I made a living by teaching English in a public school, but I hated the work. At the end of the term I handed in my resignation. With the little money I had saved I planned to keep myself in bread and coffee for a few months while I decided what to do. I had the intention to write.

(This is not the story of Valla, I'm telling the story of Murray. I don't like that story at all. It sounds just like all the other stories I ever heard, and I know the ending already. It is very sad. I have to tell the right story. I'll start again, anywhere, the middle perhaps.)

I met Valla by accident one night.

No, that really isn't so. I waited a long time to see Valla, I used to watch her walk down the street, I was too timid to talk to her, it was only by following her to her house, without her knowing it, that I found her last name, on the mailbox, and, by looking up the last name in the phone book and checking it against the address which I knew, that I found out her first name, Valla, which stayed on my lips from then on. Even then I did not speak to her. When she walked past me, my lips formed the syllables, Valla, but I made no sound. Some evenings I watched her house to see if she had a boyfriend, lover, or suitor, but she had none of these. One morning I followed her to work, and found out she was a librarian. From that day, I made it a point to go into the library once a day. It was inevitable that she should begin to notice me. I waited for the right moment to speak to her. I knew that once I had spoken the delicious period of waiting was over, and I would have either made contact or lost it. There could be no second tries, I felt.

How many times did I rehearse each gesture, each accent of my speech. How many nights did I spend, my head tightly in my pillow, thinking of the words I should say. Then, finally, one sunny autumn day when the trees outside the library window were in full color, I spoke to her, I made my move. And she answered. She smiled. I saw her lips quiver. I was beside myself, in ecstasy.

That was how it began. Yet it seems I have told it too quickly. Each moment of expectancy, of fear, of hope, each moment of longing should be re-lived. After all, it is the only love of my life. I'll have to tell it again, go over it and try to explain.

No good. It was doomed to failure. Even Murray could not bring me back to my senses after it all happened. And it was I who left her, not she who left me, regardless of what I say later on or said before, because now, telling the story, I remember clearly, I know how it all happened, I know I left her, because I was too delicate for her, for anyone, was then, and am now, because I had to leave her, the only love I ever had, the only woman who ever loved me, all because of what I could not help seeing, could not help hearing, all because of my own self, because I have been and shall always be that way.

I am that way now. I am solitary, egocentric. I know it. It's like a cloud in my brain.

The walls of my room are blue. From the yellow ceiling hangs a large bulb at the end of a slim metal chain. There is no lampshade. If my back were not to the lamp, there would probably be a lot of glare. My bed, as usual, is unmade. By my hand is a clay ashtray, orange, with three butts of varying sizes dumped in it.

The ashtray stands on three legs. Its inside is almost pink, but the rim has been blackened from having many cigarettes tapped in it. It resembles an open mouth.

The shades are up. I can see all the way to the top of the building across from mine. Most of the blinds are drawn. I expected that. People in this neighborhood keep their shades down, especially after dark. Now, even though it is not dark, most of the blinds are drawn. It gets me mad. I have always peered into windows. There's nothing wrong with it. I just like to watch people, from a distance, see what they're doing.

Some old woman is out walking. Her head is bent into the wind. She looks like a nail someone hit with a hammer. Dressed all in black, the way European women are always dressed, she looks like she's going to someone's funeral. She's going to the corner now, heading for the store to get some eggs and butter.

There's that dog again. He's following the woman. When I first came here, he barked at me, showing his yellow teeth. Now I hate him. I see him a lot from the window, and whenever he sees me he lifts his big black head and howls. During the day he lies on his owner's porch. I don't know what he does at night. Perhaps the next time I go out, if I go out for food, if I get hungry, I shall try to make friends with him. I know how to do it. A few days ago, a little girl called to him, and he came over. She stood quite still and extended one hand towards that monster. He crept closer and thrust his wet nose against the girl's hand. She did not move. Then she began to speak some kind of baby talk, and the dog listened. Within a few seconds the girl was patting his head. He was conquered. It's disgusting. Evidently it's very easy to make friends with that animal if one wants to. Now I do not think I want to, not that animal, not with his head

tilted at a slight angle from the line of the rest of his body, his eyes looking upward, his tongue lolling out, his black fur matted together at his neck, glistening, no, not at all, not that dog. Look at him following the old woman, padding along behind her. It would be funny if he ate her, but I doubt that would happen.

They are still singing. Where was I? I was telling part of the story from my youth, what kind of story, what kind of youth, negligible, insignificant, poignant only to me. It's true, about being poignant, all my stories are poignant to me, I get tears in my eyes over any of these stories, I can't help it, they're my stories, to me they're beautiful.

II.

If I am to tell stories, I shall have to apply some order to the process. I shall have to tell them from beginning to end, or from end to beginning, for that is how stories are told. It is ridiculous to try being different. After all, there are rules in everything.

I shall warm up first. This is a short story which actually happened. It will serve as the introduction to the longer, more poignant story I shall tell later, the story I can't get out of my mind even now. It is called THE EGGS.

Once, several days ago, a man, I, was hungry. It was late in the evening, after dinner, and nearly into the early morning. What was there to eat? The man went to his cabinet, took out his frying pan, and took some butter from its place on the third shelf in the ice box. He put a large pat of butter in the pan, which he then placed on his stove. The heat went as high as it would go, and a blue flame darted from the pilot to the burner and spread out fan-shape beneath the pan. The man, I, went next to the top shelf of the ice box, and returned with a small carton of eggs, half-empty. Ah, even now as I tell the story, I can feel the man's excitement, my excitement of several days ago. An egg. A beautiful, smooth egg held in one's hand. Can there be anything more lovely? Can there be anything which gives greater pleasure?

The butter was crackling in the pan, sending small yellow-brown bubbles above its hot surface. With a quick and dexterous motion, the man cracked the egg on the side of his frying pan, and, with one hand, spread the segments of shell apart so that the egg could drop, unencumbered into the pan. It fell perfectly into the hot butter. The plump yolk was exactly centered in the pool of albumin, like a yellow flower in a pond. The egg began to cook. The albumin began changing from a jelly-like mass to a white ring, like a lacy collar around the yolk.

The man discarded the eggshell into a brown paper bag at the foot of the sink. Then he reached gravely into the carton again. He chose a fine, smooth, brown-shelled egg and repeated the same ritual. Once transported to the stove, the egg soon dropped gracefully into the pan beside its brother. Both were cooking, together. It was a spectacle to behold and admire.

The man let the butter fry the edges of the eggs, and once or twice he tilted the whole pan so that the butter could trickle inwards in the direction of the yolks. When a brief few seconds had passed, he grasped a spatula in one hand and held the pan with his other. The eggs seemed done on one side. With a skillful, rapid movement, he flipped the eggs over to their other sides. Oh how they sizzled! The yolks held firm.

Ten seconds more, and he turned off the flame, lifted the pan from the stove, and deposited the eggs on a plate, which was lying on the table. What a lovely sight they made, the two eggs. Like two eyes, two breasts, two hands: two eggs. With salt and pepper and a dash of paprika the eggs were prepared further. When all seemed done, he raised his fork to his lips in a prayer of thanks. Then he lowered the fork to the plate. Soon the eggs were gone. The first egg was eaten alone, by itself, plain. The second was dispatched in the company of a modest chunk of black bread and butter.

Oh! How good it was. How lovely! How rich and creamy was the yolk, and how crisp were the edges fried in butter! The bread sopped up the remaining yolk. The plate was spotless. The meal was done.

For a brief moment, an all-important moment, the man felt as if life had a goal, a purpose, a sense to it. If only because he had eaten such eggs and might, the next day, eat two others like them, if only because of this, he was ready to go through the dark night until the next day came. There was true hope, in the shape and taste of an egg.

An egg exists to please. It does not ask to be pampered. It does not ask to be fed, to be dressed, to be considered, to be complimented. Its entire purpose in life is to be eaten and to be enjoyed. An egg is an instrument of love, there's no denying it. The egg loves whoever eats it; whoever eats it, loves the egg. There is no whining, no false promises, no placating. In short, this noble man reflected that, given a choice between a woman and an egg, only a fool would not choose the latter.

Having thought this, the man, fatigued by now from the intensity of his experience, wiped his lips and, with a last sigh of pleasure, walked into his bedroom. There he slowly undressed and went to sleep. His dreams were happy, and his sleep was unbroken.

That is one of my favorite stories. I tell it because I like it. In that short story are embodied the simple principles by which I now live my life.

Great pleasures are to be had among everyday things, if one looks for them. In the form of an egg, in the warmth of a bath, in the smoothness of clean bed-linen can be found perfect joy. The only complications in such a life come from without, such as the incessant singing noise from next door or the incredibly ugly face of my landlady. But more of that later.

Now that I have hinted at my secrets, I am free to tell my longest story. I have been remembering bits of it, more and more, during these last ten days. A scent, a color, a face, is enough to set it all off.

The moon lit up the last window to the right. It was dark, but vague outlines were visible. A silver-colored hand moved over the window-frame on its way to the arm of the sofa. And suddenly, framed by the shining glass, a face appeared.

The sun is going down in the West, and the sky is very blue. Soon it will be dark. I can already see lights behind some of the shades across the street. For some reason the singing has stopped. They seem to be listening to me next door, wondering what I am doing. Now they are laughing. Yes, and now they are going on. One of them has put a record on the phonograph at its loudest volume, and they are all singing with it, following the leader,

like a summer in Italy. She had been sitting in the chair a long time. Now she rose from it, stretched her hands over her head, leaned back. Her fingers loosened her hair from its tresses. Dark hair fell over her bare shoulders. She wanted to play a record. ("Piacere?") When it was playing, she began to dance, and her body undulated like a ten-cent hula doll. ("Lei?") Somewhere behind me the two chambermaids peeked from the half-open door, the dark one with hair tangled on her legs and the blonde, the tall blonde, who wanted to be a movie star. When she came towards me I, not knowing anyone was watching, reached out my hands towards her hips. I was accepting her invitation. We didn't speak for a few moments. We danced, and she was humming the song's melody. But then one of the chambermaids, the short dark-haired one or the tall blonde, giggled, and I turned around to see who it was. The girls ran away. When I looked back at *her*, she was laughing, too, And the record was no longer playing. The room was quiet. There was noise coming from the outside, though. Now I was blushing. ("Ebbene, cara, come si chiama?") And then I knew I had transgressed, stumbled into a situation I couldn't control. ("Sandra," she said.) The floorboards seemed to groan as she passed over them. A wave of the hand was for me. She opened the door of room number six and closed it behind her. A thin sliver of face still peeked from behind it as it closed, and I could see the expression in the one eye visible, an expression of disdain, mockery, contempt, I could feel it all the way into the parlor where I stood, not knowing what to do, by the phonograph which had stopped playing, while those two chamber-harpies clanged dishes together in the kitchen.

Why am I thinking of that? Have I then retained my memory, am I going to be taunted by scenes like that for the rest of the day, of the night, do I have to re-live all my old mistakes, the ones I couldn't help doing, the ones I was ignorant of when I did them, the ones I now understand, am I to be taunted by memory, when memory should be pleasureful and not tormenting, with the result that I am deceived by my own self, the self I wish I could forget, which I cannot forget?

Where was I? Before, before they had put on the records, when the sun was still above the top of the apartment building across from my window, whereas now it is below it so that there is no glare, but the sky is getting redder and redder all the time as if there were a fire somewhere. I was trying to tell about myself, in an orderly way, starting the farthest back, with Valla, but Valla wasn't the farthest back, that was Murray, although Murray was both before and after Valla, and Sandra was only before, or was it after, I'm not sure, all these things happened so long ago, so far ago, how can I be sure of them, how can I be sure of anything, I, who only know that I am in a room outside of which on the right is a street and on the left is another room where they sit, the ones who keep on singing, and that I am at my desk, and that if I turn my head a hundred thirty-five degrees to the left I shall be able to see the blue flame of the pilot on my stove, this is what I know, and at times I even question this, and, if I cannot be sure of the flame in the room, how can I be sure about the stories, be sure if they are so, or if the sequence is really as I think? For I may think today that Sandra came before Valla, and tomorrow that Valla came before Sandra, and yesterday it may have been that Valla and Sandra were the same person, and that is just as plausible as it is not, so how can I know, and how can I be sure? So why not take it as it comes, memory, and let the scenes follow what they will, because it's all me, I know that, it couldn't be not-me, because there is only me here in this room, and if there is also any face or any scene, then that face or scene must in some way be me, too, or else I would have to believe in spontaneous creation and worms coming out of rotten milk and things like that, which everyone knows cannot be, even I, I who am, who am in this room, who must choose now and go on, I cannot get stuck, I must go on. I started with Valla, I see her again, Valla the librarian, Valla the dark-haired girl whom I followed one day from her job, after I had spoken to her, the day we talked together, as we walked through the fallen leaves.

"My name is Valla."

I told her mine. We were on a residential street that led from the main road to a district of our town where librarians, students, and unemployed artists lived. The houses on this street were set back from the sidewalk by their lawns, and trees stood between houses and in the front yards like domestic gods. A man raking leaves waved to us as we passed. The smoke from his fire of dry leaves filled the air about us with a strong, autumnal scent. Two children were on his front porch, playing a game with some sticks. They, too, waved at us, imitating their father in the way they moved the fingers of their right hands from the tip of their foreheads just below the hair-line, upwards, frontwards, and to the right in a precise arc, while their forearms, which had thus far been bent, straightened out, until their fingers and hands were extended out towards us at the end of completely extended right arms. All this was accompanied by a large smile from each child, as it had been from the father. I smiled back, feeling very much a part of the day, the weather, the street, the people.

"They're cute, aren't they?" Valla said, waving to them.

"Yes," I said.

I had followed her out the library door that day. I walked behind her at first, but then I caught up to her. She seemed to recognize me. I fidgeted a moment, and then asked her if she'd mind if I walked a little way with her. She said it would be all right. And now we were walking together.

"I've seen you quite a bit at the library," Valla said. "You come in there often."

When she spoke, her lips formed the syllables of each word. Yet she did not speak slowly. Or, even if she did speak slowly, I was nevertheless entranced by the beauty of her voice and did not mind having to wait for the entire sentence. In fact, I enjoyed prolonging the pleasure of each word. At the word "you," her whole face centered about her puckered mouth, her eyes seemed rounder and brighter, and the sound of her voice seemed to hover in the air like a small ring of smoke. The slight down on her upper lip made this motion all the more charming by encircling her lips above with a darker band, while a dark spot just below her lower lip seemed to be a natural counterweight to it. Spot, down, shadow, and hue: all made her mouth a thrilling object. I was enchanted.

"I live to the right," she said.

We both turned down a very small street, almost an alley. The houses here were no longer suburban-type; rather, they were older and more crowded buildings. I kept step with her. She couldn't know how happy I was. In the short time we had been walking, I had told her about my family, about the job I had just abandoned in the hopes of doing something better, and about the year I had spent in Italy and France. This last bit impressed her. She had never been out of her home state. Her mouth formed an incredulous "O" when I described Paris to her.

"And you have really been there!" she said. "That's wonderful. I wish so much I could go."

"Yes. And it's everything it's supposed to be."

She shook her head. "I don't think I'll ever be able to get there."

I assured her that she would, especially since everyone was getting a chance to see Europe these days. I laughed when she laughed, I turned when she turned, I believed all my waiting had not been in vain. I did not, of course, tell her how long I had watched her from the opposite side of the street when she went walking, how I had hid behind iron gates when she passed so as to sniff her perfume, how I had waited outside her house at night watching for visitors, how I had constructed fantasies in my mind at all hours of the day, fantasies in which I would conquer her and find in her everything I had always wished to find. No, I told her nothing of that. It would have frightened her away, I'm sure of that. It would have frightened any one away, all the tricks and games I played, all my thoughts, my observations, my obsessions, no one could really understand them but myself, and that is why I kept them from her, tried my best to portray myself to her as I knew she would want me to be, she, a lovely and lonely girl, undoubtedly given to fantasies herself, but hers of a totally different order from mine, and those fantasies, hers, being the ones I had to satisfy. I had to portray myself as the loving and gentle creature of her dreams, I had to hide every part of myself that was incongruous with that picture, I had to lie, to laugh at foolish things, to pretend, to tell her about the places I had been, about places I had never been, I had to support her breathless wishes, and all because I liked her, because I had myself grown attached to the myth, to the dream, to the fanciful image that creeps every so often in youth into one's mind, threatening to blind one to the realities of the world, I had to satisfy my own dream (or disprove it) in satisfying her own. It was a sordid business. And I am happy now that it has ended. I can only go so far, in spite of what my dreams may require. After all, so far and so much, and past that no further. I say all this by way of explanation, not that I feel badly about it, for I do not, I am happy about it, but because I simply could not go further with it, it had to end, that black circle, her sensual mouth, her lips, dark and oily with cosmetics, I could only accept so much, what attracts one is usually the repulsive, and it was that way with me, I offer no excuses, I am just explaining now, about how we went walking the first day I spoke to her, when she thought I had never thought of her until I spoke, "by accident," in the library, as I was returning a book of Napoleon's *Memoirs,* and attracted her attention, when in reality, as I knew and did not say, I had planned the moment carefully for weeks, planned it even to her reactions, even to following her out of the library that day and asking to walk beside her, yes, all of it, every action, every word, was planned, as it had to be, everything was planned, and she thought it was all sudden and spontaneous, because you see, she had to think it was sudden and spontaneous, that was her dream, her myth, and it was that to which I played, sordidly, treacherously, in grandiose, hypocritical fashion.

"You know, I've often wondered who you were," Valla said. "I see you almost every day at the library."

"I see you, too. You know," I said, "I was hoping we'd have a chance to speak. And then, today, all of a sudden, everything just happened." (Here I smiled.)

"Yes," she said. "It's so funny things happen that way." (And her mouth, on the last word, "way," opened wide so I could see her teeth and gums and even the wiggly uvula far down inside.)

At this point an old man, bald and doddering, walked past us. He used a cane to support himself. For an instant he raised his eyes, as if reflecting on our identity. Then he lowered them again to the ground, where his feet, shod in a pair of dirty, torn, badly scuffed shoes, slid one after the other through the leaves which littered the sidewalk that day like confetti after a parade. Was he humming a song? I cannot remember. Let us say that he was.

Valla nodded at him. She smiled just as she had smiled at the man raking leaves. All friendliness and cheer on the surface. "Nice old man," she whispered to me as he passed. I said nothing, although I did smile. She took a deep breath and commented on the smoky smell, and on how winter was around the corner.

It was growing dark. People who had already come home from work were in their houses, and the lights were on in almost every house we passed. I had never before realized how romantic, how poignant was the twilight. The sinking sun made the sky redder and redder, and the clouds began to be filled with colors. Shadows got longer. The air seemed more fragrant.

I walked Valla home and left her at the door. It was understood that we would do the same thing the next day, meeting
at the library return-desk and then walking out together when
the clock on the wall directly over her amber-varnished desk
stretched its hands as far apart as possible, signifying that it was
six and time for the lights to be turned out and for everyone to
go home. We would walk out together, not separately as we had
done that first day, for from that first day on the contact had
been made, and it was only a matter of time as to how far the
relationship would develop, if it did not end.

After she closed the door that night, I remained outside it
for a while, thinking how I had spoken to her at last. I recalled
the many evenings spent watching that door from a doorway
further down across the street, knowing that behind that door
was my Valla, knowing that she was even then telling her mother
how she had met a gentleman coming home from work that
day, someone she had often seen in the library before, and her
mother, suspicious, saying, What does he look like, Is he rich,
Just what do you know about him, Are you going to see him
again, while she, Valla, bustled about, taking off her coat and
hanging it in the closet, going to her room where whatever mail
she had received that day was carefully laid on the fold of her bed
beneath the pillow, washing her face with warm water, wiping it
with her red towel, the one with a deep-hued carnation in the
lower corner, returning to the kitchen-dining room where her
mother was ready to ask her more questions while they both
prepared the dinner they would eat later, together, sitting one on
one side of a small wooden table and the other facing her from
the other side, with only the kitchen light on in the whole house
because they saved money that way, while outside it grew darker
and darker and the stars came out and the moon grew from a
shy silver to a rich golden color, and the street that ran right and
left from the small walkway to the door was quiet, because it was
night, and even I, who had stood for a while outside the door,
thinking, even I had gone home to my own rooms, gone away
from their street, gone away from their talk, yet knowing they

were still talking of me, knowing she was still thinking of me, just as she, Valla, was on my mind as I prepared my dinner and planned the steps I should "spontaneously" take the following day so that she would begin to like me, trust me, confide in me, even love me. And so, that night, each of us went to bed, thinking (she later told me this was definitely the case, as I had expected) of the other and wondering what the next, the following days would bring.

It is getting dark in my room now, and the story is going nicely. I have stopped because something is happening outside my window. The young married woman who lives on the second floor has come out on her porch to take in the few things she hung on her line this afternoon. She is a thin woman, unattractive except for her legs, which she usually covers with sheer black stockings. They probably excite her husband. Right now, she is attempting to take down some stockings, two pairs, from the short clothesline she has rigged up on the balcony-porch where she undoubtedly suns herself during the summer. She stretches up, her arms are reaching high over her head. This pulls her black sweater up, so that there is a narrow strip of bare skin just above her waist. I can see her belly. Her small, high teats are even smaller and tighter as she reaches up. She doesn't know I'm here. Now she reaches down into the straw basket she has carried out and puts the stockings into it. She is going to take in a few pairs of silk panties next. I watch her. She stretches again, and again I can see her midriff, again I can almost feel the tautness of her breasts and the willowy quality of her legs as she stands on tiptoe. Her face is plain, but I don't mind. These are the pleasures of life. These are my rights and privileges, to watch what goes on in the world outside my windows.

Oh. She has just noticed me. She looks angry. She has just pulled her sweater down over her bare belly, indignantly; who does she think she is, who does she think I am, where is she going? She is going indoors. That's the end of the laundry. What if she tells her husband? No, she wouldn't tell him. Perhaps she would. But what could he do, nothing, he couldn't bother me at all, and if he came up here fuming I wouldn't let him in.

Perhaps the husband is next door now, singing with the others. Perhaps the woman wasn't really taking in clothes, but just enticing me, making me stare at her, and at the same time giving a signal to her husband who was watching her from the next door window, waiting, until he too could give the signal for everyone to start singing louder, to start banging on the walls, just as they are doing now, so that I can hardly think, so that I almost forgot about my own stories which they have interrupted. Now I shall go on. I shall forget the woman with the small, high teats and the bare midriff and the willowy legs, she's gone into the house anyway, I won't even look through the window for a while, if that will be possible. If she or her husband or the people next door want to make trouble, let them, let them bang their fists against the wall, let them shout and sing, but I won't apologize, I won't stop, after all I'm perfectly within my rights, I know that, just as I was within my rights with Valla, and with Murray, yes even with Murray.

Now the dog from across the street is looking up at me through my window. I see him. What is he doing there now, staring at me as if he knew something I didn't want known. I never thought dogs had good sight, but he can always find me at my window, and he stares, that big terror of a dog.

And now the dog is lying in the street, right in the middle of the street, where the cars pass. He does this often. In a few minutes he will be rolling over from side to side, flexing his hairy paws, flapping his pink tongue from right to left as he rolls. He will snap at flies. He will feel secure on his back. He may even wag his tail. But he does not know that in a few minutes he will still be on his back, unable to move, his spine crushed without mercy into the hard pavement of the street. A car makes a dreadful mash of any animal. And from mine, I can look through the window, over the steering wheel, through the window, and see him looking up at me. I wonder if he belongs to the woman who is taking in her wash, whose husband is probably next door, banging on my wall while the others are singing. I shall shut them all out. I shall close my window. I already know how to get up from my desk, it is easy, and with my right hand I can pull the shade all the way down, steadily, just by tugging on the small circle of string tied to the dangling shade-cord, tugging with my finger in the small hole of white cord almost black from the dirt of this apartment which the old lady has not cleaned in months. And then the shades will be drawn, and I will be untouchable, safe in my dark corner.

Dimes

One day, walking along First Avenue in the low teens, Minnick found three dimes and a subway token lying on the sidewalk. He was passing a row of parking meters and it was purely by chance that he glanced down when he did. The first two dimes, black and gritty, lay at the base of one of the poles like tiddlywinks.

Minnick stopped for a minute, looking down as if to make sure of what he'd seen. Then he squatted down and reached out. The sidewalk was covered with litter—cigarette butts, gum wrappers, bits of cardboard, rubber bands. He gingerly touched the dimes, then withdrew his hand and wiped it on his pants.

The dimes were almost touching. Minnick cocked his head, then moved his hand back, fixing his thumb and two fingers around the edge of the dime closer to him. He pulled up. The dime stuck to the sidewalk. He hunched forward, still squatting, and jammed his thumbnail beneath it. This time he pried it loose. He held the coin between his thumb and middle finger and examined it, smiling. Cupping it in his palm, he curled his last two fingers around it to make it secure, then reached out for the second dime. Pedestrians passed, their feet skirting his fingers.

He picked up the second dime as he had the first, then studied them together. They were both Roosevelt dimes, one from 1962, the other from 1970. He nodded, then quickly scanned the rest of the sidewalk. The token, dark and golden, lay a few feet on, its furrowed Y-hole clogged with dirt. Inching forward, he picked it up and added it to the dimes in his hand.

The third dime was in plain view on the next square of cement. Putting his weight on his left hand, Minnick plucked it from the ground with his right. He stood up, breathing heavily, and regarded his collection, shifting his hand so the sunlight struck the coins at different angles. He cleared his throat, then slipped his hand into his pants pocket and dropped the coins in. Then he started walking again. He was a pudgy youth in his mid-twenties with a round face and blond, already thinning hair. He was wearing a brown woolen sweater, a tan shirt, dark slacks, and sneakers. As he walked, he looked from side to side, as if he expected someone to accost him.

He passed several streets where children played, then turned right along East Ninth Street, still glancing at the sidewalk, and stopped halfway down the block in front of a tenement building, its five stone steps leading to a half-opened door. Inside was a small entryway, a dim front window, and rusting mailboxes.

There were more tenement buildings across the street. Next door was a Chinese laundry, with a cracked front window and steam rising from a side vent, and a sign hanging over the sidewalk. Beyond that was a small grocery store and fruit stand.

Minnick climbed the steps and went inside. The hallway smelled of garbage and urine, fish, cabbage, and beer. The walls, paint peeling, leaned inward as if about to collapse. A slender stairway rose from the end of the hallway, a metal handrail beside it. Minnick climbed to the second floor. The light above the stairs was dim, and he could hear people shouting behind closed doors, radio music, the crashing of a dish, a baby crying.

When he reached the landing, he turned and knocked at the second door. A bushy-haired man in gold-rim glasses opened it almost at once.

"Rabor."

"Minnick, you son of a bitch. Come in. What's happening?"

"I'm not sure what's happening, Rabor." Minnick said. "That's the problem." He pumped his friend's hand, grinning broadly, then entered the apartment and looked around.

Rabor lived in a three-room flat. The front door opened into the living room, with a tattered blue sofa, two wooden chairs, two lamps, and a small green rug. The kitchen lay straight ahead, the bedroom to the left, and the bathroom off the bedroom. Piles of books lay on the floor, sofa, and chairs. Books poked out from the bedroom as well, and several stacks leaned against the far corner of the room, teetering precariously, a typewriter sitting like a hostage on the floor beside them.

"Come into the kitchen. I'll make some coffee."

Minnick sat in a wooden chair at the table. In front of him, a dirty plastic cloth supported a sugar bowl, two spoons, and a vase of fake flowers.

"The strangest thing happened, Rabor," Minnick said. "I can't make any sense of it."

"Wait a minute, wait a minute. Let me get the kettle going." Rabor took two coffee mugs from his cabinet and placed them on the counter. He spooned instant Maxwell House into them. Then he took a yellow kettle off the stove, filled it with water from the sink, and put it back on the stove. He turned the burner on high. "Just wait a minute, and it'll be ready."

Minnick smiled. "Okay, okay. So. You working hard?"

"You better believe it. My thesis is due in two months, and I've been burning the midnight oil. I haven't been out except to get groceries."

"What about Wanda?"

"Wander? Oh, she comes when she wants. She comes, she goes. She sits, she draws. She calls her friends on the phone. She sings. You know. Sometimes she takes a shower. Maybe two, maybe three showers a day she takes. She's pissed because I have to do my damn thesis. She's bored with me."

"And you?"

"I love her, man. I mean, she's a beautiful woman. When I finish the thesis, I'm going to take her out for a special dinner." He picked up the cups and put them down again. "So? What about yourself? What's wrong?"

"I'll tell you."

"I heard you lost your job."

"That's true."

"Haven't seen you in, what, three or four months?"

"I been having some heavy troubles. Bad dreams. Tough times. And then …"

"Like what?" The kettle started whistling. Rabor turned off the flame, then picked up the kettle and poured hot water into the cups.

"Losing the job. Breaking up with Katy."

"Sounds bad."

"It is."

"Well, here." Rabor put the mugs on the table, then turned to get some milk out of the fridge. "Okay. We're all set." He sat down. "So …"

Minnick poured some milk in his coffee, added sugar and stirred. "Just the way I like it," he said, as if talking to himself. His glasses were steaming up. He took a sip and leaned back. "Rabor," he sighed. "I was thinking. We've been friends for a long time. We know each other as well as anybody knows anyone."

"Of course," Rabor said. "So what's your point?"

"We go back ten years and more."

Rabor sipped his coffee. He was rocking in his chair, looking quizzically at Minnick. "I know."

"I was thinking, walking over here, how long we've known each other, how long we've been friends, you and me." He sipped his coffee again. "Like, I knew you when you were first starting to study history. I knew you when you were going out with Brenda, who you are not seeing anymore now. I knew you when you decided to write your thesis. You knew me when I was still at home. You knew my folks, my sister. You knew Katy, and you even knew Joan, who I went out with before." He paused. "You knew me when I was having a hard time and didn't know which end was up."

"So, Minnick. What happened to you today?"

Minnick leaned forward, then back again. He felt Rabor staring at him and looked away. Through the doorway he could see Rabor's bedroom with more heaps of books on the floor beside an unmade bed whose pillows had lost their shape and whose pillowcases were torn. Rabor's dirty clothes hung over a red chair: shirts, undershorts, blue jeans.

He glanced at his friend, then at the ceiling light which shone directly on the table and chairs, beaming down on their heads and shoulders. Rabor and he were sitting at right angles to each other, their mugs on the table before them, the steam rising. The tablecloth was smudged, and the kitchen table wobbled. Clasping his hands tightly together, Minnick looked up. "I found three dimes and a subway token today," he said.

"So? Congratulations."

"So what does it mean? Finding three dimes and a subway token." His expression grew intense. "What does it mean? Why now? What for?"

Rabor looked at Minnick, then into his mug. He stirred his coffee with his spoon, swirling it slowly, creating whirls and eddies which met, broke against one another, collapsed and formed again. Then he put the spoon down. "I don't understand what you're driving at."

Minnick moved closer to him and hunched his shoulders. "I don't either. But I've got a feeling."

"Of what?"

"That it means something. I have to figure out what."

"Minnick, how can it mean anything? Finding a few coins. It's an accident. It doesn't mean anything."

Minnick shook his head. He stared at the kitchen wall. It was painted a light tan and had many cracks. One of Rabor's photos hung there, a scene of the East River on a sunny day: a lone tugboat moving upstream against the tide, spray splashing. The surface of the wall was knobbly and rough. "Also, I've got to stop enumerating," he said.

"What?"

"Enumerating. Counting. Making lists."

Rabor put his hand on Minnick's arm. "Minnick, what are you talking about?"

"It's a long story. But the short version is, you have to figure out the pattern, find the order in things," Minnick said. "The world is in a state of chaos. Everybody knows that. But, underneath, there's an order. Somewhere. For whatever reason, somehow, there's an order. We just need to find it."

"Minnick, you're talking nonsense," Rabor said. "What's gotten into you? There's no order in the world. What you see is what you get. If it looks like a mess, it *is* a mess. Any sense of order is an illusion. People like you and me create the patterns."

"Maybe so. But that's our job."

"That's nuts," Rabor said.

"That may be," said Minnick. "But it's what's going through my head. Why three dimes, and not two? Why a token and not a quarter? What's the message? What does it mean?"

Rabor shrugged. "I don't hear any message," he said.

"Why a token," Minnick repeated. "Token of what?"

"Minnick, I don't know. Jesus, I'm a historian, not a philosopher."

Minnick didn't answer. He sat at the table, stirring his coffee. The ticking of the kitchen clock suddenly sounded very loud.

"Ever since I was a kid," Minnick finally said, "I've had this dream of finding money. Stacks of coins. Dollar bills. Nickels, dimes, quarters. In the dream, I get to keep as much as I can scoop up all at once, like finding a hidden treasure. Wherever I look is coins. Under every stone. Lying all over the ground. I run around stuffing my pockets like mad, filling sacks, grabbing as much as I can in my fists. I get crazy with it, thinking of all the things I'll be able to buy."

"I still don't get it," Rabor said.

Minnick licked his lips and shifted forwards. "Rabor. Everything has a meaning. A cause, a purpose. Right? Nothing exists without meaning something."

"I don't know," Rabor said. "I don't think I agree."

"But if it's true, then I have to know why I found what I found. Three dimes and a token. The token must be very significant, even by itself. Think of it. A token of what?"

"Minnick. Are you listening to yourself? You're not making sense."

"I'm on the verge of a big discovery."

"What?"

Minnick clenched his teeth, then relaxed and smiled. "Rabor, last year I was driving through this town, somewhere in New York State. I forget the name. There was a canal, and a bridge, and trees. It was just after I'd broken up with Joanie."

"And?"

"And I had a feeling that something was going to happen. Something significant. You remember, I was trying to deal with some heavy problems then. With my parents. With Joanie."

"I remember."

"Right. All of a sudden, I passed this house and felt I'd seen it before—years ago; in a dream, maybe. The name on the mailbox was the same as mine. So I took it as an omen and tried to make sense of it all—my parents, Joanie, even you. And as I was doing that, trying to put the whole answer into a simple sentence or two, I passed this large church, with an announcement in front, on a bulletin board with glass over it. And this message, just standing there, on the board of this church in this small town, this church with its old-fashioned white steeple, and a weather-vane all the way on top, with an arrow pointing with the wind, spelled out the theme of the week's sermon. 'For the wages of sin is death,' it said. That simple. And right away, I knew. I knew it was a warning. Not that I ever told anyone about it, but it was clearly an answer to what I'd been going through."

"I don't understand. What do you think it meant?"

"Not what I thought at first. What it actually meant was, I had to clean up my act. I had to stop thinking of myself first and try to think of other people for a change. My parents, my friends."

"Did you? Did it work?"

"What do you mean, did it work? Of course it didn't. But that wasn't the point. The point was I had to try. I had to see things differently. I had to look for meaning. It didn't 'work,' if you mean did it make me happy or change my life or bring me a million dollars or make anyone treat me better. Not at all. But you can't expect that to happen." He paused. "And now," he said, "I feel that finding these dimes is a message of the same order, a sign, a new set of instructions …"

"Minnick …"

"Rabor, it's as clear as the nose on your face. I found a token. A *token*. Now what's that a token of?"

"And the dimes?"

"Right. Three of them. Why three? Why dimes?"

"What kind of answer do you have in mind?"

"I don't know. Whatever makes sense. I thought about it on the way over. The dimes, take them first. Maybe it has to do with money in general. Money, materialism, making a fortune. … Or maybe it's that there are three of them. Triplets, trios, trilogies. Good things come in threes. Something about trying something three times in order to succeed. Or the number thirty, or thirty-three. That would be subtler. Like, something about what I'll be when I'm thirty. An omen of what I'll be when I'm thirty."

"You mean, maybe you'll be rich when you're thirty. Something as trite and dumb-ass as that?"

"It's not funny, Rabor. Exactly. It could mean something like that. I may have to work hard, be disappointed, scrounge around like I've been doing. Lose my job, lose my girl, have my parents give up on me like they're doing. Whatever. But in the end I'll come out smelling like roses."

"You're smelling, but it's not like roses," Rabor said.

"I can't stand it when you're crude," Minnick said, banging his hand on the table. "This is serious business we're talking about."

"You're talking random shit," Rabor said. "Nothing more."

"Things don't happen accidentally," Minnick said.

"That's a matter of belief."

"No. It's a matter of fact. There's some inner logic here …"

Minnick sat staring at Rabor, and Rabor sat staring back. A few moments passed.

"Minnick," Rabor started again. "Maybe you won't like this, but I have to ask. Why did you come here to tell me all this? I haven't seen you for almost four months. I didn't know where the hell you were, what had happened to you. I thought maybe you were angry at me. And now, all of a sudden, you show up, talking about your goddamn dimes. Speculating. Enumerating. I'm trying to figure out what happened to you, what's up with Katy, whether you've even been eating or not, sleeping or not … I mean, I can't get a handle on what you're saying. Do you understand?"

"Perfectly," Minnick said. "It's not surprising. You're confused because of my questions. Your head is all wound up in your thesis, your rational historical discourse. You just said so, you haven't been out in weeks, haven't even been able to relate to Wanda, who, if you'll pardon my saying so, is one of the most marvelous and attractive women I have ever met, and who I myself had a crush on six months ago, if you remember."

"I remember."

"So I wouldn't expect you to understand. And, no, it doesn't have anything to do with my lost girlfriend Katy, who can take care of herself now. I can deal with all that, Rabor. I told you, I'm on the verge of something very big. Very significant."

"So I must be a big disappointment to you," Rabor said. "Since I can't understand what you're talking about. Really. I hear the words, I understand that you're bent out of shape about it. But I don't *understand* it. You know?"

"I know. If you want to know the truth, I didn't expect much. I just realized, when I found the dimes and the token, that you lived nearby, and I thought I'd drop by and talk."

"Minnick, are you shitting me?"

"No, that's the truth."

"That's *not* the truth. You called me this morning and said you were coming over. I was expecting you. You didn't just decide to come over when you found whatever it is you've found."

"Three dimes and a token."

"I know what you found!"

"Then why are you asking me?"

"That's not the point. The point is, don't bullshit me about why you came here. You were on your way here when you found that stuff."

"Okay," Minnick said, grimacing. "Maybe I was."

"That's all I was saying."

"Okay. That's all you were saying. Okay." He was quiet for a moment. "So what do you think?"

"About what?"

"About my questions. About what it all means."

Rabor shook his head. "Minnick," he said. "It's simple. I'd like to go along with you, but I can't. To be honest, I think you're having some kind of breakdown. Something must have happened since I saw you. Something with Katy, maybe. Or around losing your job. I don't know. But you're not making any sense."

Minnick bit his lower lip. He looked away from Rabor and stared at the wall. He stared at the jagged cracks which ran in diagonal and irregular paths; he stared at the chipped paint, at the loosened plaster; at the window and at the window frame, twin rectangles subtly and marvelously fitting into one another. He stared at the curtains ruffled by the breeze which came through the open window, watching them blow into wavy shapes, oval and cylindrical shapes; at the bookcases by the wall, their contents overflowing; at the books, the pamphlets, the paperbacks and hardcover books; at the different colors on their bindings, the reds, greens, mostly browns; at the rectangular books, the thin ones and the thick ones, at the art books, the poetry books, the history and the fiction books; at the records loosely stacked beside the record player, a light brown box with two light brown speakers; at Rabor's bed, at the socks on the floor, the underpants, the shirt on the chair; at the kitchen alcove, the table, the light hanging from the ceiling, the yellow kettle, the mugs, spoons, sugar bowl, the carton of milk with the picture of a cow on it, the cow smiling, red, the dairy's slogan beneath it; at the picture on the carton of two children drinking milk, both smiling, innocent, the name of the dairy written beneath it; at Rabor, across the table, staring at him without saying anything. The room was silent except for the clock ticking and some water dripping into an open pot in the sink.

Rabor suddenly stood up and reached for the coffee mugs. He carried them to the sink, washed them and put them in the dish strainer to dry. He came back, took the milk from the table, and returned it to the refrigerator. Then he came back to the table where Minnick was still sitting.

"Minnick," he said. "I don't want to get you upset."

"I'm already upset."

"I know. But I don't want it to get worse. I'm sorry if I don't understand what you're talking about. Really, Minnick, for Christ's sake, you're an old friend, but you've always had a talent for getting everything backwards and upside down. What can I say?"

"I don't want you to say anything."

"Minnick."

"I mean it. If you can help, help. Otherwise, just listen. I know I've got to figure this thing out myself. I know that. Nobody else can help me. It's like the old folk song. I've got to 'walk this lonesome valley by myself.'" Minnick started to sway back and forth in his chair, singing the words of the song.

"Minnick. Stop it," Rabor said.

"All right. All right."

"You want to talk, talk. I'll listen. But don't start doing vaudeville in my kitchen."

Minnick nodded. "I don't have anything else to say," he said.

"I just have to organize things in my mind."

Rabor nodded, waiting.

"Everything has a meaning. Start there," Minnick said. Rabor sat still, his jowly face intent, his gold glasses framing his eyes, his curly hair pushing over his ears, his shirt smudged and sloppy and open at the neck so that his chest hairs were poking out. His bushy head was tilted back.

"I think I'm afraid," Minnick said.

"Of what?"

"Of what I'm going to find out."

Rabor shook his head.

"But I can't be bothered by that," Minnick said. "The main thing is getting at the meaning, getting the sense ..."

Rabor nodded. The clock was ticking loudly. Minnick looked up.

"For example, why are you and I friends?" he said. "What do we have in common? Why do we keep seeing one another, even after we've changed and grown different from the people we used to be when we started out being friends, even after we don't share what we used to share any more, even after we've started making new friends, developing new interests. What does that mean? Another example along the same line: why am I here now? Why here and not somewhere else. Why with you and not alone. Another: why did I find the dimes, why the token, and what is it a token of? Another: why is your wastebasket standing there and exactly there, in precisely that location and no other, at precisely this time and none other, not earlier and not later, over by the windowsill to the right of the desk, why there and not somewhere else, what is the significance, the overall meaning of that wastebasket, in relation to the desk, to the window, in relation to your life? What is its destiny, for if we have a destiny then to be sure the wastebasket also has its own destiny, and if so then what is it, the wastebasket, sitting there and nowhere else? What is the sense of your room, arranged exactly as it is, and exactly now, the bed where it is, and the chair where it is, and the clothes where they are, and the pillowcase and the sheets and the books and the kitchen table, all of them, where they are, and the mugs and the spoons and the kettle and the sink, everything where it is, there and nowhere else, now and no other time, and you sitting where you are and being you and no one else, and me sitting where I am and being me and no one else. And the misery outside, the children in the street, the old women, the grocery store, the laundry, the drunks, the whores, the people walking with canes and crutches, the mothers with their purses and the workmen with their lunch pails, all of them being who they are, themselves and no one else. Do you understand? Each example goes on and on, unravels, telescopes forwards. Each door opens new doors, each room opens new rooms. It all intertwines, fits together, spins in circles. Everywhere you look, more examples pop up. The wall. Those books. Your glasses. My shirt. Why is it all arranged the way it is arranged? Everywhere, there's an order to be grasped, a significance to be probed, unraveled."

Rabor pulled his pipe out of his shirt pocket and reached for his tobacco pouch. He filled the pipe, then tamped it down and lit it, drawing the smoke through his mouth and releasing grayish-brown clouds which rose, shifting and spiraling, towards the ceiling. He put his match down on the table.

"I don't know," he said. "But let me ask you a question. Let me play Devil's advocate, if you will. How can you figure out the 'meaning' of everything? What can they possibly be, these 'meanings' you're looking for, why a mug or a wastebasket is where it is or what it is. Things are what they are, Minnick. If there's a mystery, then it's a mystery. There may be things beyond your ability to figure them out. How can all of this have any other meaning than just being there? What are you *looking* for, beyond that?"

"The universe is alive," Minnick said. "Inanimate objects becoming animate, filled with hidden significance, while people are losing their humanity, are starting to be like robots and things. The whole world is shifting. Don't you feel it?"

"Those patterns are in your mind," Rabor said. "What are

you really looking for?"

"When I find it, I'll know."

"Who says your answers have any validity?"

"Not God," Minnick said.

"All right. Not God. So who, then. You, Minnick? Do you say what everything means and what the patterns of the world are all about ...?"

Minnick looked down at the table. "Of course not. I can't make something true by myself. You're missing the point, Rabor. I have to *discover* what it means. There's a meaning somewhere, and I have to figure it out. That's why it's so frightening. I can't just ... make something up."

"Then how do you do it?"

"By following the clues. The clues."

"The clues."

"Yes. By following them towards the deeper meanings of things. Then, by following further, slowly coming to see how everything works. Events, relationships."

"Like unwinding a ball of string."

"Exactly," Minnick said. "Like unwinding a ball of string. A long piece of string, knotted and tangled, all looped around itself."

Rabor shook his head. "Forget it, then, Minnick. And forgive me. Even though I'm your old friend, I think you should see a doctor."

"I don't need a shrink," Minnick said.

"I'm *worried*." Rabor said, raising his voice. "I don't know what's happening to you, Minnick. I don't know where your head is. I think you should see a doctor, I really do. Take it as friendly advice."

"You don't understand," Minnick said. "I knew you wouldn't." He banged his fist on the table. "I knew it! I knew."

"Minnick, why are you shouting at me?"

"Because you don't understand. Because you're not even trying to understand. Sure, Rabor, you're my old friend, but you don't understand this at all." Minnick shook his head. "You're my old friend, who I came to see to help me out. But you're more interested in me seeing some doctor than about the *puzzle* here, that you could help me figure out, if you tried."

"Minnick, I'm trying. But you're not making sense."

"That's because you don't understand."

Rabor looked at Minnick for a minute, then away. Minnick was hunched over the table, leaning on his elbows, his lips clenched. In the corner of the kitchen, next to the window, was a huge green plant, its broad leaves quivering in the breeze that came through the slit of the window sill. It reached almost to the ceiling. Rabor abruptly got up, went to the sink, and took out a large glass jar from the cabinet beneath. He filled the jar with tap water, then brought it over to the plant and poured water into its base, soaking the dirt, drenching it until he had emptied out the whole jar. Then he brought the jar back to the cabinet, replaced it, and sat down again across from Minnick, whose expression had not changed.

"Minnick," Rabor said. "Old buddy. Something's going on with you that I don't understand. Okay? And I don't think you have the faintest idea what it is yourself."

Minnick stared at him.

"Minnick? You hear me?"

No response.

"Minnick, I'm talking to you, damn it! Do you hear me?" Rabor leaned across the table so that his face was right up against Minnick's, his bushy head, now beaded with sweat, pressing close against Minnick's cheeks, his nose almost touching his face. "Do you *hear* me?"

Minnick closed his eyes. "You don't understand," he said.

Rabor stared at him, his bulky arms hanging down by his sides, his hands gripping the side of the wooden table, just below the edge of the tablecloth.

"Why the dimes?" Minnick said. "Why?"

Rabor took a breath. "Minnick," he said, more forcefully. "Maybe I can't understand you, but I do know it isn't up to you or me to figure out the patterns of the whole universe. Please. Go see a doctor."

"Why the dimes?"

"Minnick, you know what I'm telling you."

"Dimes."

Rabor suddenly lunged at Minnick, grabbed his shirt, and shook him. "Minnick!" he shouted. "What's happening to you?"

Minnick shut his eyes.

Rabor banged his fist on the table. "Then go," he cried. "Go kill yourself for all I care. Drown. Blow your head into a million pieces. Jump off a bridge. I don't care. *Don't* see a doctor. Just leave me alone, please. I've got a thesis to write. Please get the hell out of here with your crazy talk. Okay?"

Minnick stared at the wall, saying nothing.

"Minnick. Please. Out." Rabor leaned forward, his hands raised in a supplicant gesture. "I can't help you."

"All right," Minnick said, after a long pause. "If that's how you want it." He stood up.

"And don't turn this into *my* failure," Rabor said. "I had nothing to do with it."

"If you say so." Minnick stood up slowly, pushing his chair away from the table, and started towards the front door.

"Minnick!"

Minnick turned around. Rabor took a step towards him. His hand rose a few inches in the air, then fell again. Then he shook his head and turned.

Minnick stood still for a moment, then moved to the door, opened it, and stepped out. The door closed. Minnick's footsteps, descending the creaky stairs, echoed through the empty hall.

Rabor stayed standing, looking at the table and listening to Minnick's steps, one after the other as he walked down the stairway, one, then the other, left, then right, step after step, left, then right, down the stairs, down the first-floor hallway, more faintly now, faint and fainter, as he moved towards the front door, the mailboxes, the open doorway. His steps grew fainter still, even though Rabor cocked his head, straining to hear. Then they stopped. They disappeared and were audible no more, even though Minnick had continued on, had descended the five front steps and then stepped onto the sidewalk, walking now along East Ninth Street, over the concrete blocks of sidewalk, the pavement on which he resumed his course once again.

Flamingoes

[handwritten margin notes: "on vacation", "disturbing", "guy", "sounds", "bird", "a people are fucked up story"]

They had booked an eight-day "ABC" vacation, and now, having spent three days in Aruba and three more in Curacao, they were ready to visit Bonaire. They thought it a bit odd to take a jet for a ten-minute trip, but there it was. The 727 took off, rose quickly through the clouds, and then immediately descended. Dropping quickly, it cut back through the clouds and landed at the Bonaire airport before they had even settled in their seats.

A small taxi dropped them in the center of town, and they walked two blocks to the small hotel Stan had chosen from the guidebook. Their suite had a balcony that overlooked the ocean and western sky. After unpacking their luggage and changing their clothes, they walked back to a cluster of stores, rented a mini-jeep, and set out to tour the island.

"There's a tropical rain forest on the north end," he said, pointing to his map, "where a channel cuts the island in two. On this side, there's a turtle pen and a reef where you can go snorkeling. The far southern tip, which is virtually deserted, has a large salt flat and a famous flamingo preserve. And there are beaches everywhere."

"Let's just drive around and see what we like," Vera said. "Then we can come back and explore the town."

It was nearly one in the afternoon and close to ninety degrees. The air was dry, the sky clear, and a warm breeze was blowing from the southeast. They were both in T-shirts, shorts, and running shoes; and Vera had on her sunglasses.

"Climb in," he said. "Let's see if I can get this thing going."

The mini-jeep was bright red, with a canvas roof and tiny wheels. Its sides were open, and the floorboard was covered with sand.

They drove to the forest end of the island. The road cut through a thick glade of tropical plants, large-leafed rubber trees, palms, trees with needle-like fronds, banana trees, and flowering shrubs. Stopping at a high bend, they looked down at the winding channel. Large orange and red boulders marked its course; slender hills, lavishly greened, rose from its banks. Overhead, the sky was a scrim whose pale tint augmented the island's deeper colors.

They drove to the narrow end of the island and stopped at a beach beneath a bluff of sandy hills. Rippling waves purled along the shore. The beach was deserted.

"So peaceful," she said.

"Want to take a swim?" he said. "There's nobody around."

"Sure." She had her bathing suit beneath her shorts. "Are you coming?"

"Of course." He hesitated. "I was thinking of going skinny dipping."

"Go ahead if you want." Then, as he seemed unhappy, she added, "I'm just not up for that, Stan. Not now." She put a hand on his shoulder. "Okay?"

"Sure. I mean, it was just an idea."

"Let's just enjoy the water. It's so hot out. A dip would feel fine."

He started untying his shoes. She headed towards the water, towel in hand. "You got a towel for me, too?" he said.

"There's one in the back."

"Okay." He returned to the jeep and found it, then stripped to his bathing suit and followed her.

Vera was floating on her back, the sea calm and buoyant. "Come on in. It's lovely."

He started in after her. "Cold."

"Not really, once you get in."

He splashed some water on his legs and thighs, then patted his stomach. "Jesus!"

"Don't be a sissy."

He grimaced, then suddenly plunged in, sending up showers of spray, and swam after her. She was still floating on her back, smiling, the sun on her face. When he reached her, he put his arms around her, encircling her back with one and her legs with the other, and pulled her against him. He nuzzled her shoulder, nipping the skin at the upper part of her breast.

"Stan. Don't."

"I love you, that's all."

"I love you, too." She pecked at the corner of his mouth and squeezed his back with her arm.

The beach was dazzlingly white, dotted with large brown rocks and clumps of green and umber seaweed. Small bits of blanched wood lay about, singly and in heaps.

They swam for a while, then clambered out of the water and stretched out on their towels, their faces towards the sun. For some time they were silent. Slowly, the water evaporated from their bodies, leaving a scratchy coating of salt. Stan lit a cigarette and sat up, tossing the match onto the sand. "This is the life, huh?"

"Yes."

"Want one?"

She shook her head.

He exhaled a stream of smoke. "So. Are you happy?"

"I'm okay."

"What were you thinking about?"

"Nothing."

"It must be something. You were quiet a long time."

"Not really." She looked up.

He was staring at her. "What?"

"Well, all right. I was thinking about Josh. Wondering how he's doing with your folks. I hope he's all right."

"I'm sure he's fine. Jesus! You can't even be away from him for a couple of days …"

"Ten."

"All right. Correction. Ten."

"It's a long time. I was just thinking about him going to bed with his 'yallow manket.'"

"I'm sure my mom can handle him."

"I know." She shook her head. "I know."

"Then, what?"

"Nothing."

"Something bothering you?"

"No. Really. No."

"You sure?"

"Yes! I just wish you'd stop deciding what I'm feeling. I'm fine. I was just starting to relax …"

"But wait. I don't understand. How can you relax if you're worrying about Joshua?"

"I didn't say I was *worrying*. I just said I was thinking about how he's doing. And, anyway, you're the one who asked. I was happy in the sun, just thinking about one thing and another, letting my mind drift."

"You said you were thinking about Joshua."

"Well, that, and some other things. I don't remember."

"Okay." He paused. "Look, Vera. I'm sorry"

"Okay."

Vera was thirty, fair-skinned and freckled, with shoulder-length straw-colored hair and hazel eyes. Her lips had tiny sores where she'd bitten them when she was tense. Her bathing suit was a baby blue two-piece affair with a floral print.

Stan was a year older and dark-haired, a bit paunchy in his dark green bathing suit. He finished his cigarette, then twisted the butt in the sand, flopped over on his stomach, and cradled his face in his right arm, eyes closed.

"Don't fall asleep," she said. "You'll get burned."

"I won't. But wake me if I do."

She nodded. He nestled further into the crook of his arm and then was still except for the rhythmic movement of his breathing. She stared at the sky for a while, then sat up and looked at the ocean.

Several clouds had begun to form in the west. A wind was developing. The sea remained calm, gently heaving. The waves made rolling, tumbling sounds as they reached the beach and a sucking sound as they receded.

Stan had fallen asleep. Vera took a Winston out of his pack and lit it, then stretched her legs and began piling sand over them. The tip of her tongue jutted out from the corner of her mouth, signaling her concentration.

When he awoke, her legs were completely buried. A cloud was crossing in front of the sun, and it had suddenly gotten cooler. "Hey," he said. "What's happening?"

"The wind's been blowing in for about ten minutes."

"I guess the weather changes fast around here." He stood up, brushing the sand from his legs and stomach. "Hey, look." He pointed to a group of dark clouds moving rapidly towards them. "That's not just your run-of-the-mill clouds ..."

"Is it a storm?"

"I hope it's nothing serious."

"Look." She pointed. "You can see little sheets of rain beneath the clouds."

"You can see the whole damn horizon. Jesus! And there's one area the clouds are coming from ..."

"A tropical storm?"

"More like old-fashioned rain, I'd say."

"Is it coming this way?"

"I think so. Maybe it will just miss us."

They watched the storm approach. To their right the sky grew dark purple, then almost black. The clouds thickened and clumped together. Sheets of dark grey mist trailed from the bottom of the cloud bank, moving closer. The wind turned chill. It blew sand against their arms and sides and kicked up brush along the beach.

"Cold?" he said.

"Yes."

They pulled their towels tightly around their shoulders and he pressed her to him. The clouds moved closer, drifting in front of the sun and blotting it out.

"The sky's still blue over there," he said.

"And the sun's shining on the water." She snuggled against him, shivering. As she moved, small cracks appeared in the sand covering her legs.

The storm swung closer. A strong breeze rose to their right, bending the palm trees and spinning sand about. It blew their socks off the blanket and rolled them on the beach like tumbleweeds.

"Here it comes," she said. "You can smell the rain."

Suddenly, the cold, grey sheets enveloped them. Wind lashed them, then moved past; great globs of rain splattered down. The heavy drops turned finer, then became a steady stinging spray. They were completely drenched, wind-whipped, sodden.

"Oh, Jesus!" he shouted. "I don't know whether to hide or jump up and dance."

"It's cold!" Vera cried, kicking free from the wet sand and throwing her arms around his shoulders.

They huddled together. The rain fell torrentially. Then, as suddenly as it had come, the storm passed. The last grey clouds soared overhead. The rain slowed, then stopped; there was a little sprinkle, then it stopped again. The line of mist moved away, needling the ocean. The sun re-emerged, beaming down on them.

"I've got goosebumps," Stan said. He craned around. "I wonder if there's a rainbow."

"I don't see one."

"No. Me either."

They let the sun dry them off. Then she took another swim

and lay on her towel while he had another cigarette. "It must be late."

"True. Hungry?"

She nodded. They gathered up their wet shoes and towels, walked to the jeep, and drove back to the hotel.

Later that afternoon they sat in reclining chairs on the balcony of their hotel room, watching the sunset. The porch had a clear view of the beach and the sea. He had bought a bottle of rum, and they were drinking it with Coke out of a can.

"So peaceful here," she said.

"I know. We should have done this before."

"But we haven't had the time, the money ..."

"But it's so *nice*. Compared to the rat-race in New York. God! We ought to borrow a thousand bucks every year, book a flight, and come on down, just for our sanity."

"Do you really think so?"

"Yes. We get so drained by running around the city all the time. Me still in training, you taking those courses and managing Josh. It's not easy. Maybe that's why we've been sniping at each other a bit."

The sun was a brilliant orange disc hovering above the ocean, just off the horizon in a cloudless sky. The air was warm and balmy. Cooking smells drifted up from the kitchen below: cinnamon, onions, and garlic.

"Deep down, we still love each other," he said.

"You really think so?"

"Of course."

They were silent. "So ..." She paused. "You still want to work it out?"

"Of course."

She looked away, tears forming.

"What is it? Tell me."

She shook her head. "Nothing."

"How can it be nothing?"

Suddenly she was laughing and crying at the same time. "I don't know. It just is. Maybe I'm just tired. Maybe it's hormones."

"We haven't gotten much sleep." She nodded, sniffling. "I mean, but here we are on our *vacation*, finally. We ought to be able to have a good time."

"I'm *having* a good time," she said.

"It's a beautiful sunset."

"I know."

"What more could we ask for?"

"Nothing. I've got everything I need right now." She sniffled again. "You got a Kleenex?"

"There's a towel."

She pulled the towel from the back of her chair and wiped her eyes and nose. "It's just, sometimes I wonder if there's any foundation left in our relationship. Sometimes I worry we've used it all up and there's nothing *there* anymore." Her voice cracked. "Like we haven't taken good care of it, and there's nothing left to fall back on."

"Vera, the bedrock is there. Really. We just need to take the time ..."

"You still feel that?"

He nodded.

"I hope you're right."

It was quiet. She drained her rum and Coke, and he refilled her glass. "The sun's so beautiful," she said. He sipped his drink, lit a cigarette, rocked in his chair.

"I had this horrible dream, Stan, just before we left. I dreamed we were living in this huge house. It was too big, not comfy at all. And you were gone, I don't know where, but I was alone in the house, just me and Joshua. And suddenly I realized there was a fire somewhere. I smelled smoke, but I didn't know where it was coming from. I ran upstairs and then back down. Then I ran down to the basement, and the whole cellar was on fire. I didn't know if I'd be able to get out. Then Josh started crying, and I grabbed him and headed for the door. I was really frightened. We made it through the door and ran across the lawn to a grove of trees, and we sat on the ground there, watching the house burn down, which it did, completely, down to nothing."

"That's awful," he said, refilling his drink. "God."

"I know." She was quiet. "What do you think it means?"

"I don't know." He shook his head. "But it sounds upsetting."

"Yes," she said. "It was."

He took a deep breath. "Vera. Look. The sun's dipping into the ocean."

She looked, then sighed. "Feels like we're at the end of the world ... like the water doesn't end. It just joins the sky somewhere. And the island's just this tiny dot in the ocean. You feel how helpless we are."

He was silent. Then: "They say that if you look at the sunset, you can sometimes see this uncanny green light flashing across the whole sky, almost like magic, just when the sun goes under."

They sipped their drinks and watched the sun set until the glimmering orange ring had slipped completely beneath the sea.

"Did you see it?" he asked.

"No."

"Neither did I."

After dinner at a Cuban-Chinese restaurant, they strolled around the small town center, peering into shop windows. Stan bought a local newspaper. "This will tell us what's going on," he said.

"I'm tired," she said. "I'd like to go to bed early."

"Sure. I know we didn't get enough sleep in Curacao."

"Not with that guy wheezing and coughing all night. What was his name? Mr. Nickerson?"

"Nachmansohn."

"Anyway." She gestured. "That's what we get for choosing a rooming house instead of a hotel."

"It looked interesting."

They walked hand-in-hand back to their hotel. The sky was almost completely dark. An ovoid moon, part-way up the eastern sky, illuminated a few low-lying clouds. A sultry breeze was blowing in off the water. They entered the lobby and nodded at the night clerk, then walked up the stairs to their room. Stan unlocked the door and let them in.

They put down their bags. Vera took a shower and brushed her teeth, then put on her pale pink nightgown. She sat brushing her hair by the window for a long time before going to bed. Stan was there already.

"That flamingo flat here is supposed to be the largest in the whole western hemisphere," he said.

"Let's see it tomorrow, then."

"Fine. We can also go by the turtle farm if you want. Or take a swim. Or just sit around and read."

"I'd like to send some postcards. I haven't sent any to Aunt Mabel or my sister."

"You'll be back before the postcards get there."

"I don't care. It's the idea …"

"I know. Well, anyway, it's up to you."

She slid into bed beside him and turned out the light. "I'm bushed."

He lay there motionless, waiting. She turned towards him, moving her leg so that it touched him. He pressed closer and put his arm around her shoulder. She nestled against him, her mouth against his shoulder, her arm around his neck. He rolled over and placed his right leg across her thighs. Neither of them moved.

"So, you still love me?" she said.

"Mmm-hmm."

She sighed. "I'm not invincible, Stan. Not made of bronze."

"What?"

"I can be hurt, you know."

"What are you talking about?"

"You say things that hurt me sometimes. You put me down in front of my friends. Like what you said in front of Rita."

"Rita's a fool."

"She's my friend."

"I'm just kidding."

"You put me down in front of my friend. That's not right."

"I'm sorry." He began brushing his leg up and down across her legs, then moved his hand under her nightgown and started stroking the small of her back.

"I don't mean to be difficult. But I need you to respect what I say, what I feel …"

"I do …"

"Let me finish …"

He rolled away and pulled his leg back to his side of the bed.

"I know the things you do are important. But my work is important, too. I don't mean to threaten you …"

"I'm not threatened."

"I just want you to understand. You can be so critical …"

"I've been trying *not* to be critical."

"But …"

"Vera, what are you talking about, specifically?" He shoved his arm beneath his pillow. "I mean, this is our goddamn vacation, and you're starting the same thing all over again."

"We've got to discuss it sometime. I can't just roll over and make love. I have to feel right. And right now, I don't. Yes, things are bothering me."

"Like what?"

"Like how you act around my friends. Like at Jim and Rhonda's. Okay, so Jim's just a file clerk. He's not an intellectual or a lawyer or a doctor. But he works with me, and I like him. He's easy-going and natural. And I like Rhonda, too."

"Rhonda," he said, scornfully.

"That's what I mean. You don't have to like her. But you should act decent because she's my friend."

He sighed heavily.

"How many times have I had *your* friends over, cooked them dinner, gone out for drinks. I don't complain."

"My friends are …"

"Your friends are your friends, that's all. You see them in the hospital, and you like to hang out with them. That's how I feel about Jim and Rhonda."

"But Rhonda's such an empty …"

"She's a good person, Stan. Rhonda's been through a lot, and if you took the time to talk to her, you'd realize it."

"I don't think I'd ever like her."

"All right. So you'd never like her. But I do, and I didn't like your being nasty to her. You were putting them both down all night long."

"They didn't know it."

"I think they felt it. And even if they didn't, why would you *do* it? Why would you be mean to them? Does it make you feel like a better person?"

"No," he said.

"Then I wish you'd stop it. It's not like you. You used to be kinder …"

He was quiet for a few minutes. Then: "Okay. Maybe you're right."

"All right." She put her arm out towards him. They lay together, tentative, each facing a different direction, but breathing in synch.

"Vera," he said, moving closer, cupping his body against hers. She made a small, whimpering sound. "Vera. Are you crying?"

"No."

"I do love you."

She turned towards him, reaching out once again. They kissed. He ran his hands over her body, pressing her buttocks, her ribs, her breasts.

"Stan." She drew him closer, pressing his head against her

chest. He sighed, murmured, kissed her neck and breasts. He put his arms around her and entered her. The bedsprings sounded like crows.

"Do you think anyone can hear?"

"No."

They awoke to another clear day. Sunlight streamed through the front window, but the air was cooler. They dressed without talking. He picked up his paper from the day before. "So, you want to see the flamingoes?"

"Sure."

They ate their breakfast downstairs in a little cubby area— fresh papaya, pineapple, coffee, and rolls—then walked out to the jeep.

"The map's still on the seat."

They drove along the only highway, past the edge of town. The air was still and clear, the ocean quiet. A few fishing boats moved out to sea, leaving ripples in their wake. The white sand intensified the sunlight.

"It's like the French Riviera," he said. "The light, the colors. I could forget about everything and stay here forever."

"Could you?"

"Yes. I get tired of the rat race sometimes. The same hassles. I'm sure that's why I've been nasty …"

"I'm glad to hear you say that."

"Maybe people weren't made for such complexity."

"Maybe not."

The sun caught him in the eyes. "Damn! I knew I should have bought some sunglasses!"

They passed an area of empty wooden shacks and a large abandoned house. Wooden planks lay in the sand, broken and blanched, their paint peeling like sunburned skin. There was a small lighthouse, a cluster of poor homes, then more beach.

He lit up a cigarette. "Our last day," he said. "We'll get some sleep tonight. Tomorrow morning we'll have to leave early."

The far end of the island stretched out before them, flat and very white. The shoreline curved slowly, cutting left and then right again. In the distance, the air shimmered. There was a bright glistening area far ahead which trembled with a pinkish tinge.

"That's it," he said. "The flamingo flats."

They drove closer. The shimmering intensified. Off to their left was a broad salt flat, covered by a thin skim of water, in which appeared thousands of pink dots.

"There they are," she breathed. "Oh, Stan. Look!"

"There's a million of them."

"Can we get close?"

He drove further. The pink dots took shape, lengthening into tall pink birds. They stood in lines, in groups: wading about, dipping their beaks in the water, preening.

"They're beautiful."

"You'll never see so many again. I heard they were on the decline. They might even be extinct in a couple years."

They parked the jeep, got out, and began walking toward the birds. There was a gentle sound, like the rustling of bones.

"Do they talk?"

"They don't talk, but they do make sounds to communicate. Like cranes, I think."

The birds nearest them moved away quickly, beating their wings.

"I don't think they'll let us come too close."

Now they were on the edge of the marshy flat. The birds stood at a distance, only one or two bothering to look at them. She looked down. "Stan, what are these? Eggs?"

He bent down. Oval objects the size of mangoes lay scattered in front of them. "Looks like it."

"Are they going to hatch?"

"I don't know. A lot of them probably won't. You've got a lot of duds in nature. For every one that hatches I think there are two or three that don't."

"Really?"

"I think so." He reached down and touched one of the eggs. "It's warm, but you can't tell if that's from being sat on or from the sun."

"Maybe it's the sun that hatches them anyway."

"Maybe so." He picked the egg up in his fingers. "It's heavy, you know."

"I guess it would have to be."

"I wonder if it's a dud."

"Stan ..."

"What?"

"Leave it alone. Why not put it back?"

"I'm just curious ..."

"We don't need it. It belongs to some bird."

"But we can be curious, can't we."

"I don't like it."

He balanced the egg in his palm. "Vera, I'm not going to *hurt* anything."

"Then put it back."

"I want to see what's inside it."

"It's just an egg."

He looked to either side, then placed the egg back on the ground and picked up a small rock.

"Stan. Don't."

Squatting down, he began tapping the shell with the rock. A piece of the shell broke off. Then another. "It's tough," he said. "Not like a chicken's egg. And there's this membrane ..."

The egg cracked open. Thick yellow juice spilled out, oozing onto the thin skim of salt water and sinking down to the sand beneath. There were bits of blood, strings of red tangled in clots of yellow and white stuff. Inside the egg, a miniature flamingo lay curled into a ball, its beak and features perfectly formed, its feathers glistening wet.

"Stan!"

"What?"

"Look at what you've done."

He looked up. "I didn't know it was alive. How was I supposed to know it was alive?"

"Stan. It's a little *bird*." She stood up and ran away, heading back across the sandy flat towards the jeep.

He dropped the egg, then ran after her. "Vera!"

When he reached her, she was sitting on the sand near the jeep, her back to him, the sun harsh against her neck. She was hunched into a ball, elbows resting on her knees, head tilted forward, her face cupped in her hands, and she was crying.

On Being On

Once again, I am on. It's my duty, and I accept it. Every third day I assume my post for twenty-four hours. I must be within reach of the telephone's clang, ready for the operator's nasal voice and primitive laughter. I must carry the sound box with me at all times. It's my duty to be available.

I am on. Enclosed now in my narrow call room cubicle, I feel helpless. I am at their mercy. If the plasto-electric signal on my sound box buzzes, I must reach for the phone and dial 111. The operator will answer and direct me to my task. For twenty-four hours straight, I must do what they say.

The operator dials my number or makes my sound box buzz whenever she chooses. Sometimes she calls me for the fun of it, just to make me squirm, wake me, or interrupt my train of thought. She seems to know whenever I have something to do. Just when I begin to dictate one of my summary notes, she'll interrupt me. Just when I decide to take a walk, she'll make the sound box buzz.

Sometimes, when I answer, she laughs and recites nursery rhymes, or she says she's sorry, she actually wanted someone else and dialed my number by mistake. But the damage is done. I know she's done it on purpose.

I cannot rest. She seems to know every move I make. If I reach for a volume from the rickety wooden bookshelf or try to find a moment's peace staring at the matrix of cracks and peeling paint on my ceiling, she knows it and interrupts. If I move towards the porcelain toilet bowl, wishing to relieve myself, she rings my bell. I cannot count on being left alone for a minute, I'm her prisoner.

They've furnished my call room in poor taste. The bed sags. The sheets haven't been changed in a week. The yellow spot I saw six days ago, midway across the bed at waist level, is still there. The blanket is thin and doesn't keep me warm on cold nights. The desk rocks from side to side whenever I lean on it. The overhead light is dim, and the tantalizingly shiny desk light has never worked. The chair is hard and uncomfortable. The dresser drawers are so crammed with other people's things, there's no room for my own. They've left a standard set of reference books on one wooden bookshelf—The Merck Manual, pharmacopeia, propaganda leaflets, cardiac arrest protocol, military annals, emergency room statistics. I know I'll be quizzed on these next June.

Now, as I knew it would, the phone rings, startling me from my thoughts. No: startling is too soft a word. I am jammed, jangled, uprooted, knifed in the heart. My temples throb. My blood pressure rises. My face gets red. My stomach tightens, and I feel like throwing up. The doctors have said this is a simple stress response. Fight or flight. Something like that. But I don't care. They say I should learn to relax: meditate, hum to myself, block out the shock. But I can't. Let them preach to themselves.

They've said this is an apprenticeship, but I don't believe it. I know it's a torture. I'm being punished for something I did, but they won't tell me what it is. They talk double-talk. When they say how things will be for my benefit, I understand it means how things will be for their benefit. I'm nobody's fool in this. If I have to put in my time, I'll do it, but I don't have to believe the lies they tell me.

My duties aren't clearly defined. I'm simply on call. If anything in this gigantic complex goes wrong, I'm called to deal with it. At once. They judge me on how quickly I can get to the problem. If I don't show up within ten minutes, I get a pay cut for that day. If I miss a call entirely, I lose the entire day's pay. It's not a good contract from my point of view.

But I've been a good worker. I've always been on time. I've

gone to their staff meetings and heard them insist that the public's safety and well-being depend on our response, and I've pointed to my own record and to the three decorations I've received. I've saved lives, I'm sure of it. Once with a man who was vomiting blood. Twice with heart attacks. I can be relied on to make the right decision.

They say our work is a serious matter. Our hospital complex is a vital cog in the community's welfare. That's why, for twenty-four hours, I'm not allowed to stray from the buzz of my sound box. I have to carry it clipped to my belt or dangling from my collar.

The official bathroom is down the hall, smelling of stale cigars, sweat, and cleaning powder. I know the daytime staff abuses it. Its water is rusty. Its toilet flushes so vigorously, I always count on being sprayed by the ricochet. The paper towels and toilet tissue are substandard. An attendant is supposed to look after this, to replace what's run out, fix what's broken, mop up what's messy, but he doesn't. He doesn't care. He does as little as he can get away with, and they don't police him the way they police me. His post is a sinecure. He's been on the city payroll for years. He knows people. He'll have his post long after I've been discharged. No, the attendant doesn't have to be concerned. His twenty-nine seniority credits make him invincible. If I were to complain, of course, I'd be fined for insubordination and given a lecture on tact. It would be foolish for me to challenge the system. The rules must be obeyed. I do what I must do. I'm on every third day. If there's a problem, I must deal with it.

Sometimes I think of peeing in my sink instead of going to the bathroom down the hall. Its smooth enamel surface is less than waist high. Standing on tiptoe, my trousers unzipped, I can dangle my organ into its clean white hollow. When I feel daring, I actually go through with it, letting my hot yellow stream splash along the smooth white surface. Of course, I'm careful to wash away any telltale drops. The real trick is to pee in the central hole, so that nothing lands on the bowl. I'm always hesitant to do it because I know the sound box will buzz before I finish.

Sometimes I grimace in the mirror. If they only knew....

But of course, they do know. They tolerate me, tolerate my idiosyncrasies. I'm sure they do this because, in spite of everything, I've been a good worker. They need me. I'm the only one who works faithfully every third day. I take no sick days, no holidays, make no excuses. For all my worrisome, rebellious tendencies, I'm the most dependable one they've got.

My room is separated from the rest of the complex. They've provided an on-call lounge nearby and supplied it with a visual-connector. But I rarely watch it. I've seen all their programs. More than once. I prefer to sit in my room and peruse the books on the rickety bookshelf, finger the medicines in the emergency kit, lean on the green blotter on my desk, read the inscriptions my predecessors and comrades have inked on it.

Still, the phone's shrill ring and the sound box's abrupt buzz frighten me. I always jump when they sound.

They call me for various repairs. A lettkenat has broken on 18-R-3. A Myrill key is jammed on 66-P-1. The IV has run dry on 46-Y-2. The patient on 78-F-6 needs a bedpan. I hurry to the designated location, evaluate the degree of distress, flip open my ever-ready repair kit, take out what I need: medicines, electronic tools, needles, sedatives, plastic couplings.

When the supervisor on 39-S-1 has an upset stomach, I'm summoned to treat it. I'm summoned to find the correct antidote, the right remedy, in my medical tray. I have to examine his stool and palpate his abdomen, take his blood pressure, count his breaths and heartbeats, check for fever, and then dispense the correct pack of chewable white tablets with the proper instructions.

If the night aide on 28-C-2 has forgotten her password, I must go to the dentition-identification center, find her nose- and fingerprints, check the X-rays of her teeth, tabulate her identogram from the vibratory pattern of her voice. "Check it out," as the manual says. Then I can give the password to her. They'll place the aide on the lecture list for next week, for forgetting. She'll have to pay.

I'm called to 44-K-3 to witness a routine photo-interrogation. A secretary on 20-N-2 pages me to check her addition. The Emergency Room needs another unit of blood typed and cross-matched, and I have to draw 500cc from my own arm to meet the deadline. I must wind the clocks on the different floors, or they'll all run down.

Being on is like Chinese water torture. At every instant, I'm in suspense, wondering if the next moment will bring an interruption.

I count the hours to mealtime. As soon as the cafeteria staff open the door, I rush down the corridors from my call room (running is forbidden) and join the line of employees picking up their trays. I look for the most palatable food available. They pay for my meals. I eat, almost always alone, at a corner table. The electro-announcer, its voice emerging from the network of loudspeakers on the dining room walls, calls out the numbers on page: "3297-J. 3297-J. Report to 13-C-2. 1382-B. 1382-B. Contact 79-R-4." The announcer's voice is harsh and metallic. The speakers are so loud they make the walls shake. It's impossible to think during a meal, and talking is forbidden. Nonetheless, I can at least eat. And eat and eat. Even so, each page which begins with my own number, 8-, makes me cringe, and my stomach goes into spasms. I'm sure they know that I'm eating, and they deliberately create counterfeit 8- calls.

Everyone has to wear a uniform. Mine is bright green with black sleeves. I also have a green and black striped helmet. My badge is pinned to my shirt. My number is stamped on both the helmet and the shirt, but not on my pants. My pants are too large, and they droop. The laundry service is slow, and I've often had to steal pants from a drawer filled with other people's clothes. It's not funny, though. If I were caught stealing, I'd have to forfeit my pay for a week and lose one quarter of a seniority point. And then they'd force me to attend six weeks of lectures on stealing.

After being on for twelve hours, I feel like a machine. But I don't complain. I don't scheme. I simply stop thinking. I go on "automatic." I move from bed to toilet to dining room to 44-TR-3 to call room to pee hole to 67-N-2 to the Intensive Care Unit: from task to task. I lie down exhausted, knowing they'll call me. Then they call. I can never sleep. I have waking dreams of being chased, of being ripped with animals' claws, of floating. My brain turns into cotton and my mouth dries out. I behave as I've been trained to do: automatically.

Even when I'm done, I must still work a ten-hour day. Even after the twenty-four-hour shift, I have to put in another ten before I can sleep. Every fifteenth day I get a weekend free, but it's not enough. I can never get caught up.

All in all, they say, it's a good job. Seniority points are easy to come by, and the pay is good in comparison with others on call elsewhere. The complex pays for food and uniforms. Every year I can take a two-week vacation.

After eighteen hours, I feel as if I'm outside myself. The phone or sound box invokes a paroxysm of palpitations and flushing. I start peeing every ten minutes. My back sweats. My face gets greasy. I become obsessed with the urge to sleep, with a shapeless anger, a sense of helplessness. I have impulses to destroy my bookcase, smash my mirror, defecate in my bed. With great effort, now as in the past, I can control myself.

I see faces on the wall, hear voices from my past. And I enjoy them. When I'm called, I still respond efficiently. Even if I walk with a glassy stare. The others seem jealous of my skill and position.

I'm flooded with sexual feelings. I see one woman every other Sunday for four hours, and another, one Wednesday a month. They work hard, too, it seems. Sometimes I have the sense that one of them may be the telephone operator who provokes me with wrong numbers. Perhaps she's only teasing.

I fantasize, but the phone interrupts before I can get going.

It's my duty, being on. I get paid for it. It's my livelihood. They've said I may soon qualify for a promotion to a supervisory rank, proof of my excellent efforts. But I don't believe them. I don't believe it will happen. I know they'll probably keep me at this job forever. Why would they switch me and then have to train someone else?

I hate the ring of the phone, the buzz of the sound box, the oppressive, tasteless food, and the metallic-voiced speaker. In spite of it all, I endure the days and nights. I maintain control. I follow my pattern, doing what I'm trained to do. They stimulate me: I respond. I've been well schooled, and I'm ready. My lips automatically stretch into the requisite smile. I am on. I do my duty. Every third day, I enclose myself in my call room and hold the sound box to my ear, waiting for it to buzz. It becomes more and more simple. I am on.

The Schedule

ugh

You know, it's not really fair. Look at yourself. You work as hard and as diligently as any of them. You observe the proper rituals. You smile at your superiors and praise their ideas. Whatever is laid on your desk, you complete quickly and accurately. Your skills are unquestioned. Why then have you been consigned to a second-rate desk? Why mired in a second-rate position? Why is it your superiors never return your smiles?

I am quite serious. You are as qualified as the others, if not more so. Yet there can be no doubt about it, you have failed to receive the rewards that they gather in right and left: the medals, the promotions, the honorary scrolls, the vacation trips, the parties, the gold watches.... I can see that it must gall you.

No, please don't deny what must be true. I can see that it must gall you. It must. Let us leave it at that.

You must be livid at times with indignation: bubbling over. Yet you do not show it.

You have your own ambitions, your own plans. You have not resigned yourself to such treatment forever.

I have heard about your Schedule.

You seem surprised. It may be a secret from the others, from your superiors; but I have heard about it. Quite ambitious. Rigorous, one might say. And yet you have followed it faithfully. Every day. Amazing.

Please don't be bashful about it. Don't pretend to be bashful. I know on good authority that deep down you are proud of it. Quite proud. You grit your teeth when you think about it. You clench your fists. Your heart pounds faster in your chest. You imagine your power. Oh yes. I have heard about your Schedule.

What? Whose side am *I* on? Well, of course, I agree with *you*. Is there any doubt that you have received a raw deal? The whole affair is shameless. Certainly. If I were in control, let me assure you, I would change things.

Ah, no. You have misunderstood me. I myself have no power.

No. Not even the desire for power: I am not like you.

You have *potential* power. And you know it. No: look here, you must be honest about these things. At least with me. What is your entire Schedule about, if not the assumption of power?

The Schedule is magnificent. Each detail has been analyzed, dissected, understood. Each moment has its purpose. No effort is wasted. Even as your superiors look the other way and nod blankly, your position is being strengthened. What irony that they think you are at an impasse, when in fact you are closer than ever to your goal.

But you have planned it this way.

Each morning you wake up early, when it is still dark outside. You wash quickly and set the coffee on to perk. You dress in your studying clothes. Your breakfast is simple: a cup of black coffee, a piece of fruit, some toast. Then you move to your desk. You turn on the light. Your books are already in place.

First you read your three pages of dictionary, which sharpens your logic. Then you read the pages of your encyclopedia and note down ideas and quotations in the blue-backed notebooks you have bought for this purpose. When this is complete, you are ready for another half-cup of black coffee: your mind is awake.

You follow the encyclopedia with the requisite portions of the Texts. Goaded on by the wisdom of your Brothers, you are able to sift ideas and mold new thoughts.

All this takes exactly an hour and a half. If you begin at 4:30, it ends at 6:00. The majesty of the Schedule is in its blanketing every waking minute: nothing is overlooked; nothing is excused.

It is a blade which pares existence to the bone.

You continue. You move your bowels, ridding yourself of the residua of the past. You exercise, straining each muscle to its limit and sweating like an animal. You rub your body with oil so that it glistens.

Then you take your long black velvet robe from its special place in the closet and put it on.

It will now be past 6:40. The morning will be going well. Wearing your official robe, you can begin your official tasks. You sit down again at your desk and take out your writing paper from the third drawer on your left. Your pen and pencils are by your right hand. You draft, first in pencil and then in elegant dark blue ink, letters to your correspondents, speeches you will some day be called upon to give. You map out strategies.

When this is finished, you take off your official robe and hang it back in its special place in your closet. The day progresses to more prosaic concerns: the morning newspaper; preparation for your job.

You get dressed in your working clothes and walk outside, down the stairs, out the front door, a block and a half from your lodging. The news dealer knows you. He hands you the morning paper as you hand him your dime; you tuck the paper under your right arm; you wave goodbye to the news dealer and retrace your steps back home. Quickly, you scan the morning news. Then, more carefully, you search the entire paper page by page for any article of significance.

Before you leave your lodging again, you straighten your desk. All the papers go in their places. The folders are replaced in your files. The books go back on their shelves. You leave no clues of your activity.

Then, your morning is ended. You surrender yourself to your job: to the second-rate desk and the second-rate position and the second-rate bored glances of your superiors.

You leave your lodging again, down the stairs, out the front door, and wait in the cool morning air on the corner for your bus.

When it arrives you climb aboard and pay your fare. You move to the rear of the bus where there is always an empty seat.

You reach the job two minutes before the hour. You go to your desk and sit down. The swivel chair will overturn if you lean too far back. Your desk, equipped with blotter, pens, ink, eraser, tally sheets, slide rule, and white office stationery pads, is made of old walnut. It is chipped in many spots. Its drawers are large and heavy. On your left, just before your copy of the Company Style Manual, stand the IN and OUT baskets. Your work piles up in front of you.

Your desk is the last on the aisle, in a dim corner away from the window. The next time you are promoted, they say, you will be moved over by the window.

There is an alcove to your right, set off from the rest of the office by a little wooden gate. A secretary sits there, at the end of a thick blue carpet. Her desk always has a vase of flowers on it. Beyond her, hidden from view by a set of sliding doors, the superiors sit in their plush offices. The secretary keeps everyone away.

When the superiors want you, they ring for the secretary on the special inter-office phone. She gets up from her desk and walks back to the sliding doors. They open, and she disappears inside. Soon afterwards, she walks out, her feet mincing a straight line, and steps out onto the blue carpet which leads to the gate. She opens the gate. Entering the main office area, she rings a small bell which hangs on the wall; everyone turns around. The secretary announces in her flat, nasal voice that the superiors want you; and then you step in front of the secretary and walk past the wooden gate, onto the thick blue carpet, past the secretary's desk, to the sliding doors which open as you approach. It is up to you to enter the superiors' home territory. They are, after all, the superiors, and it is their privilege.

On rare occasions, the superiors appear in the main office among the staff. They laugh and tell jokes and slap people on the back, all the time bending over their shoulders to check the accuracy of their computations. They extol the best workers and urge everyone to imitate them. Ah, but it doesn't fool you, that big act. You are not impressed.

No. I did not mean to imply that you might be fooled by them. You have misunderstood me. Really, you are too quick to take offence.

Your time is valuable. You do not waste it, do not gossip with the others. How can you interest yourself in their chatter of women or cars or sports or beers, when every day they treat you like a hired hand? They treat you like a servant, your fellow workers.

You detest them. One day they will learn.

You devote all spare time to thinking about the Five Main Points of the Schedule.

You spend your lunch hour outside, watching the others pass by. Your meal is sparse: some vegetables, some clear soup; perhaps some cheese. On a rare day you recognize a friend and exchange a few words with him. You walk through the working area downtown. This will be your stronghold, someday. Your head throbs.

Afterwards, you return to your job. The afternoon passes like the morning: the petty tasks, the others' bemused glances, the superiors' nods, the dimness of your corner.

At five o'clock you leave, tucking the stray papers into place before you do. A neat desk impresses your superiors. You walk outside and return to your lodging, avoiding the others.

You are again your own master. The evening begins. You cook dinner: a chop, some salad greens. While the chop heats, you review the Schedule and calculate your progress.

Most of the evenings, you study. You plan.

Every day, every night, the Schedule is a little closer to completion. The time for action approaches. The superiors and the others have no idea what is about to happen.

Ah yes, it is a dangerous game you play. You understand that quite well. Yet, you play it well. It is quite clear that you are someone to be reckoned with.

You seem surprised how much I know about you. You are flattered. And you are afraid. Please believe me, I could not think of revealing your plans to your superiors; or worse, to the others. I would not jeopardize your position. You should trust me.

You are still wary.

Ah, you are not leaving now! Of course, I know the moments are precious to you. But we were having a nice chat. I find it admirable, you know, how you continue to concentrate, even when you must be exhausted. But then, you have a goal.

You want to dominate.

You do not want acceptance from the others. You plan to set terms for *their* acceptance.

You maneuver. First, you make yourself indispensable. You become secure in your second-rate post. Then, while the superiors revel and dissipate their power, you watch them. You learn their weaknesses: their belief in their invulnerability. You make notes. You can allow them their fun, even if you are excluded.

Oh yes, they will speak to you: about business. They will ask your advice: about money. But they will not confide in you. They will not invite you out for a beer. They will not trust you.

They prefer to tell their tawdry tales to each other. You are not privy to their inner circle. Their misfortunes and their happinesses are concealed from you. You are not honored to receive them.

And what would they tell you, if they spoke? What exciting tales would they spin? What delicious experiences? Their mistress is sick and their fun is curtailed. They had a simply lovely time at the opera. They are considering a divorce. Their kids are doing poorly in school. Their daughter is pregnant. They have no money. The market is uncertain but X___ is a good buy at 33 ¼. R___ will have a party this week, and H___ will be drunk.

Their confidences would bore you.

You are glad that they avoid you. But you are jealous that it is their choice, not yours. You envy their secrecy.

Ah, but you have your own secrets. Better than their tales of domestic intrigue.

The Schedule.

What can you expect? They are different. Totally different. They have never had to struggle the way you have. It has been easy for them. How then could they comprehend the obstacles you have overcome, the impediments? Their lives have been easy and simple: linear. They have never suffered.

Not like you. Oh yes, perhaps a father has died; or a promotion has been long in coming; or they have had poor digestion for years; or their wives do not love them. But this is not the kind of suffering you mean.

Yours is a deep, rancid suffering. It is a suffering with every step. You have had to remake yourself every day, have had to reorganize the chaos of your life every day, have had to surmount the barriers every day. Your life is rooted in suffering like a tuber in the earth. You grow on it.

No one knows your past.

Look. Even now, at my merely mentioning it, you turn away, your face blanching, your jaws tightening. Your past. How could any of them understand?

Your childhood: poverty and filth. Your parents: ineffective monoliths; the man eager to smash you down to his own level, the woman weary and weak, religious. What could they do for you?

You have had to do it all yourself.

The humiliation, the mocking, the epithets: you have endured them all. The past does not imprison you.

You cannot even remember your siblings. And it would serve no purpose if you could. You could construct them now out of cardboard as easily as out of memory. You could make them up, and the reconstructions would be accurate. See: A tall youth with glasses and close-cropped hair, stuttering, his arms dangling at his sides, who disappeared when you were six; and that would be a brother. A short girl, fat, with a greasy face and pimples, stupid, who fornicated with the neighborhood boys on the coal pile in the cellar; and that would be a sister. A skinny girl chewing gum, her long fingers stuck in her mouth, humming; and that would be a sister, too. A helpless child with bulging eyes who could not walk, who drooled all the time, who was thrown down the stairs one day at an early age, who died; and that would be a brother. It does not matter. How could it matter? You cannot even remember your siblings.

It is no wonder your face no longer shows fear or sadness, no longer smiles. You have adopted the perfect mask. You have become rigid and automatic. Your face conceals your plotting.

Your years of adolescence are forgotten. It is for the best. The turmoil, the continual striving to pierce the web, the repetitive disappointments, the taunts and pummelings, the superiors' early rebuke.

You had to learn to play the game first.

Well: you have learned.

Even then you had your goals. But now they are within your reach.

The great danger is that one of the others will find out, that your plans will be undermined before they can succeed. You are understandably cautious. If anyone knew, you would lose your second-rate post, you would be denounced. They might even choose to make a lesson of you. It would be the end.

That is why you always lock your files before you leave your home. That is why there is nothing extraordinary in your desk at work. You do nothing to arouse suspicion.

You are wary of being watched in the street. Yet you are able to tell if you are in jeopardy. The Voices will warn you.

You will not become what your family has become: living from day to day, living and barely living; scraping and bowing; accepting; cringing and apologizing when someone else steps on their feet.

They are thankful that they have not starved to death, that they are allowed to live quietly in a single room with the tattered sofa, the peeling paint, the putrid odor.

They feel much progress has been made.

Yet you have scribbled in the margin of your Texts: "Progress is illusory. We are falling behind. Only the Schedule brings hope."

You will not bow before the present gods. Their legs are weak. Their legs are hollow.

You anticipate your power.

The tinseled gods fall to the ground, their heads cracked apart. All places of refuge and sanctuary are disrupted: banks, churches, country estates. All crumbles. You pre-empt the profits for yourself. Chaos fills the streets. Death is everywhere. You stamp your feet in the blood which fills the gutters. You laugh.

The liberated crowds march under your banner. Your picture is on every corner.

You make the laws.

You punish the wrong-doers.

The others fall before you on their knees, begging for mercy. The old executioners, unmasked, tremble. The torture experts writhe. The simoniacs, the grafters, the nepotists: all collapse. The old system ends.

You are the king.

You are the uncompromising sword; you are the cleansing fire. You are the king.

Your system begins a new era. All is remade. But first, you take revenge. You scourge.

Please, I insist: don't pretend to know nothing about this. I know. I know your secrets and your goals. Please be honest enough to wipe that incredulous grimace from your face. I know. It is simple. I know the goals of the Schedule.

What else could justify the years of suffering, the years of preparation? What else could keep you going from day to day? Ah, no. Please do not grimace like a clown in a minstrel show. I know.

My source of information? That's *my* secret.

Yes. But I assure you. You are not threatened. Who would I tell? Who would believe me? And besides, I am on your side. I have nothing to gain by betraying you.

You are quite correct. I am not one of your Brothers; nor do I claim to be. My identity is, after all, irrelevant. It is you, is it not, who have the ambition, the fire, the Schedule?

You are still afraid. Of course. You must think I am one of the others, one of their spies. Ah, really: that is going too far.

Be careful. Your superior is looking this way. His face shows no concern, but it is not clear what he is thinking. He seems to be merely surveying the office. All is still safe, is it not? Your position is preserved. Your superior continues to play the fool. See: even now, he is nodding at you. The others remain ignorant.

But you must be careful. That is my word of advice. You must always watch out for discovery by an unsympathetic one.

If you were discovered and exposed … it would be all over. The plan would crumble. You would lose your post, be cast into the street. You'd be chained, beaten, tortured. You might even be lynched.

So take care.

I shall be watching your progress.

The Seventies

"Arleen," my mother used to say. "You'll never make a good mother." It wasn't a putdown, but a fact. Kids—they're a lot of work and a lot of responsibility, and too much can go wrong. Mother thought I was too selfish to care for anyone else, and I tended to agree with her. After growing up with two sisters and a brother, I wanted space for myself. When I left that house, I found it. I enjoyed it and am *still* enjoying it. No need to muck up my life taking care of anyone else.

To keep me off-balance, especially when I failed to praise her sacrifices, she'd add, "You probably won't listen to me, but if you ever *do* have kids, you'll understand what I'm talking about." You can't argue with someone like that. By the time I was sixteen, my mind was set. I'd never be a mother, and I informed both Mother and myself of that fact (and for good measure decided I'd never get married, either).

Then, of course, she'd come at me from the other side: "But how can you be a *real* woman, Arleen, if you never have kids?" By her account, I lose either way. But by then I was fine.

Not that I dislike kids. I like them, so long as they're not mine.

A dog, maybe. Yes. I have a dog, because dogs provide companionship without wringing your soul dry in return. And I'm not anti-social. I have friends, and I love them and try to be good and decent to them. I just don't like too much responsibility. I need to be able to walk away.

But having kids. It's a huge commitment. You have to be on

⟩ of your game every moment, whether you feel like it or not. I'll tell you what I mean....

When I was younger, I lived in Somerville with a couple and their two kids. This was back when there were communes, food co-ops, hippie skirts, sandals, and beads. I was twenty-six and had a dog, Princess, and she and I were living with a guy named Roy. Inspired by the counter culture, Roy and I started talking about moving in with some other people, which is how we met Matt and Brenda Marks.

Roy knew Matt from his men's group, and some women I knew were in a consciousness-raising group with Brenda. We mentioned our idea to them, and they said we should get together and talk, so we dropped by their house one evening after they'd put their kids to bed. The place was on a street near Porter Square. We hit it off famously, talking until one in the morning. Of course, a little weed helped. They said they'd bought the house six months ago. It had an apartment on the third floor, their tenant had just left, and as far as they were concerned, we could move in whenever we wanted. We'd have our own apartment, but we could all cook and share meals together.

It was just like that, smooth and low key. They asked if Roy and I would help out with their kids, and we said yes.

As it turned out, things didn't work out that way. Roy split after six weeks, riding his motorcycle to New Mexico to join some old back-to-the-land buddies, and I was left in Porter Square with Princess, a one-year lease, two new friends, and their kids.

I had a job as a secretary at Channel 4. It had taken me months to find it, and I wasn't going to give it up. My plan was to eventually get to the newsroom. The thought of trailing off to the Southwest after Roy or crawling back to hometown Milwaukee did not appeal to me in the least.

And I liked Somerville. I could take the T to work, and we lived near enough to Fresh Pond for me to take Princess for a run after work.

Matt and Brenda had been living with their kids in Brattleboro, but they wanted to be part of the Cambridge scene. Brenda's dad, the only doctor in some North Carolina mill town, had given her twenty-three thousand dollars, which was big money back then, and she bought the house outright. It was a three-decker, painted white, with porches on every floor. There were rose bushes and a privet hedge in the front, and a small yard in the back, just right for a garden.

Matt was an intense, wiry man in his early thirties, originally from New Jersey, who taught physics at the local high school. Brenda was more laid back. She had a willowy frame, but was still carrying some weight from her pregnancies, and she was an inch or two taller than Matt. She had a fair complexion, with pale, almost transparent skin, and straight blond hair. When I first saw her, I thought she was Norwegian or German. Since leaving the South, she'd been doing one thing after another—crafts, psychology, photography, pottery—but now she was mainly a mom. The thing I remember most about Brenda was her fingers: long, like a weaver's or a harp-player's.

The kids, both boys, were great as far as kids go. Ivan, five, was his dad's favorite: dynamic, bright, and a bundle of energy. Jonathan, two and just out of diapers, was quiet, sweeter, more like Brenda.

After Roy left, the three of us had a house meeting. Brenda and I insisted on Matt's doing his share of childcare and housework; but because of his teaching schedule, most of what he did was on the weekends. One of us would cook every three nights. Matt did the grocery shopping. Brenda did the laundry. I put the kids to bed Tuesdays and Fridays and sometimes babysat so Matt and Brenda could go out. Although I had my own space upstairs, I was free to use the downstairs living room and kitchen whenever I wanted.

Brenda had found day care for Ivan, but it was harder for her to get something for Jonathan. So, since they had space on the second floor, they and two other couples with toddlers hired a teacher to care for the kids in a large room they'd made into a nursery. We called her the "crèche person." So Jonathan was on the second floor each weekday until one o'clock, and then he was with Brenda.

When you look at it now, the situation was crazy. This was the early Seventies, and the counterculture was in full swing. Protests against the War, underground newspapers, lots of weed, and lots of sex. Matt was having an affair with a modern dancer named Shoshona, and Brenda was sleeping with the father of one of the kids in Jonathan's playgroup, Derek. Plus, they were still sleeping with each other and trying to be parents to their kids. They hadn't told all this to Roy and me when we met, but it was obvious after a few days. They both thought it was okay, so long as everything could be "openly discussed." But whenever they "discussed" it, they'd fight.

"How can you be involved with two men at once," I asked Brenda. "Especially if you're living with one of them?"

"Men do it all the time," Brenda said. "What's the problem?"

"I'd feel awkward as hell," I told her. "I could see it if you were living by yourself and dating different guys; but, living with one man and having sex with another … it seems like you'd have to choose one sooner or later."

"Matt and I discussed that," she said. "He started with Shoshona first. It really freaked me out when I discovered it, and I told him he'd have to break it off. He asked me what my problem was. He said our marriage was primary for him, and Shoshona was not. He felt he could handle it emotionally and didn't want us to break up, but he did want to keep seeing her. I said that if he really wanted it that way, he'd have to agree that I had as much right as he did to have other relationships, and, if he did, then I'd go along with it. So we agreed we'd each be free to have other relationships, so long as everything was open and above-board, we didn't threaten the marriage, and we continued raising the boys together."

"Sounds like a lot of work," I said.

"It's something we both wanted and agreed on."

"And there's isn't any jealousy?"

"Not until recently," she said. "Not until I started seeing Derek."

"Ahh, Derek." I said.

She nodded, looked upwards and smiled. "I know. I'm getting very fond of Derek ..."

"You and Matt are always fighting," I said. "How can you keep it up with so much tension?"

"What do you mean?" she said. "I think we're doing all right."

I couldn't believe what I was hearing. "You fight over what the kids should eat, you fight over their bedtime, you fight over how they should be disciplined, how much television they should watch ..."

"Okay, so we do have different ideas on some things," she said. "But mainly we agree. We agree on *how* to raise the boys. Our arguments usually come down to the same few things. Matt thinks I treat Jonathan better, and I think he's easier on Ivan than he should be. But we've been discussing that."

"What's 'discussing,'" I said, "about the way you argue?"

"A lot," she said. "We talk about the different families we came from, about the different patterns we learned growing up. Matt brings stuff up in his men's group. I talk to my friends. And we use our arguments as a way to learn more about ourselves, the way we handle things. Like, I was a younger kid, for instance, with two older brothers, and Matt was the older, with a younger brother. So naturally he identifies with Ivan, and I lean more towards seeing Jonathan as my own kind of kid. Some of that's unavoidable, but it's what we have to deal with."

"Don't you ever just want to haul off and hit him with a pan?" I asked.

"Not really," she said in her bland, Southern voice. "I might, if we didn't discuss things. But I've agreed with what we're doing. It's not happening behind my back."

Frankly, I thought she was asking for trouble. "So his being with Shoshona doesn't bother you?"

"Okay. It bothers me," she said. "Of course, I'd prefer if he *wasn't* involved with her. But now I'm involved with Derek, who I like, and things seem to be working out. I have to trust Matt. He says his relationship with Shoshona is only a sexual thing, and he still loves me. I talked to Shoshona, and she says it's that way with her, too, just a sexual thing, and that's all she wants. She doesn't want Matt all to herself. She just enjoys being with him now and then. And, like I say, I've got this thing with Derek." She gave this dreamy smile again.

"I must be old-fashioned," I said. "Because all this gives me a headache. I'm even glad Roy left, because I have more time to myself. You know? It's great to be able walk around Fresh Pond, go to a concert, see a movie, without having to worry about whether someone else is enjoying it."

"I know what you're saying," she said. "When I was twenty-four I spent a year living in a big commune in Baltimore, and we could spend time alone, and no one was tied down to anyone else. But then I met Matt."

"You fell in love?"

She nodded. "Uh-huh. And I think we're still in love with one another ..."

"Beats the hell out of me," I said. "But if you can handle it, more power to you."

This may sound funny, but I liked them both. I liked Brenda because I could see her trying to be a stronger and better person, and I liked Matt because he was trying to be honest. It might have been a crazy way to live, but it had its moments, and neither of them seemed to expect more than what they were getting. I think they were each genuinely trying to support one another, even though it hurt, and I found that impressive.

Sometimes, though, watching TV in the living room after the kids were in bed, I could hear Brenda crying alone in their room, when Matt had gone off to be with Shoshona. And some-times, when Brenda was off with Derek, I'd hear Matt slamming a door or throwing stuff around the bedroom. But usually, they seemed to hold whatever worries they had inside themselves.

One October evening we were all at the dinner table. Matt had cooked chicken curry, and there was ginger ice cream for dessert. Jonathan was strapped into his high-chair next to Brenda, making a mess of himself, as usual. Ivan, in his blue booster seat (everything of Ivan's had to be blue) was asking for more ice cream.

Coffee was brewing and everyone was mellow, so I decided to stick around instead of heading off to give Princess her eve-ning run. Moments like this made me happy I'd chosen to live communally.

"Ivan, wipe your face," Brenda said. "It's getting covered with goop."

"What about Jonathan?" he said, tilting his head to one side and grinning.

Brenda scrubbed Jonathan's face with a napkin, holding him while he tried to pull away and frantically shook his head from side to side. "No, no!" he was squealing.

"Now Jonathan's all clean," she said. "So how about Ivan?"

"O-kay," Ivan said, pushing his napkin jerkily across his face. "Now I'm all clean, too." He drained his cup and began banging it on the table. "More milk, please!" he crowed.

Brenda and Matt each sat in their seats for a minute, then both started up at the same time. I stood up and motioned them back into their seats.

"Relax. I'll get it," I said. "And I loved hearing that lovely 'please,' Ivan."

"Mommie tol' me," he said, wagging his head up and down. "Say 'please' an' you get what you want."

"See? Then it works." I filled his cup, then left the milk on the table. The coffee smelled great, so I got myself a cup.

"So how's work, Arleen?" Matt said, when I sat back down.

"Not bad. Same thing."

"You hear from Roy?"

"No. And I don't expect I will, either. Roy's not the writing kind."

"I 'member Roy," Ivan said. He imitated a motorcycle rider. "Whhrrooom!"

"Right. You got it. That's Roy," I said.

"Are you going to marry Roy?" Ivan asked.

"I don't know," I said. "Probably not."

"Mommie's married to Daddy," he said. "But she's *frens* with Derek. An' Daddy's married to Mommie, but he's *frens* with 'Shona." I waited for him to finish.

"But you're right, Ivan," I said. "You don't have to be married to be friends. And you can even be by yourself for a while."

"Like you an' Princess," he said.

"Ivan!" Brenda said sharply.

"Right," I said. "Like me and Princess. Does it confuse you sometimes?"

"Yes," he said, nodding mightily.

"Confuses me, too," I said.

"But then Mommie or Daddy talks to me and I get ... I don't get confused no more."

"*Any*more," Brenda said. "Don't get confused *any*more."

"*Any*more," he repeated dutifully.

"Whose turn is it to put the kids to bed tonight?" Matt said, his tone implying he hoped it wasn't him.

"Daddy's!" Ivan shouted.

"He's right. It's yours," Brenda said. She smiled, and her smile seemed to irritate Matt.

"Does that mean you're going out?"

"Mmm-hmm. With Derek. We're, um, going to a movie."

"Another 'movie'! Jesus, weren't you just out with him three nights ago?"

She shrugged. "Maybe. I don't remember exactly. Why?"

"No reason. It just seems the two of you are getting pretty close."

"And weren't you with Shoshona last night? What about that?"

Jonathan started crying. "Mommy and Daddy, don't fight." Ivan said.

"Look, *I'll* put the kids to bed tonight," I said. "You can both go out."

"It's not that," Matt said.

"It's your turn and you ought to do it," Brenda said. "That's what we agreed on."

"I don't know."

Just then, Ivan spilled his milk. He toppled his cup with his elbow, and the milk went flying across the table. It formed a big puddle that reached from Ivan all the way across to where I was sitting, and then began dripping onto the floor.

"Ivan!" Brenda shouted. "Can't you watch what you're doing."

"Accident!" Ivan said. "It was a' accident."

"It was an accident," I heard Matt saying at the same time. "He didn't mean to do it. Come on, Ivan, let's get some napkins and clean this up."

Ivan scrambled down off his seat, grabbed a handful of paper towels from the kitchen counter, and avidly began mopping and drying. Matt got the sponge from the kitchen sink and swabbed the table.

"If you were just a little more careful …" Brenda said.

"I'm sorry, Mommy," Ivan said. "I didn' mean to be bad. It was a' accident."

The magic of Ivan's most newly acquired word melted her, and she relaxed. "All right. But just watch yourself next time."

Matt winked at him as they tossed away the wet towels. "Thanks for helping, Ivan," he said. "I know you'll be more careful next time."

"Anyway, I'll put the boys to bed," I said. "You two do what you want. I'll take Princess out later on."

A few days later, I was talking to Matt. We were in the living room. The kids were watching Spiderman cartoons on TV, and he was grading his students' tests. Brenda had gone off to do some errands.

Matt was in his favorite beige sweater and slacks. His hair had grown long and was curling down below his ears. He had a skinny neck: his Adam's apple jutted out as if he'd swallowed a rock. And he had an oval head, like a balloon that was starting to deflate. His eyes were deep brown, and I noticed that whenever he was tense, they darted from side to side, jerking like he had some kind of chemical imbalance. Other times, though, he'd stare at you, eyes unmoving, focused on what you were saying. The overall impression was one of precariousness and intensity at the same time.

"I want you to know, I really appreciate your staying here, Arleen," he said. "I know you didn't have to, after Roy left."

"It's no big thing," I said. "I needed a place."

"You know what I mean."

"I don't mind being here," I said, "so long as I don't get used as a buffer. That's not my role. You know?"

"I know." His eyes were going back and forth. "I know."

I glanced at the TV where Spidey was climbing a wall with that peculiar glint in his eye.

"I love the kids," he continued. "If you want to know the truth, that's the main reason I'm still here. The only reason."

"I get that."

"I want to be with them growing up. That's important."

I didn't say anything, and he didn't either for a few minutes. But then he shifted in his chair and put his test papers down. "See, when I was growing up, me and my brother, my dad was very … unpredictable. He worked in an auto plant in Rahway. It was a hard, physical job, and he wanted peace and quiet when he was home. But sometimes my brother and I got a little raucous … and then he'd lay down the law." He paused.

"And what was that like?" I said, tentatively.

"Not good," he said. "My dad had a temper on him. And he would strike out." He shook his head. "It was not good. Which is one reason I want to stay with Brenda and the kids. I want to make sure the same thing never happens to them."

"And is that hard?" I said.

He nodded. "Sometimes, yes. But, you know, deep down, I think I'm more like my mom. I enjoy domestic things, like cooking, doing dishes, cleaning. I enjoy talking and listening. I like putting the kids to bed at night—the way they smell, the way their skin feels."

"Sounds like you have more control than your dad," I said.

"I do. But you're right, it's not easy. And sometimes, with this stuff going on with Derek, I'm not sure I can handle it." He paused. "You know what I'm saying."

"I know," I said. I thought for a moment about the *I Ching* reading Roy had done on Matt the week before he left. Roy had an obsession with the *I Ching*. He often tossed the coins and consulted the book to figure out how to handle a problem. He also did readings for his friends: he'd take the coins out of his special case, open the book, throw the coins onto the rug, and draw the hexagram. I'm not up on all the details of that ritual, but I do remember that Matt got six "solid" Yang lines in a row, which Roy said stood for great power and intensity.

"This guy doesn't look it, but he's a volcano," Roy told me. "He's got tremendous force and strength, but he's constantly got to control it. If he lets himself go, he could easily overreact."

"And did you tell him that?" I asked.

"More or less," he replied. "And he said he agreed."

It sounded like macho jargon to me, but I could relate to the issue of self-control.

"You know," I said to Matt. "I asked Brenda how she could be … carrying on with two men at the same time. She told me the two of you had talked about it."

"We have. It's right out there on the table."

"So she said. But …"

"What?"

"But I wonder if you don't get upset anyway. I mean, does this seem like a stable situation to you?"

"Nothing seems stable to me," he said. "If it wasn't for the kids, I'd be out of here in a minute."

I waited for him to go on.

"There's a lot of tension, yes. Obviously, I don't like Brenda running around with Derek, even if I agreed to it. And I know she's not happy about me being with Shoshona. But that's the price we pay for staying together with the kids."

"It's the Seventies," I said. "Smash the old stereotypes. Scuttle about for something to replace them. Hope your new things are better than the old. Only, you never know."

"All we can do is try," he said. "Try to live our values. If we do that, our lives will make sense. If not …"

"I don't expect life to make sense," I said, thinking of my mother. "You just get from one end of it to the other."

"I think we owe it to ourselves," he said, going on with his thought, not listening to what I said, "and to our kids. To try."

One evening soon after that, we were again at dinner, and Brenda and Matt started carping at one another again. It was about six-thirty. The kids had already eaten. Ivan was in the living room, playing with his Legos. Jonathan was on a blanket on the kitchen floor. Brenda began by criticizing Matt's lack of ambition. Then he criticized her cooking.

"Fine," she said. "If you really want to get things off your chest, then let me get something off mine. Let's talk about your friend Shoshona. Here I am, knocking myself out day after day to keep the kids clean, keep them fed, keep the house decent, and what thanks do I get? None. But Shoshona, your magnificent free spirit over there, whom I call flighty, can pursue her career and do whatever she wants. And you want to know why? Because she gets whatever she wants from men. And you know why that is? Because she puts out, that's why. She's a social parasite."

"That's nonsense," he said. "Do you hear yourself speak? How jealous can you be? Shoshona works fifty hours a week on her dancing. You think that's living off of men? You make her sound like a petty whore or something."

"Well?" Brenda said.

"Well, that's bullshit. Shoshona works hard at her career. That's her choice. And, yes, she goes out with men she likes, and she lives in her own space and not with any of them. That's how she keeps her independence. There's no pretense about Shoshona. Which is more than I can say for you or your friend Derek."

"Meaning what?"

"Meaning you make your affair sound like 'just friends.' As if everyone doesn't know what's really going on."

"And just what do you think is going on?"

"You want to talk about home wreckers? Well, let's talk about them. It's not Shoshona. She's got no stake in coming between you and me. But Derek's another matter. He's essentially already left his wife."

"Not true!" she cried. "He's …"

"He doesn't give a shit about his family," he went on. "He's just looking to make trouble in mine. He'd like nothing better than for you and me to split, and for him to move in here. Don't think I'm blind."

"That's not true at all."

"If you believe that, you're fooling yourself. Derek's not even living at home now. And he doesn't give two shits about his daughter. I'm telling you, he just wants to make trouble …" I could see his face getting red and a vein bulging in his neck.

There was a ruckus from the living room. Jonathan had crawled over from the kitchen and knocked down the tower Ivan had been working on. Ivan gave him a push, and he was bawling.

"Can you kids keep it down?" Matt shouted.

"Jonathan ruined my tower," Ivan complained, pushing Jonathan again. "Get *away*, Jonathan!"

Jonathan, tired and outraged, wailed loudly. Brenda rushed over and picked him up. Come on, Jonathan," she said. "It's time for dessert and a quick bath." She turned to Matt. "We can finish this later."

She ran a bath for Jonathan, fed him some ice-cream, and brought him to the bathroom and undressed him. Matt went over to Ivan and started rebuilding his tower. Everything seemed domestic once again. Matt and Ivan seemed to be quieting each other down. Brenda was bathing Jonathan. I was putting dishes in the sink.

When his bath was over, Brenda wrapped Jonathan in a thick towel and brought him to the kids' bedroom. She put him in his pajamas and then into bed.

"Matt, will you give Ivan his bath?" she called.

"Don't *want* a bath," Ivan muttered.

"Ivan, get ready for your bath," Matt said. I could see he was still wound up. He went into the bathroom and started running another bath, with bubbles, then came back and snapped his fingers. "Chop, chop, Ivan," he said. "Legos will have to wait until tomorrow. Get ready." He moved Ivan's tower to a corner of the room and dumped the Legos in their bin.

"O-kay," Ivan groaned and headed to the bathroom.

Matt undressed him and went to get his favorite bath toys. When he came back, he threw the toys in the frothy bath and pointed Ivan to it. "In you go, buddy," he said. Ivan climbed in and happily began deploying his rubber duck, submarine, and little foam creatures.

Matt came back to the kitchen table, and Brenda returned from putting Jonathan to bed. I was making coffee and setting out some fruit for dessert.

"He's wiped out, poor guy," she said. She sat down and took some fruit.

Matt shifted in his seat. "I'm not done with this, Brenda,"

Matt said. "Realize that *you* are Derek's escape plan. He has no money, but he knows your daddy's rich. He wants to bust us up and move in, and I won't have it."

"Do you really want to talk about this *now?*" Brenda said.

"I do. Derek doesn't even have a place of his own. Jennie's thrown him out. He has a tiny room. When you get together, he comes over *here* ... in *our* house ... when I'm out ..."

"Derek may be falling in love with me," Brenda said. "It's true."

"If you think he's falling in love with you, you're blind," he said. "He sees you as a life preserver."

"That's not fair, either to Derek or to me," she said.

"But, in any case, this isn't what we *agreed* on!" Matt said. "We agreed to keep this family together!"

"We're going to keep the family together," she said. "What I hear is that you're jealous of Derek and me, jealous that I'm enjoying someone who finds me attractive, and it's *you* who are trying to break *us* up."

"Not so," he said.

Just then there was a loud splash from the bathtub, and Ivan started laughing.

"Ivan," Brenda called, "What's going on?"

"Nothing, Mommy," Ivan answered, then giggled.

I went in to see what was going on. Ivan was sloshing back and forth in his bath, and there was water all over the bathroom floor. "It may be time for Ivan to come out," I said, "and we've got to mop up."

"I don' wanna get out," Ivan said.

Matt got up and went into the bathroom. I went back to my coffee. "Ivan," he said. "Just look at this mess. Time to get out, buddy."

"But I'm playing with Ducky!" he said.

"Ivan, get out of the tub," Brenda called from the kitchen. "Now."

"Don' wanna," Ivan muttered. "Five more minutes."

Matt was mopping the bathroom floor with a towel. "Matt, can you get him out of that bath?" Brenda called.

"Don' wanna," Ivan repeated, more loudly. "Five more *minutes!*"

"Matt!" Brenda repeated. "He needs to come out."

"We can give him five minutes," Matt said.

Brenda looked at me, angry and distraught. I shrugged. "If you want him out, he should come out. You're the parent," I said.

"Damn it, Matt," Brenda cried. "Get him out of the tub. He's made a mess in there and he needs to get to bed."

Matt leaned over to Ivan. "Come on," he said. "You need to get out now."

"Don't wanna!" Ivan yelled. "Five minutes!"

"Now," Matt said.

"Can't you discipline your son?" Brenda shouted. "Who's the boss? Get him out of the tub now!"

"Dammit, Ivan, let's go," Matt said.

"No!" Ivan said.

Matt picked him up under his armpits and started hauling him out of the tub. Ivan, slippery, twisted away and fell back into the tub, and another wave of water gushed over the edge of the tub and onto the floor. "Come *on*, Ivan," Matt said, reaching for him again.

"I don' wanna. Make me!" Ivan shouted.

"Matt," Brenda called from the kitchen. "What's going *on?*"

Matt grabbed Ivan with both arms and pulled him out. Ivan wriggled and squirmed. "Dammit," Matt shouted, trying to keep hold of him. "Your mother wants you out! Arleen wants you out! You have to do what you're told!" He picked Ivan up in the air, holding him tightly around his chest while Ivan continued wriggling, then plopped him squarely on his feet and tried to wrap a towel around him. Ivan was crying, "I don' wanna. I don' wanna." He twisted free from the towel and kicked Matt sharply in the shin. "Dammit, Ivan!" Matt said. "When we say something, you *listen!*" And he drew back his hand and gave Ivan a sharp slap on his naked bottom. Ivan began shrieking.

"Do I have to give you what you're asking for?" Matt shouted, smacking Ivan again. The sound echoed through the house, like a door suddenly slamming shut in a storm. Ivan shrieked. His rump blanched where the hand had hit him, then flushed scarlet red, deep red, like a flame.

"You want more?" Matt shouted, his voice strangled in his throat.

"Daddy!" the boy cried. "Dad-dee!" And he screamed the most god-awful scream I've ever heard, like a flayed animal.

Matt's face registered total horror. "See what you've made me do!" he screamed at Brenda.

It was more than I could take. I jumped up and ran into the bathroom. The floor was sopping. Matt was standing there with the towel. Ivan was screaming.

I saw the look in the boy's eyes: panic-stricken, terrified: the look a dog has when you whip it. His mouth was open and he was screaming one long continuous wail.

I took the towel from Matt and wrapped it around the boy. Matt was trembling now, his whole body shaking. I held Ivan until he'd stopped crying, then handed him, wrapped in his towel, back to Matt, who grabbed him tightly. He knelt down and clutched his son, their faces touching. "Ivan," he whispered. "Ivan, buddy. I'm so sorry. Let's take deep breaths ... both of us ... and I'll get you dry."

Ivan hugged him and let his father dry him off. The two of them were there together. I went back to the kitchen where Brenda was sitting, slumped in her chair, dazed and speechless, and sat down myself. I think we were both looking at Brenda's fingers.

Nobody said anything for a long time.

Making Friends

Kid in poor hood fights more than boyfriend

Andy hadn't wanted to move. All his friends were in the old neighborhood. But Ma said they had to, 'cause she wasn't going to be beat up again by that crazy Warren who already attacked her twice.

The week before, he'd broken the door down to get at her. He was out of his mind, strung out on drugs or something. And he'd got it in his mind that Ma was "his woman," just 'cause she'd been nice to him once or twice. And then, 'cause she wouldn't go along with it, he tried to teach her a lesson.

So Ma said they all had to move, and no one could know about it. Annie helped them find a place, and one night after dark they moved everything as quick as they could, with Annie and her husband and another friend to help, and left their old apartment empty, with the doors open and the keys in the locks, and the floors all littered with garbage and broken toys.

They didn't leave a forwarding address and they didn't tell anyone where they'd gone.

Andy begged to go back just once and explain to his friends where he'd gone and why. But Ma said no. She didn't want anyone knowing, or else Warren would be breaking down their door again.

The day after they moved, she took him and Sharon and Chrissie and registered them in the school down the street. "But how'm I going to make new friends?" he cried. "You can't just come into class in the middle of the year. It's hard!"

"I know it's hard," Ma said. "And I'm sorry you got to do it.

But that's the way it is. So we might as well all try and make the best of it."

"All right," he said, but he wasn't happy. "I'll try. But it won't do any good."

"Just try."

It wasn't a question of trying. Andy always tried hard at what he was supposed to do. He was afraid of failing. Deep in the back of his mind was a grinning monster with a pock-marked face who kept saying over and over again he'd never amount to a hill of beans, and that's what bothered him.

The new neighborhood was tougher than the old one. The kids were all different types—Black kids, Spanish kids, Irish kids, kids with Italian names and kids with American names, and kids with weird African names like Nbulu and Nkomo that sounded like coconuts knocking against one another.

The Spanish kids were always fighting the other kids, and the Blacks were sensitive if you said the wrong thing. Sometimes a couple of them would push against you for no reason and threaten to "cut your dick off."

There was lots of name-calling in the street and in the school. And lots of fighting. Especially on Friday afternoon and Saturdays. As far as he could tell, most of the kids came from the same kind of homes he did. There wasn't much money for new clothes and shoes, and kids wore hand-me-downs from older brothers and sisters, or cousins. Nobody had much money to spend, and the little kids were always holding their dimes and quarters tightly in their fists.

Some of the other kids' mothers were on welfare like Ma. A lot of families were messed up. A lot of fathers drank. It was like Cambridgeport, but worse.

School was a joke. During lunch, the kids threw food around, snapping peas with their spoons and trying to flip gobs of vanilla pudding or creamed spinach on the ceiling. There was a lot of noise, with some kids grabbing other kids' lunches and racing around. The aides wouldn't stop them, cause the tougher kids said they'd beat them up if they tried, and anyhow they were just old ladies with arthritis and swollen feet.

During class, some of the bigger kids would stand up when the teacher turned her back and make loud sucky noises or squeeze farting sounds against their armpits. The teacher would spin around and get mad and the whole class would be in trouble, and no one would have recess because the class had "been bad."

Sometimes the principal would come in, shaking his fat sweaty head, and tell them that none of them were going anywhere without education, and here they were, wasting the one chance they had, and if they didn't straighten up and "clean up their act," then they'd wind up in jail, or working in stinky factories like their Ma or Pa, or being on welfare with a bunch of ungrateful kids like themselves.

That kind of talk bothered Andy. He didn't want to wind up in jail. He didn't want to wind up without a job. And he didn't want to get stabbed to death in the street or killed in some race riot.

It was often hard for him to concentrate. Thoughts would suddenly rise up in his mind like dinosaurs coming out of some swamp, and he'd forget what he was doing. Or else his thoughts would get thin, like all the sense was going out of them, and they'd start floating away and he couldn't grab them back.

And he worried about being dumb.

He'd never made good grades, and now he was in the worst part of the class because of mistakes he'd made his first few weeks. This school had different rules than the one he'd been in before. Like writing his name on the left side of the page instead of the right. Or putting the name of his school underneath his own name instead of next to it. Or underlining the titles of his themes.

Because he started off doing things the way he'd been taught in his old school, the teacher yelled at him and made him feel stupid. And once the teacher yelled at him, the other kids felt they could tease him, and they did.

Talking to Ma about it didn't help. "Look, Andy," she'd say. "Just try. Sit there with the book in front of you and *concentrate*."

"I *do!*" he'd shout. "I *do* try! It don't do any good!"

"I don't want you ending up like me," she'd say. "I never learned to read, all through the tenth grade. They kept promoting me, but they didn't do me no favors. Now look at me. I can't get a job, and I got to stare at the paper for half an hour just to read one lousy story."

He hated it when she started on that.

"An' you're just like I was," she'd go. "You started out seeing your 'b's and 'd's backwards. You didn't know whether to write with your left or your right hand." She'd shake her head, then smooth her stringy sand-colored hair with her skinny fingers. "An', God knows, you don't get nothing from your Pa!"

The she'd lean forward and fix him with those staring blue eyes: "If it takes a little more time, you go ahead. You ain't smart like Chrissie. An' you ain't got the spunk *Sharon* has. So you got to work five times harder for anything you get."

It was like living under a curse. She had this problem, so now he had it, too. It was in his blood, he couldn't get away from it. And the teacher didn't care if he learned anything at all.

His teacher wrote home that he had a spelling problem, a reading problem, and a conduct problem. He threw the note away and told the teacher Ma had seen it. She didn't even call to check up on him.

What worried him most was getting along with the other kids. In the beginning, no one had wanted to play with him. Every kid already had a best friend, and there wasn't any room for him to break in.

When the teacher came down on him, the kids started calling him "Dumbo," and "dead stupid." They'd gang up on him. Two guys would come up behind him, one on either side, and bump him with their hips. Or try and knock the books out of his arms. Or take his hat. Or knock him down the stairs.

Once he punched a kid hard in the ribs, and the kid left him alone. But it didn't make him a friend.

Two kids who jostled him a lot were named Steve and Poke. Steve was slender like himself, but Poke was chunky, with little pig-eyes staring out of a smooth pink face. One day when they'd tripped him up for the two-thousandth time he turned on them. "All right," he shouted. "I'm *sick* of you guys teasing me all the time. You think it's *easy* to come into a new school and try and make friends, well you're wrong! So you can just stop *bugging* me or there's going to be trouble!"

"Trouble," Poke said, imitating him and wagging his head from side to side. "There's going to be 'trouble.'"

"All right! Stop laughing!" He clenched his fists. "All right! You asked for it!" He threw himself at Poke, swinging wildly.

Poke, who outweighed him by about twenty pounds, grabbed him around the waist and squeezed. Then he threw Andy on the ground and fell on top of him.

"Goddammit!" Andy yelled, kicking and clawing. "Get offa me!"

Poke squirmed to stay on top of him and punched him in the gut.

"Atta boy, Poke," Steve shouted. "Give it to him!'

"You fat blubberhead!" Andy yelled, unable to move Poke off his chest.

Poke ground his stumpy fingers into Andy's ribs. "Give up? Give up?"

"No."

Poke ground his fingers into Andy's ribs again.

"All right, all right," Andy shoutcd. "Just get offa me!"

Poke got off. His face was sweaty and bright red. "You're a tough little fucker, aren't you?" he said, breathing heavily.

"I just don't like being bugged all the time."

"Okay." Poke stood up and brushed himself off. "So the little guy don't like being bugged." Then he grinned and held out his hand. "No hard feelings?"

135

Andy looked at him, puzzled, then shook hands. "Okay."

"Well, I guess that means you're okay, then," Steve said.

That was how Andy made his first two friends.

Steve and Poke were both white. They told Andy they hated "niggers" and they hated "spics." If they had to, they'd get along with them in school, but they hated them just the same. "Some of 'em can't even speak English," Steve said. "What the hell good are they?"

"Like, what do they want here?" Poke said. "That's what my dad wants to know."

"The spics come to get welfare, right? That's what *my* dad says. An' then they bring their whole family," Steve said.

"That's why we got to stick with our own."

"Is that really true?" Andy asked.

"Sure. You think about it. You'll see."

Andy didn't like the way the others made fun of the Black and Spanish kids, but he went along with it because Poke and Steve were his only friends. He wasn't even sure *why* he didn't like it. It just didn't feel right. Maybe it was because he'd gone through a lot of teasing himself, and he didn't think any kid should be treated that way.

One night he asked Tom, the man who'd started coming by the house to see Ma, what he thought about it. "See, they make all these jokes, like. And try and get everyone to laugh. Only I don't think it's funny. But I don't know what to do."

Tom was a big burly guy with round shoulders and a tired face. "Just keep your mouth shut," he said.

"Why?"

"'Cause you just got here, that's why. If you want to fit in, then you got to fit in with what the other kids do. If you want to be different, then you'll be different all by yourself."

"But it ain't right, is it?"

"Kid, I don't know what's right and what ain't any more." Tom took a deep breath. "There's been a lot of trouble here between white and Black, and with the Spanish. You know? You got to understand these things." Tom was leaning so close, Andy could smell the beer on his breath. "Know what I mean?" he said.

"I don't know." Andy stopped, feeling the man's eyes on him. "I mean, yeah. Yeah, I understand."

"All right then," Tom said. "Then you don't have to ask any more questions. Anyway, what I hear is that you got enough to keep you busy, just doing your schoolwork. Ain't that right?"

"Un-huh," Andy answered, feeling put down. The monster was laughing again. He realized it had been a mistake to talk to Tom in the first place.

One day, after school, he sat on the front steps and watched what was going on. His sister Chrissie had already made friends with the girls on the street and was out with them. His other sister Sharon was nowhere in sight. A bunch of kids his age were playing football in the street, three against three. One or two others were riding bikes.

The street was made up of three-decker houses, jammed right against each other, none of them with driveways or yards. Almost every house had a front porch (many had porches on every floor) and a couple of steps going down to the sidewalk. The roofs of the houses were completely flat. Down at one end of the street, to the right, was a small convenience store where everyone went for bread and milk, ice-cream, and smokes. There were some more stores across the street: a drug-store, a laundromat, a meat market, and a bar.

All the kids on his block were white. Two blocks over, they were mainly Black. And the Spanish lived somewhere nearby, but he wasn't sure where.

It was getting on into November. Somewhere, someone was burning a pile of leaves and the smell filled the air. It reminded Andy of the time they'd visited Grandma and Grandpa in New Hampshire. That was a long time ago, a couple years after his Pa had left. Ma had taken him and the girls to visit Pa's family and ask for some money to help them out. Grandma and Grandpa still lived on a farm. He remembered the place smelled of apples, manure, and burning leaves.

That was the only time he'd seen those grandparents. They hadn't given Ma any money, and she'd never gone back. They never wrote or kept in touch. They never sent Christmas presents or cards on the kids' birthdays. It was like they didn't care.

It was getting cold. On days like this, the sky had a way of turning icy blue, without a cloud to spoil the color. He could see it over the flat rooftops, the dome of the sky, arching overhead. And it was already getting dark. He noticed that when it got dark in the late afternoon it was like someone dimming the lights bit by bit, so that at first you wouldn't even notice it cause your eyes were adjusted to it, and then you'd suddenly realize you couldn't see down the other end of the street, or you'd try to catch a football and find out you couldn't follow its path through the air any more, and it would be like a fine grey cloud drifting down over the whole city, heavier and heavier, until you had to squint just to see a few houses away. And then the streetlights would go on, and the kids' mothers would be calling them to come in for dinner, and the streets would empty out except for the older kids leaning against the sides of the buildings, smoking weed, and the men coming home from work.

He asked Ma about it one day. "Where do all the Spanish kids come from, and why do they come here?"

"I dunno. Same as everyone else, I guess."

"But why don't they stay in their own country?"

"Andy, think about it. It's probably better here."

"The kids say they all want to go on welfare."

She sounded her hard, dry laugh, more like a cough. "Andy, I never knew anybody crazy enough to *want* to go on welfare. Not even if they was Puerto Ricans."

"The kids say the same thing about Black people."

"I hear it, too. Lookit, maybe they ain't got nothing where they are, so what we got looks like a lot. But when they come here, they see it ain't all that great after all. But then they got to make the best of it."

"Yeah," Andy said, thinking it over. "That makes sense."

Ma sighed. "Don't seem to me we get so much outa welfare we ought to worry about someone else getting it, too, you know."

"But the kids call each other names, and there's an awful lot of fighting and all," he blurted out.

"Well," Ma was quiet. "You just got to deal with that, too. You got to figure out what you think is right."

He nodded.

"One thing you got to remember. No matter who you are, if you're hungry, you got to eat. If you're sleepy, you got to sleep. There's a whole lot about people that's the same." She paused, lighting a smoke and tossing the match into the round glass ashtray on the kitchen table. "I guess there's lots of differences, too. But they never hit me as the most important part." She inhaled.

"Ma, don't smoke," he whined. "It ain't good for you."

"And you … don't tell your Ma what to do."

The next day Andy looked at himself in the mirror. He was scrawny: no doubt about that. Sharon was slender like Ma. Chrissie was supposed to look like their Pa. But no one could say who *he* took after. He had a tight mouth and a sharp, upturned nose. His hair was sandy brown like Ma's. His eyes were hazel. He noticed some freckles on his nose: and nobody in the family had freckles. And his ears stuck out. Looking more closely at his face, he saw a few pimples.

"Startin' to be a teenager," Tom had teased. "Only eleven, and he's already getting started on his acne."

"Shut up," he said to himself in the mirror. He didn't like the things Tom said. He pursed his lips, then made a scary face; then combed his hair over his eyes, trying to look cool.

It didn't work.

He tried combing it off to one side …

"Andy!" Ma called. "What're you doing in there? You want

a snack?"

He went into the kitchen. Ma was in a blue blouse and jeans, heating water and smoking again. He didn't say anything.

"You want something to eat?"

He shook his head. "Naw. Thanks."

The kettle rumbled, then began whistling. Ma turned the flame off before the whistle became shrill and poured some steaming water into her cup, then plopped in a tea bag and put the kettle back on the stove.

"So how's school going?"

"Okay."

"Learnin' anything?"

"I guess."

She nodded. "Listen, I might be getting' a job. Maybe next week."

"Going off welfare?"

"Well … not yet. But if this works out, maybe I could."

"Uh-huh."

"Anyway, I want you to start keeping an eye on Sharon. You got to be the man of the family. Chrissie can take care of herself. She's pretty mature. But I'm worried about Sharon. I don't know what she'll get into next."

Sharon had already been getting into trouble, but he didn't want to tattle. She was twelve, a year older than him. And Chrissie was thirteen.

Sharon had been telling Ma she was going to school every day, but in fact she was playing hooky and hanging out with kids down on Dewsnapp Street, doing smokes and who knew what else. But Sharon was always getting into trouble. Last year, she'd been stealing from Kresge's. And the year before, there was a whole thing about her taking rides with strange men and almost getting into real bad trouble.

"Okay. I'll keep an eye on her," he said.

"Good." Ma sat down at the kitchen table.

"Ma, you look tired," he said.

"Believe me, Andy. I am."

He leaned forward. "Are things okay with Tom?"

She didn't look up. "I guess."

"Is he going to be our new dad?"

"Jesus, Andy!" she cried. "I don't know. I just barely met the man."

"He spends a lot of time here."

"So?"

"So nothing." He shrugged and stuck his hands in his pockets and looked at the floor. "I just wondered."

"Do you want him to be your dad?" she said after a while.

He pursed his lips. "Not really."

He jabbed her smoke out in the ashtray. "I guess we'll just have to see."

The kitchen was quiet except for the refrigerator humming. He knew he had homework to do, but he didn't want to.

"Ma."

"What?"

"Do I look like my Pa?"

She examined him with an odd expression on her face. "Like your Pa?" For a minute she looked sad, like she was seeing old photos. "I dunno. I guess, in some ways, you do."

"What ways?"

"Jesus, Andy! What do you want? I dunno. Maybe your eyes. And the way you walk. A little." He nodded. "Why?"

"No reason. Just wondering." He shook his head. "I mean, do I *act* like Pa?"

"What do you mean?"

He waved his hand. "I don't know. I don't know *what* I mean. I'm just asking." He didn't have any other way of putting it, 'cause he wasn't sure himself just what he wanted to know. "I mean, after all, I don't even remember him. I don't know what he was like ... or anything."

141

She was quiet. "Maybe in the way you're so stubborn. He was like that. And he kept to himself an awful lot. You'd never know what was going on in his mind." She became quiet again, getting her distant look and rubbing the side of her nose.

The refrigerator motor clicked off. There were shouts from the kids outside.

"I don't know," she said, abruptly standing up and bringing her empty cup to the sink. "I don't want to talk about it anymore." She was getting angry.

He felt he should stop, but he couldn't. "How come he don't ever write or call?"

"I don't know that, either," she cried. "Some day when you find him, you can ask him!"

"Don't get mad."

"What am I supposed to do, when you sit asking me a bunch of dumb questions …?"

The words stung. "That's right. Whatever I say is dumb. Whatever I do. Thanks a lot." He turned and headed for the door.

"Andy, I didn't …"

"Forget it!" he shouted. "Sorry if I *bothered* you." He pulled the front door open, went out and slammed it shut.

He felt bad as soon as he'd done it, but he was angry. How was he supposed to figure out who he was and what to do, if everybody either put him down or didn't care, or wouldn't answer what he asked or … what the hell!

Kicking every stone or can in his way, he headed for the playground, where most of the kids hung out. It was a grey day, a fine mist coming in, making everything damp. He could even smell the ocean.

He'd forgotten to wear his jacket.

It was chilly, but he didn't care. He had on his flannel shirt, and a T-shirt under that. And besides, he didn't care.

When he reached the park, none of his new friends were around. Some older kids were smoking weed by the benches, and a few Black kids were playing basketball. Other than that, the park was empty. He sat on a concrete wall and put his head in his hands. "What a life," he said, half-aloud.

A bunch of Spanish kids came up the sidewalk towards him, then veered off to the side where there was a grassy area. One of them was carrying a soccer ball. When they got to the area, they started kicking the ball back and forth, laughing, and chattering to one another in Spanish.

Andy watched them.

The sky was a dark, dingy color, the color of city streets. A breeze stirred up from the east. Now it was beginning to rain lightly. Parts of the playground already had puddles from rain that morning, and the grassy area was muddied up.

One of the kids kicked the ball over towards Andy, and he bent over to get it and throw it back.

"Hey," one of them said all of a sudden. "You want to play?"

"What?"

"Yeah. You. You want to play?"

One of the other kids said something in Spanish, and a bunch of them laughed. He didn't have to understand Spanish to know they'd said something about him. Probably that he didn't know how to play. Or that he was too skinny. Or maybe just that he was white.

A flash of fear went over him, and he wondered if they were going to beat him up or something. "Aw, what the hell," he said to himself. "The way this day has gone, I don't care if they do …"

The kid who'd spoken to him came closer and asked him again.

"Hey, thanks. But no thanks," he said, feeling stupid. "I don't know how to play. Football, maybe. But not soccer."

"It's easy," the kid said. "And, anyway, you'd make the sides even."

"Yeah? Well, okay then." Andy slid off the wall and joined the others.

"See. This is all you do," the kid said. "Kick it with your feet.

Can't touch the ball with your hands. But you can use your head if you want. See?" He bounced the ball off his head, high in the air.

"Neat," Andy said, wondering how the kid could do that without it hurting.

"You all set, then?"

"Sure."

"Okay. You're on our team."

They started playing. Once he got into it, he found it wasn't so hard, and soon he was running and sliding and kicking with the rest of them.

The kid's name was Carlos and he was from Puerto Rico. One of the other kids, from Colombia, somewhere in South America, was as dark as any American Black man.

They played until it got so dark they couldn't see. Then they stopped. They were completely soaked.

"Thanks for the game. See you later," Carlos said.

The kids moved off in different directions. It struck him that this was the first time since he'd moved that anyone had asked him to join their group.

When he got home, dinner was on the table. "Where you been?" Ma said.

"Playin' ball."

"Well ..." It looked like she was going to say something, but she didn't. "Just sit down and eat your dinner. Wash your hands first."

"Okay." He sat between Sharon and Chrissie, across the table from Ma.

He hadn't been eating more than two minutes when the phone rang. It was Sharon's teacher. Suddenly Ma was yelling at the top of her voice. "What! Not for two weeks? Yes, I will. Yes, you bet! Thank you very much for calling."

She hung up the phone and stalked to the table.

"What?" Sharon said, squirming.

"You know damn well 'what'," Ma said. "You ain't been going to school for two weeks. Maybe more. What *have* you been doing? That's what I'd like to know." She grabbed Sharon by the back of the neck.

"Nothing!" Sharon screamed. "Nothing! Just smoking with some of the girls."

"I don't want you smoking in the street!"

"All right. All right. I'll stop!"

"And what *else?*"

"Nothing! I swear. You can ask Angie."

"I ain't asking nobody!" she dragged the girl into the bathroom and started hitting her with both hands. "Now that's enough!" she shouted.

Chrissie ran to the bathroom door. "Ma," she pleaded. "Please stop."

"Goddamn lying ..." Ma cried. "That is one thing I will not take!" She grabbed a hairbrush and started hitting Sharon with the flat end.

"Ma!" Sharon cried. "Ow! Ma! Stop!"

Ma was beside herself. "I'll stop when I'm good and ready."

"Ma," Chrissie said again. "Please. Please stop. She'll be good."

"Go ahead and kill me," Sharon suddenly cried. "You don't care anyway. Move here! Move there! Get yourself this boyfriend, that boyfriend. What do you care about *us?*"

"Whatever I do don't mean you can lie to me! I never lied to *my* mother!"

"You ain't listening!"

"You go to school!" Ma screamed. "You hear me. Every day. I don't want you knocked up at fourteen, going on welfare yourself. Okay?" She shook Sharon by the shoulders. "You understand?"

The door opened, and Tom stepped in. Ma didn't see him.

"Okay," Sharon said. "Okay. Okay."

"I'm disgusted with the lot of you," Ma said, turning towards the kitchen again.

"All of us? What did I do?" Chrissie wailed. "Jesus Christ! I didn't do nothing!"

"All right. So you didn't do nothing. But the bunch of you's is driving me crazy."

"What's going on?" Tom said.

"Nothing," Chrissie said.

"I just found out Sharon ain't been going to school for two weeks," Ma said, holding her hands out helplessly.

"So? What's the big fuss?" Tom took a step toward the table.

"You've been drinking!"

"I'm hungry."

She rushed towards him, like she was on fire. "No! Get out! Get out of here, Tom. Right now!" She pushed his arms and chest, trying to turn him around and shove him out the door. "I don't want you here now. Get out!"

"I ain't even moved in, and you're throwing me out?"

"I don't want to talk about it. Just go, Tom. Please go."

The children had all gathered behind her, standing between her and the table.

"Christ, what did I say?"

She pushed him towards the door. "Just go."

"I'm going. I'm going." He stumbled the few feet towards the door, then braced himself against the jamb and turned around. "But I'm not going to forget this. You had one man and lost him. You had another man and lost him. And now I'm starting to understand why ..." Then, anticipating an assault, he turned again and began down the stairs, stumbling and leaning against the wall for support.

Ma slammed the door shut and ran into her room, her face in her hands.

The following afternoon, Andy went back to the park. Steve and Poke came with him. It was a dismal, chilly day, with grey clouds low in the sky, looking like it was going to rain some more. They hung around the benches for a while, talking about school. After a few minutes, Andy spotted Carlos entering the park from the other end. Poke saw him, too. "Hey! More fuckin' spics in this park ..."

Steve looked up. "You're right."

"Look," Andy said. "We don't have to talk like that. Do we?"

"Why not?" Poke said. "Don't hurt anyone."

Seeing Andy, Carlos moved hesitantly toward them. "Hi, there," Andy said, waving.

"You know him?"

"Uh-huh."

"How come?"

"Just 'cause."

Carlos reached them. Andy shook his hand. "How ya doing?"

"Okay." He hung back, hands in his pockets.

"These are my buddies, Poke and Steve."

Carlos nodded. "Hiya." He extended his hand. Steve grunted. He looked at Poke. Poke didn't hold out his hand. "Hiya," he said in a flat voice.

A cold breeze gusted past them. For a few seconds, no one spoke. Andy felt his features tightened up.

"Yeah ... Well ..." Carlos took a step backwards like he was going to leave.

"Hey ..." Andy said, his mouth suddenly dry.

"See you later."

"Hey," Poke said. "Does your Pa have a job? Or is your whole family on welfare?" Andy stared at him.

"What did you say?" Carlos said.

"What kind of answer you got?"

"Hey," Andy said. "Wait a minute ..."

"Wait a minute, yourself," Poke said. "I want an answer." He paused, looking at Carlos. It was suddenly very tense.

"You want an answer?"

147

Poke nodded slowly. "Uh-huh."

"Okay. Shove it up your ass! That's my answer."

"Hey! Nobody talks to my buddy like that," Steve said, pushing Carlos with the flat of his hand.

"Then he shouldn't talk to me like that!"

"Take it back!" Poke shouted.

"Fuck you."

Poke swung at Carlos, but missed. Steve jumped forward, grabbing him by the chest and pinning his arms behind him. "OK, Poke," he cried. "I got him. Teach him a lesson. Pop him one in the gut."

Poke shoved a fist into Carlos's stomach.

"All right! All right!" Andy yelled, throwing himself at the three of them. "You guys cut it out!"

Poke shoved his shoulder in his face. "You stay out of this."

"Cut it out!"

Carlos twisted around and kicked Steve in the shin, just as Andy was pulling him back.

"Oww! Son of a bitch!"

"Come on! Break it up!"

"He kicked me!"

"Forget it!"

"I won't!" Steve grabbed Carlos again and pushed him to the ground.

"Leave him alone!"

Poke turned on him. "Hey, what in hell are you doin', anyway? What do you care what happens to him?"

"I'm sick of all these fights and name calling, that's all. It makes me want to puke!"

"It does?" Poke turned to Steve who still had Carlos down. "You know what I think, Steve? I think Andy has a streak of spic in him. That's what."

Steve looked up. "You know? You just might be right. Isn't that right, Andy? You got a little spic blood in you?"

Something inside him gave way. "You guessed it!" Andy cried, hurtling through the air against Steve and knocking him over. "That's right! You guessed it!" He was kicking and clawing, trying to pull Steve off Carlos, ramming his shoulder into Poke's side. "I'm a spic, too. Him and me, we're brothers. Ain't we, Carlos? That's right. I'm a spic, too. A fuckin' spic."

Poke hit him in the back of the head, and he winced. For an instant he was dizzy; then it passed. He swung back, connected, took a punch in the mouth, swung back again.

With each punch, the monster was taking a beating.

"You want to beat him up, beat me up, too!"

Selfish?
I Don't Think So

I'd gone to the City Hospital to visit my grandfather, an old man who'd worked a sewing machine in the Garment District most of his life. Now, sick with arthritis and pneumonia, he was lying in a busy eight-bed ward staring at the yellow walls, his twisted fingers fumbling with the plastic call-button the nurses had tied to the bedrail. His half-eaten dinner was on a movable tray over his chest. He said he hoped to be well enough to go back home in a few days.

The guy in the bed next to him, an elderly fellow with a hollowed-out face who'd suffered a stroke, lay still, his eyes wide-open and terrified, making throaty sounds.

I was talking to my grandpa about "little things"—the kids, my job at the deli—when my cousin Martin appeared. Martin works as a manager in some specialty shop selling fancy olive oils and balsamic vinegars. He was wearing a natty three-piece suit and carrying a huge bunch of flowers, which he plopped on the small table next to Grandpa's bed.

"Well, and how are we doing?" Martin said, patting the old man on the shoulder.

Grandpa coughed. "Not bad, Marty. Not bad." He pulled himself up, propping his back against his three pillows.

"Good to see you," my cousin said peremptorily to me, extending a hand. His tone set my teeth on edge.

I shook the hand. "Uh-huh," I mumbled.

Marty drew up a chair, sat down, and started telling Grandpa about his latest successes. He was managing an important store on Lexington Avenue. His son had been admitted to Stuyvesant High. His wife was raising lots of money for the United Way. In his spare time, he was playing the stock market. In the past ten months, he said, his stocks had out-performed both the Dow-Jones Average and two of the top mutual funds.

"Doing pretty well for yourself, Marty. Aren't you?" Grandpa said.

"I think so," Marty said. "And that's what it's all about, Grandpa, isn't it? Looking out for Number One. If you don't take care of yourself, who the hell will?" And he laughed at the truth of his cliché.

I couldn't compete with this, so I wished my grandpa a speedy recovery and stepped out into the hallway.

I was planning to go right home; but just outside the hospital, I saw a group of people, so clearly ordinary Joes like myself that I wanted to stop and listen to what they were saying. It was a way of washing out my mind after Marty, so to speak.

Turns out they were members of the hospital union now on strike, talking with a reporter, and waiting for news of one of their leaders, who'd been beaten by the cops on the picket-line. "It's a heavy scene," one of the workers was saying. "We've only been out for ten days, and four folks have already been hurt."

"The cops charged the picket line."

"With no provocation."

"They knew what they were doing. They picked Bob out, and three of them went after him."

"If they think this'll make us give in, they're wrong!"

The reporter pointed his pencil at one of the workers. "You say the cops deliberately attacked Mancuso?"

"No question about it!"

"They claim he was keeping the line from moving and creating a disturbance."

"That's a load of bull!"

"They went after him. We all saw that." There was a general nodding and agreement among the group.

"Yeah. Well ..." The reporter scribbled a few lines, then put his pad in his pocket. "Okay. I guess I got your side of it."

"Do you know if Bob's going to be all right?"

"He's still unconscious."

The workers looked very worried. One of the women was crying.

"I don't know what you're so upset about," the reporter snapped. "You knew this could have happened when you began this strike. Right? *You're* the ones calling the shots."

"We're fighting for our rights," one of the older workers said. "The working man's always fighting just to catch up."

"That's what *you* say," the reporter said. "But, face it. You're not really concerned about the other guy. Even Mancuso, getting his head clobbered. He's taking a risk because he wants something for himself."

"Well, what's wrong with that?"

"Nothing. Only, it's the way the whole country is run. Everybody's out for himself. You guys are no different."

"Bob's a great human being. He *does* care about other people," one of the women said. "That's the whole reason we're out on strike. 'Cause it's not just one person. It's all of us."

"You'd have to convince me," the reporter said. "So far as I can see, you're just like everyone else. You, Mancuso, whoever."

"Is that so?" one of the younger workers said, stepping forward.

"That's how I see it."

"Then let me tell you what kind of people we are. Especially Bob Mancuso. Something most people don't know."

"Go ahead," said the reporter.

"This happened, maybe three years ago," the young man began. "Bob was on his way downtown to a meeting, and he was late. It was around four. The subway station was hot and dusty. He'd just come from a session with the union organizing committee, and he was mad 'cause the hospital was harassing them. Rumor had it they were going to be fired on phony charges. The hospital had a vicious anti-union campaign going, too, mailing every worker pamphlets on how horrible things would be if the union won, and so on.

"Plus, Bob was also having trouble with the union bureaucrats downtown who were ready to drop the drive if there was any trouble or put themselves in the drivers' seat if it went well.

"Bob was juggling all this in his mind, trying to figure out what to do. He knew the workers needed a union badly.

"Finally, the train came. He went in and took a seat. They went down to 145th Street, then 125th Street, each time letting some people off and taking a few on. Like I say, it was hot and sweaty. The fans weren't working.

"Then, picking up speed, the train began that long run between 125th and 59th Streets.

"Bob was thinking about what to tell the bureaucrats when, out of the corner of his eye, he saw a guy moving at the end of the car. The guy pulled the door between the cars open, and hot air blew in, sending dust and papers flying. There wasn't any motorman in sight.

"Then this guy—a kid, really—stood on the platform between the cars. The train was reeling from side to side like a drunken sailor, and the wheels were screeching on the rails.

"As Bob watched, the kid started climbing the chains connecting the two cars. He was lurching this way and that, trying to hold on as the train hit a curve.

"Bob suddenly realized that the kid was going to jump. He looked around the car, and saw other folks looking at him too; but nobody was doing anything about it. It was like they were all waiting for something to happen.

"The kid was on top of the chains now, holding on to the railing.

"Bob moved into action. He jumped up from his seat, ran to the platform, and flung his arms around the kid's waist, pulling him down.

"The kid resisted. 'Goddammit, lemme go!' he shouted.

'Leave me alone!' and he was punching Bob and kicking at him.

"But Bob wouldn't let go. No, sir. 'Get down from there,' he yelled. 'You can't solve anything that way.'

"The kid fought him, but Bob won. He grabbed him around the shoulders, with the other people in the car still watching, and led him over to the seats, and he sat down with him. And he asked him what was going on, and why he'd be doing something like this.

"The kid started crying. Turns out he couldn't find a job, couldn't face his family. Couldn't see how he could marry his girlfriend. Too much was piling up, and he'd decided to end everything and kill himself.

"So Bob talked with him. He said the kid wasn't to blame for his problems. It was the system behind all that. That was the cause. And the kid was lucky to have a good family behind him, and a girl who loved him and all, and he ought to stand up and keep fighting, and not give up and let the system beat him down.

"Make a long story short, Bob made a real impression on the kid, this guy he'd never seen before in his life. He not only saved the kid's life, but he brought him into the struggle.

"Selfish? Thinking only for himself? I don't think so!" And he looked around at the others for confirmation.

The others said, "That's right," and nodded their heads.

"Well," the reporter said, shrugging his shoulders. "That's a fine story. Could've made it up, though, as far as I'm concerned."

The young man grabbed him with both hands and pulled him right up to his face. "How do I know? Because *I'm* the kid Bob saved. That person was me."

The newsman's face grew red, and he started stammering something that didn't make sense. The workers started pushing at him and talking to him all at once.

As for me, I felt like going back to Marty to tell him something I'd just learned.

A Meeting

I met Miss Bishop, my second-grade teacher, on Sixth Avenue. She recognized me right away. "Danny Altman, third seat back on the second row." she said. "Tell me everything that's happened since I saw you last."

She hadn't changed. Still wearing that blue frock that reached to her ankles, she was holding a yellow number two pencil in her right hand, its tip pointed skyward, while her left hand curled nervously around her neck.

I was surprised to see her on a crowded street eight hundred miles north of her home. It jarred my memory. I looked down at my feet, half-expecting to see my scuffed, dusty brown loafers, but my neatly buffed cordovans shone back at me instead, ovoid and unblemished on the hot Yankee pavement. I could see my maroon socks just above the leather's edge.

"Well?" she said. She was bending forward at an angle of about twenty degrees, her hips thrust back, like some buzzard from Valdosta County. The wrinkled corners of her mouth drooped tenaciously downwards. Drained of color, her face was a slab of Elberton marble.

"Well," I said, then blushed at beginning a sentence with an adverb. "A lot has happened. I started writing longhand in the third grade, then got addition and subtraction pretty much in hand and moved on to the multiplication tables."

She nodded. "Very good."

"Then, harder things. I started geography in the fourth grade and, even though my conduct and penmanship were uninspired,

I made great progress with spelling."

She nodded again, saying nothing, continuing to stare at me with her sharp grey eyes. Her hair seemed dried-out by the afternoon sun, its sparse shoots straggling in various directions.

"Other things, too, I guess," I continued. "Diagramming sentences. Learning Georgia history. I memorized 'The Song of the Chattahoochee,' but now I've forgotten it."

"That's not very good," she said, barely moving her lips. "You were always poor at retention."

"That's not fair. I won the spelling bee three weeks running," I said. "Three weeks. No one else ever did that."

She sucked in her cheeks and worked her jaws up and down.

"All in all, I've progressed," I said. "The sixth and seventh grades were easy. I mastered long division, could multiply two two-digit numbers together in my head, and took a course in music appreciation. Fractions were a breeze. After taking Georgia history I moved on to American. In high school I studied world history from the cave man to the atom bomb. I spoke in prepositional phrases. Shall I go on?"

She shook her head, examining me closely. "What about fifth grade?" she said. "I heard about that."

"With Carol Warner? That was a misunderstanding."

"I heard it was shocking."

"Some people did get upset," I allowed. "Carol's mom and dad, for instance. But she was partly to blame., She said she'd show me hers if I'd show her mine, so I did."

"Stupid," she said.

"I couldn't agree more. All her friends were watching me, too. She'd told them," I said, "Even Frederica, who I had a little crush on at the time. They were all staring, but I thought I had to go through with it."

"Big mistake."

"To top it off, Carol didn't go through with her part of the bargain. I felt played for a fool."

"Probably not the last time," she said. "But go on."

"I never got better in conduct, I'm afraid. I'd get demerits for the craziest things."

"You never could keep your mouth shut. That was the problem," she said. "Always wriggling around to talk to the person behind you."

"True," I said. "The person behind me always fascinated me. If they were a girl, I'd flirt. If they were a guy, I'd fight. But, funny thing, I never cared about the person in front."

"So," she said, changing the subject. "What are you doing in New York?"

"I came here for school and stayed," I said. "And you?"

"Sometimes I travel."

"Are you still teaching?"

"I'll ask the questions, Danny," she said, poking my jacket. She smelled of stale gardenias. "What's this?"

"Dacron," I said. "Everyone's wearing it. Keeps its shape and it's great in hot weather. A hundred nineteen fifty at Macy's."

"Hmm," she said, sniffing. "I suppose you have some kind of job somewhere."

"Of course." I cleared my throat. I didn't look my best. My dark black suit was creased, and my green and white striped button-down shirt had wilted. Plus, my ballpoint pen had stained the lower edge of my shirt pocket. I "ahem-ed" again. "I pursued an academic, pre-college course in high school. You know the subjects. Algebra, geometry, chemistry, Latin ..." I paused, but she rotated her right hand quickly, motioning me to go on. "I took chemistry when the labs were in the old building, you know, with Miss Rutledge, who kept spilling sulfuric acid on herself and was always running to the lounge to rinse it off, but it didn't matter because all her dresses had holes in them anyway."

"I'm not interested in Miss Rutledge's wardrobe," she said, sniffing again. "Nor in the irrelevancies of your secondary school career. Nor, might I add, am I impressed with the overall appropriateness of your comments so far. Besides," she said, raising her right hand, the pencil's tip pointing to the top of the Time-Life

Building, "Miss Rutledge passed several winters ago, of a severe and progressive ailment."

"Oh," I said. "I'm sorry to hear that." I paused, not knowing how to go on after such news. My nose had started tickling, which happens when I'm upset, and I knew that I'd soon have to grab my handkerchief out of my back pocket and wipe up the watery mucus which was already forming on the inner border of my left nostril. I felt indecisive.

"Go on, go on," she said, waving her hand like a prune on a stick. "I'm sure you have more to tell."

"Well, not much," I said, then stopped, embarrassed at having started another sentence with "well." "High school went quickly. New languages, new sciences. I was ambitious. Went off to college. You've probably heard it all."

In spite of the afternoon heat, a deathly chill emanated from her body: she disapproved. "I heard," she said.

"Look," I said. "The schools away from home were better. I couldn't hang around Valdosta all my life. And even Atlanta wasn't so impressive then. If I went north, I'm glad if it."

"You *came* from the north, as I recall," she said. "Your family was Yankees. You stayed south just long enough to get some local color, a little sugar in your speech; and then you were off again. That's carpetbagger tactics. You didn't know a good thing when you had it."

"Maybe. But I didn't think about it at the time."

"Perhaps," she said, looking away.

"I went off to school, and that's that," I said. "It was enriching." I tugged my jacket so it hung straighter. I was losing confidence. "I took courses in poetry and logic, art appreciation, calculus, and sociology. One of my roommates is now running a bank. Another is a judge."

"Hmmph."

"I even knew Ivan Dalby, who became a famous artist. He was a friend of a friend. Truth was, he thought I was a nerd. But we hung out together once or twice."

"Never heard of him," she said.

"I don't regret what I've done," I said. "After college I went to medical school, got a good internship and am now associated with one of the finest hospitals in New York."

"I see," she said. "Spell 'separate.'"

"Right now?" I said.

"Right now."

"S-e-p-e-r-a-t-e," I said, then realized my mistake. "It's been a long time."

"Apparently so," she said, as if she were speaking through a reed. She glanced away at the pedestrians who, without so much as a nod at us, were heading uptown and downtown, their faces red and perspiring, their clothes damp from the heat, their arms swinging like pendulums. She looked back at me. "Whatever happened to R.A. Wilshire? I thought you and he were friends."

I sensed she was feeling out of place. That was probably why she was asking about Valdosta folks I hadn't seen in years. Leaning towards me, she seemed frail, her pale blue frock falling loosely over her frame, a lone strand of fake pearls dangling around her neck. A scratched yellow pin I remembered well clung to the left side of her dress, just beneath her collar. I could understand why she was asking about people I'd almost forgotten.

"Sorry. I'm not sure. R.A. …? I haven't seen him in years. Not since the fifth grade at least. His mother had a breakdown and the family left town. We never wrote." My nose suddenly released a glob of mucus towards my lip. I wiped it with my sleeve. My eyes were itching. I could see her frowning. "Sorry," I muttered, reaching for my handkerchief and blowing my nose. "It's like this every August."

"Why don't you take some pills?" she said.

"They make me drowsy."

"Maybe you should try some others …"

"It's not so easy!" I cried. "Nothing's as easy as you think. The spirit is willing, but the flesh is weak."

"No need to be dramatic," she said. "A more rational approach might be more productive."

"No doubt," I said, blowing my nose again and wiping my lip with the handkerchief. "You know, if you want to know the truth, I really didn't like R.A.. Everyone thought I did, but I didn't. He was a bully. I just played with him because he lived up the street. He threw rocks at me after school in third and fourth grade," I sniffed, not haughtily, like her, but to keep my nose from dripping.

"And did you throw any back?"

"Sometimes. Mainly, I was ducking. Look, it's easy for you to say what I could have done, but he was throwing rocks as big as your hand. He could have split my head open or put an eye out. That's what my mother said."

"Unlikely."

"He threw straighter than me. I could have been killed."

"Mmm," she said. "And what about little Benny Sewell? You were fond of him, I think."

"I liked Benny a lot. But he died in a car crash when we were in high school. You must have heard about it."

She looked at me vaguely.

"It was very sad. We went to his funeral, all of us from the Top Hat Club. We sat near his mother and told her how shocked we were. Everybody was crying."

"Benny had a good deal of promise in the second grade," she said, sniffing elegantly. "His handwriting was precocious, and he was quick at analogies. Very quick."

There was a long silence, during which I watched her jaws work. I wondered if she was chewing gum, but she wasn't. My nose had calmed down.

She suddenly jabbed me in the side. "And so. Where are you going in your fancy Dacron suit, eh? What has all this education led up to?"

"I was waiting for you to ask," I said, stiffening and making sure my tie was straight. "I'm done with school now. Living in

Ossining. Married, with two kids. Junior partner in a booming practice."

"Why 'junior'?"

"That's just the term. It's a huge opportunity ..."

"Hmmm."

"I have two weeks' vacation every year, a profit-sharing plan, time off for meetings."

"It all sounds very nice."

"Sally and I might buy a summer place," I said. "Never a dull moment."

"But then," she said, "you were always a busy child. Couldn't sit still. Passing notes when you thought no one was looking. Writing humorous phrases on the blackboard during recess. You had trouble with self-control."

"I got a lot of demerits. But I'm better now. I have a better perspective on things."

"Perspective without control isn't enough," she said, squinting. "You always had trouble knowing when to stop." She nodded at her own words, then looked to the left, a little like the MGM lion, just like she'd done a thousand times before, after answering one of our questions. I remembered that the windows that looked out on our schoolyard were on her left, and she always tended to gaze out that way after she'd finished one of her "pronouncements," fixing on some spot far beyond where the rest of us could see. And then, suddenly, my second grade classroom came back to me in great detail.

It was hot in the winter, breezy in the spring and fall. Odors of soap, chalk, and crayons hung in the air. We thirty pupils sat at wooden desks in rows of six, the front of one desk linked to the back of the next, like parallel trains pointing to the front of the room. Miss Bishop would be at her desk, a massive wooden block on the teacher's platform in front of the room, which was elevated from our floor by a single step. The desk would be covered with our spelling papers and compositions and lined by her own books—a Webster's Dictionary, a spelling primer, and several textbooks, as well as a volume of Georgia poetry from which she quoted at irregular intervals.

On the right of her desk sat her daily calendar, a thick rectangular wad of sheets, one for each day, covered by a red embossed leather flap. One day in March, R.A. Wilshire and I had scrawled an obscenity on it, on a page well into the next school year, when some other class would be before her and we would be safely elsewhere, in a third-grade classroom. I was never sure if she'd found the message. The thought crossed my mind that she might buy a new calendar every fall, instead of in January, and that she'd never seen it. On the other hand, she might have had the habit of scanning the pages every Friday and found it only a few days after we'd written it. Still, I wondered for years if, on some October morning as she tore the preceding day's page from the top of her calendar and settled in to write the day's lessons, she hadn't seen our vulgar phrase. What shock would her features have assumed, and what quick search of culprits would she have undertaken in her mind. Would she have discovered it during class? Would her face have turned stony as she stared out over her hapless second graders, wondering which of them had defaced her sheet? Would she have questioned the class over and over, trying to get someone to confess, keeping them after school for a week, insisting on a confession from one before she would stop punishing them all? R.A. and I had been so afraid of her wrath that, when the time for the message to be discovered approached, we studiously avoided every second grader, and didn't ask anyone about it lest some indication of abnormal interest on our part prompt them to wonder how we had prior knowledge of the event, and lead Miss Bishop to discover our authorship.

Outside our classroom, the sun would be shining. The sky would be blue, and the playground would be peopled with seventh graders, the boys formed in two football (or baseball) teams, some of the girls acting as cheerleaders, leaping and chanting their rhymes, clapping their hands, kicking their heels, their skirts whirling about their knees, while other girls, more standoffish, jumped rope or gossiped in twos and threes by the bushes.

The voices of the children outside on recess while we were still indoors were like darts piercing our brains, barbs which hooked our attention, which drew our minds and eyes out towards the grassy field and the distant trees, the wall, the sets of swings, the sandy flat where the girls played jacks. At times like these, Miss Bishop, noticing our thoughts wandering, would sit, gazing reflectively over our heads towards the clock in the back of the room, counting the minutes until our own recess or time for lunch. Her black-gloved hand would drop its yellow pencil on her desk, and she would touch the small false pearls which, linked together, formed a chain around her neck, its curve dipping towards the thin fabric of her pale blue frock.

The image vanished, and I was again aware of her squinting at me.

"So here I am," I said. "I'm on the other side of long division and algebra, and I got an A in my college course on religion. That must count for something."

"I'm not criticizing," she said.

"I won an award in med school for some research I did."

"You always needed to be first," she said. "You were first in line for lunch, first one out for recess. First to finish your sums at the board. First to sharpen your pencil by the bookshelf in the corner. First to arrive in class. First to raise your hand."

"I'm not so pushy now," I said. "but you're right, I've always been a real competitor. The spelling bee was no accident."

"No," she said, significantly.

"I'll be in line for full partnership soon. My report cards were always excellent. Life may not be a bed of roses, but at least I'm going in the right direction. What else can I say?"

She shook her head. "Nothing. The handwriting's on the wall. It seems you'll always fall a little short."

"How can you say that?" I cried. "I've gotten almost everything I ever wanted. I won the History Prize in high school."

"Yes. 'Almost.' But you didn't win the Math Medal, which you wanted very badly."

"I know you can't win them all," I said. "I've scaled down my ambitions. I'm learning."

"Too little, too late," she said. "You should have stayed in Georgia. You got out of your element, and you won't find it again."

"Someone has to live in New York."

She scoffed.

"If you had your way, no one would do anything different," I said. "It would be a boring, predictable world."

"That's not necessarily so," she said; and for a minute I saw her as a jaded jazz singer, putting me on by referencing the Gershwin song. I grinned, but one look from her cut me short. It wasn't funny.

"I've got a lovely wife. My kids are smart. I told you about the summer home. I still phone my parents every week. So what if I haven't been back to Valdosta?"

"It's not enough," she said.

"How can I fail?"

"It's a sure thing," she said. "It's in the cards. Take my word for it."

"I don't believe you."

"There's not even room for doubt."

"But, then," I stammered, my nose itching again, "then what's the point of going through all this, of making all the effort?"

"You tell me that, Danny" she said, immobile, smiling at my jacket. "You'll have to figure that out for yourself."

"But it isn't *fair!*" I cried. "I can do fractions in my head."

"Danny Altman," she said her voice dry and scratchy. "Who says anything has to be fair? I thought you'd already learned that."

"No," I said. "I haven't. I'll never learn that. I don't believe it."

"Maybe I should have kept you after class a bit more. More dusting the erasers."

"I don't believe you."

"You were headstrong," she said. "It's a matter of self-control.

Greed, in some sense. A lack of subtlety."

"You can't condemn me for that," I said. "People have to work with what they've got."

"But there's a limit ..."

"Things can change," I said. "Didn't you always say that? And change for the better ..."

She shrugged, then let the heavy corners of her mouth droop into a tragic mask, saying nothing.

I'd been talking rather loudly. Lowering my voice, I rubbed the sides of my slacks. "Things have been going well for me," I said, confidentially.

"That may be. But no matter what you do in Westchester County, your soul will be as dry and as grey as my hair. And that's the whole of it."

"You don't belong in New York," I said. "Why don't you go back to Valdosta."

She was unmoved. "You watch your manners," she said. "That's just what I've been telling you. Self-control. Try to keep a sense of perspective."

"Sorry."

"And don't apologize!" She paused, the yellow number two pencil pressed against her cheek. "It's just too late."

I hung my head, staring at my cordovans and maroon socks. My cordovans seemed to have gotten scuffed by walking on the sidewalk. "Then that's it?"

She sniffed. "Don't go asking me. You're the doctor."

I studied my shoes a little longer. There didn't seem any more to say. I consulted my watch. "Well," I said, "I guess I've got to be going."

"Mmm. Always enjoy seeing a former pupil again," she said, her jaw set.

"Yes. I can see that." We were both silent. "Well," I began again, "I'd better get going. It was nice to see you."

"Speak the truth. I should have kept you after school more. No doubt about it," she said, looking at my shoes. "But even

167

then, it might not have helped."

"I did learn penmanship pretty well," I said.

"All right. Glad to hear that. Goodbye, Danny Altman."

"Goodbye. My regards to Valdosta." I held out my hand.

She had already turned, however, and was walking uptown, away from me, her body bent forward, her face turned upwards at an angle towards the sky, her pale blue frock brushing about her legs, her pencil still in hand. "Say what you mean," I heard her say, "And don't pass notes when you think no one is looking."

I let my hand fall to my side and, taking a deep breath, started walking downtown. After I'd taken five or six steps, I turned to look at her one more time. We were already separated by a throng of pedestrians. All I could see was a grey frizz of hair bobbing among the heads, now visible, now gone, now visible, now lost, as the distance between us continued to grow.

Donna
and the Doctor

The Chadwick Family Practice Center was bustling. One of the aides pointed Bigham towards an examining room down the corridor. "Your next one's in there," she said. Bigham took the chart out of the rack, glanced at it, and knocked. A voice said "Okay," and he went in.

A young woman in her twenties was sitting cross-legged on the chair. She was in white shorts and a loose-fitting yellow halter that bared her shoulders and cradled her breasts.

"So, Miss LaGrava," Bigham said, reading her name off the chart. "What brings you here today?"

The woman gave a quick smile, then shook her head and winced. "I been havin' these wicked pains in my stomach?"

"For how long?"

"I don't know. Weeks at least. Months. See, I had an abortion a couple years ago and got infected. They had to put me in the hospital an' operate, an' I was on intravenous and all. That was the beginnin'."

He took a seat beside her, dropped her chart on the desk in front of him, and turned towards her. "And now?"

She leaned towards him, hands clasped together, an urgent look on her face. "Now I been gettin' the same kind of pains again. Sometimes they're so bad, they make me cry. I have to lie down, hold my stomach, get somethin' for the pain."

"Something like what?" Bigham tilted his head. He'd been having trouble with the drug addicts in town lately. Everyone was coming in and asking for Valium and Percodan, making his life miserable. He hoped she wasn't another one.

"I had this doctor?" She said it like a question. "He tried me on all sorts of pills. But the only thing that ever worked was Percocet."

Bigham shook his head. Whenever he heard "the only thing," he assumed the patient was looking for drugs. But for some reason today he decided to give this woman a chance. Maybe because it was a hot muggy day in June, and he'd been running from room to room for the last seven hours and was bone tired. Maybe because life was hard enough without having to mistrust everybody. Maybe because the woman looked like she'd been through a lot and could use a sympathetic ear. Anyway, he was a doctor, not a detective, and he thought he'd hear her out. "Okay. So, tell me. Why can't you take anything else?"

"I just can't. Like, my stomach gets even worse with other pills. An' I can't take anything with codeine. It makes me wicked sick, and I get all bound up." She suddenly looked embarrassed. Then, leaning forward, she put her hand on his knee, and said, confidentially, "This doctor tried me on Darvon and Tylenol, and a lot of pills like Motrin and Naprosyn. You know? But they just made me sick in my stomach and gave me an awful taste in my mouth." She pulled a small brown bottle out of her purse and plonked it on the desk. "See. Here's the last prescription I had. Forty Percocet, and they lasted me two months. You can see for yourself, there's still two left inside." She shook it like a rattle. "I don't take it unless I have to. Really, I hate takin' any kind of pills. I wouldn't ask for it if I didn't need it."

The bottle looked legitimate. Bigham recognized the doctor who prescribed it. Doctor Michaelson had recently retired. "Okay," he said. "Tell me about your pains."

She told him about her abortion, her infection, the operation she had afterwards, her X-rays, her visits to several clinics. ...

"All right. Look, I'll need your medical records from all these places."

"Sure. If you're going to be my doctor, I'd want that."

Bigham asked about her life. She told him she lived with her five-year-old daughter in an apartment nearby. She had a boyfriend, but the relationship was on the skids. She wanted to get well so she could get a decent job, be a better mother, do something with her life. Her main problem was the belly pain she'd had ever since the abortion. Also, she had a discharge and her periods were irregular. Bigham scrawled some notes. "They've already checked your weight and blood pressure, and you don't have any fever. So let me examine you." He handed her a green cloth gown. "Miss LaGrava …"

"Donna," she said.

"Donna, put this on, and I'll be back." Then he left the room. "Becky," he called from the hall. "I need a chaperone in Room Four." And he went to see another patient.

When he was finished, he headed back to Room Four. One of the aides, Lisa Serrani, was sitting in the corner and Donna LaGrava was on the examining table in the green gown.

Bigham listened to her heart and lungs, felt for glands in her neck. He held a wooden tongue depressor in his right hand and a penlight in the other. "Say 'Aaah.'"

When she did, there was something strange about her throat, but he couldn't say what. Something oddly … permissive. He didn't need the blade: she opened her throat completely, widely, for him. The walls of her pharynx were glistening wet and contracted sharply when he touched her tongue with the blade. It was almost uncanny. Everything else checked out. He asked her to lie down on his examining table and palpated her abdomen. She grimaced when he pressed her left side. "There!" she cried. "You got it! Right there!"

Bigham sighed. "Okay, Miss LaGrava. Look," he said. "I'm going to need to examine you down below. Lisa, can you set this up?" He pulled a screen around the table.

"What?" Donna said. "Why do you need to do that?"

"You've got pains down there and a discharge, your abdomen is tender, and you've had a bad infection before."

She hesitated, then nodded. "All right."

"While I'm at it, I'll check your breasts, too," he said. "It's part of the same exam. Then I'll get a Pap smear and examine you for infection."

"You want me to sit up?"

"Please."

While Lisa was setting up for the pelvic exam—examining tray, rubber gloves, speculum, jelly, swabs, slides, culture tubes, fixative spray—Bigham stood at the side of the examining table. Donna had taken the top of her gown down and the size of her breasts surprised him. They were pendulous and as swollen as sacks of wine. "All right, let me check you," he said. He lifted her left breast with his left hand and pressed the fingertips of his right hand against its upper part. The skin was smooth, but the breast had the texture of a bunch of grapes: fluctuant, like a waterbed.

"I got implants," she explained. "I was a dancer. I thought it'd help my career."

"And did it?"

"Nah. I had a lot of trouble. I thought the doc made my boobs too big, which was not what I wanted. And I didn't feel comfortable with all those pigs tryin' to touch me ..."

Bigham felt each quadrant for lumps, but all he could feel were globs of thick, squishy stuff. After checking the left breast, he palpated the right. Same thing. And then, without under-standing why, he felt aroused. Which made him uneasy. Bigham never got aroused during breast or pelvic exams. He regarded it as inappropriate.

"Well," he said, turning away. "Aside from those implants, your breasts seem healthy enough. Do they hurt when you get your period?"

"Yeah. They ache wicked bad."

"And have you ever taken anything for that?"

"Like I said, Motrin. But it only made me sick."

"Okay. Miss LaGrava. You can close the top of your johnny."

He stepped to the other side of the screen and put on the rubber gloves. "Lisa, will you get her ready?"

Lisa guided Donna into a reclining position, pulled the metal stirrups out of the base of the table, and slid Donna's feet into them. Then she went to the head of the table and held Donna's hand. "You just relax, honey. You'll be fine."

Bigham moved to the foot of the table. "Okay, Miss LaGrava. You'll feel something cold. This won't take but a few minutes."

Donna held the side of the table with one hand and Lisa's hand with the other. Bigham shone his gooseneck lamp on her vagina and picked up his speculum. "All right." Her labia were puffed and puckered, light orange like an apricot, and set in relief by her pubic area which was shaved almost completely bare. He spread the lips apart, then slipped the speculum inside. "I'll take the PAP smear first," he said. He focused the light, then spread the speculum blades and looked in. "There's definitely some discharge here, so let me get a culture first." He picked a clean cotton swab off the metal examining tray, scraped the cervix, then put the swab into a culture tube. Then he picked up the wooden PAP smear spatula, spread the speculum blades again, and looked inside again. The cervix was round, pink, and gleaming. He took the PAP smear, then removed the speculum and put it on the metal tray. Then he spread the specimen onto two slides and laid the spatula aside.

"Ouch," she said to him. "That hurt."

"Sorry ... Okay, now let's see what's going on. I'm going to look for any sign of abscess or infection. Did you say you had one of your ovaries out?"

"Yeah. The right one."

He slid his gloved second and third fingers into her vagina, moved them to the right and felt for a mass. Then he felt the contours of the uterus. "Does that hurt?"

"No."

He moved to the left side, palpating the ovary. "And over here?"

173

"Ow! Yes. Right there."

"Okay. You're right, your right ovary is gone. But you've still got the left one and it seems very tender."

"That's where it hurts," she said. He probed the area further with his gloved fingers. "Ouch! Yes. Right there!"

"Okay," Bigham said. He removed his hand and crossed to the other side of the screen. "You can get dressed now." He took the gloves off and tossed them in the waste can. Then he prepared the slides, spraying fixative on them and securing them in a brown slide holder. "I'm not sure what's going on," he said. "You might have an infection. You might have a cyst. I think you need an ultrasound."

"An ultrasound. I had them before."

"Right. We'll talk about it after you're dressed."

He took her chart with him into his office and wrote some notes. When he returned, she was in her clothes again, on the chair. He sat down beside her. "I'm not really sure what's going on. I'd like some blood tests, urine tests. Routine. And I'll need records from the other doctors you've seen. And then you'll come back for another visit."

"Okay," she said. "So can I have my medicine?"

He looked up. "What?"

"Some Percocet 'til these pains go away."

Bigham didn't like to prescribe narcotics. When he did, it was only for a brief period of time, like two or three weeks. But Donna LaGrava did seem in pain. And he'd done a thorough exam, ordered tests. "All right," he said. "I guess I can for now. At least until we know what's causing all this." He scrawled a prescription for thirty Percocet. "When you come back, we should have some answers for you." He smiled.

She put the prescription in her bag. Then she put her hand on Bigham's hand. "Thank you, Doctor," she said.

Bigham stood up. "The receptionist will make your next appointment. I'll see you then," he said.

Bigham sat in his office, completing his note. Donna LaGrava was now his patient. He'd taken a history and performed a physical exam. He'd touched her body, her private parts, a ritual that bound them together, patient to physician, physician to patient. The laying-on of hands.

He thought about how doctors were supposed to examine patients in an impersonal, "professional" way. Any straying from that detachment was inappropriate. And yet, he reflected, years of intimate experiences were compacted in his hands—reassuring, probing, greeting, caressing, making love. How could his hands examine people's bodies without invoking those other experiences? How did he manage to touch one woman's breasts (his wife's) "lovingly" one moment, and then, hours later, another's (his patient's) "professionally"? He knew the usual answer: it wasn't what the hands, but what the brain felt that mattered. It was all in one's attitude. But still …

Sometimes, during an exam, he'd had flashes of past experience. He might have been touching a patient's breast or stomach, or stroking their arm, when a sudden memory emerged, the remembrance of some other body, someone else he'd touched in almost the same place, or in almost the same way, but at a different time and perhaps for a different reason. And, along with that memory, he'd sensed again the feelings he'd had at that earlier time. It amazed him, it was a mystery, but it was also unsettling.

He wondered how Donna LaGrava made a living. She'd said she'd been a dancer, but what was she now? Was she still a dancer, perhaps even a stripper, or did she have some other job? She seemed oddly comfortable showing her body. Then he remembered having been aroused during the exam and he felt confused, guilty. Bigham didn't like ambiguity, and he didn't like feelings that couldn't be explained and acknowledged.

But that night, making love to his wife, Bigham flashed to Donna LaGrava's breasts and to her up-tilted thighs the moment before he'd inserted his fingers, and he imagined embracing her, a breast in each palm, and entering her wetness below.

Donna appeared at the Center two weeks later, dressed again in shorts, and a halter without a bra. Her blood tests, urine, and Pap smear had been normal, and the culture had grown out normal flora. She hadn't gone for the ultrasound, so it had been rescheduled. She told Bigham her pain had been so bad she'd had to take all thirty Percocets.

"An' I fought with my boyfriend. I think he's leavin.' Just talking about it makes me want to cry. I hate being alone, just me an' my daughter ... But I don't have no one to turn to."

"There must be someone in your family. A parent. A brother or sister. A friend."

"There's no one. My mom's dead. I never knew my dad. I got a brother in Cleveland I haven't seen in years. And friends ...?" She scoffed. "I don't think you can trust nobody." She started sniffling and reached for a Kleenex. "I know my privates are sick, I'll never have any more kids. ..."

"Come on," Bigham said. "It's not that bad. If there's something wrong, we'll find it out and help you feel better."

"But what makes it hurt so bad?" she sobbed. "I get so scared. I don't want to be sterile." She put her hand on his arm. "I'm sure something horrible's happened. First, I had the abortion and got infected, and they took out my ovary. Then I had a miscarriage. I don't think I told you about that last time, but I did, and I had to have a D and C to clean me out. I haven't been right since. My periods are all messed up. I took birth control pills, but they made me bleed all the time, so I had to stop them. And now I don't know what's happening, with these wicked pains ..."

Bigham felt battered as if by waves in a storm. "Look," he said. "Miss LaGrava. I don't know what to say. We need to get you an appointment with a gynecologist, and I still want the records of everything that's happened, and that ultrasound. I can't tell you what's going on until I get all the information. You know?" She nodded, blew her nose. "Give us a chance. Let us look at your records. You get the test. See what a gynecologist says. I'm just a family doctor, you know."

"And what about the pain?"

"What about it?"

"I need somethin.' I can't go on."

He hesitated. "I can't keep giving you Percocet," he said. "It's too easy to get hooked on."

"But what if the pains keep up and you can't find the reason?" she said. "I been to gynecologists before. They can't find anything. That's why Doctor Michaelson was giving it to me."

Bigham felt uncomfortable. Something wasn't right. But the woman looked so incredibly distressed. "If the pains continue and we don't come up with an answer, we'll have to consider other alternatives," he said. "Maybe a referral to a pain center. You can't take narcotics for the rest of your life." He shook his head. "But we're getting way ahead of ourselves. Let's see what the gynecologist says. Maybe you need a laparoscopy."

"What's that?"

"It's when they look into your belly with a little scope to see what's going on."

"Oh, no. I don't want another operation!"

"I'm just saying it might be an option ..."

"I don't care. I don't want to be seeing a whole lot of doctors again."

"Okay, look," he said, sighing. "All right. I'll give you thirty more Percocet for now, but I can't promise any more." And he wrote out the prescription.

"And something for my nerves. Please."

The request irritated him. He'd already given in on something he usually wouldn't do, and now she was pressing him for more. But he had three or four people waiting to be seen, and he didn't want to get into another long discussion, over tranquillizers this time.

"All right. Something for your nerves. Just for now." He dashed off the prescription, tore it off the pad, and spun it across the desk. "But look, I want that ultrasound done. And you'll see the gynecologist. And I need those records." He made a note to discuss medication the next time she came in.

"They won't have to operate, will they?" she asked.

"I don't know."

"I don't want no operation."

"I understand. Just get the ultrasound, and I'll see you after that."

"All right." He showed her to the door, and then she was gone.

Bigham had been working at the Center for seven years. When he finished his residency in family medicine, he'd decided to find a job in an underserved community, caring for poor, hard-working folks who needed it. He'd been raised in Tennessee, by strict Appalachian people, and he felt an almost religious calling to help folks who were "doing without." His God-fearing parents sent him to private elementary and high schools at great cost to themselves, so he could get a good education. His grades won him a scholarship to Davidson, and from there to the Medical College of Virginia. All through his residency he thought about where he should practice, and then he made his decision.

After completing his military service, his first job was with a series of clinics in rural Iowa. That was where he met his wife, Ina. Growing up, Bigham hadn't had much experience with women, and his mother, Effie-Ma, had frequently warned him about getting involved with them, especially the "wrong" kind of girls. But Ina seemed different. She was serious. She was a Presbyterian, too, and she wanted her life to be of use. They fell in love and got married after a year.

After five years in Iowa, Bigham was ready for a change. He thought of working in an urban setting, and Ina encouraged him. She wanted to get out of the Midwest and had always imagined being in New England, so he accepted Chadwick's offer. He felt he'd made the right choice. He liked and respected the other physicians there. He liked the nearby hospital. And so he and Ina had formed a life for themselves in the suburbs north of

Boston.

They lived in a small house a few towns from Chadwick. Ina taught third grade. Without children, Bigham felt they had a simple life, structured by their religious convictions and sense of service.

The records from Donna's other doctors did not arrive. In the middle of the next week, she phoned Bigham's office, frantic. Her boyfriend had broken into her home. He'd beaten her up, ransacked the place, and thrown her pills down the toilet. "He don't believe I'm sick," she cried. "He said he don't want me takin' pills. What am I goin' to do now?"

Bigham's stomach churned. The story sounded hokey. "Look, Miss LaGrava, Donna," he said. "I feel awful. And I'm so sorry to hear this has happened. But I can't refill your prescriptions."

"But I'm in horrible pain," she moaned. "I'm all beat up …"

"I'm sorry. I can't."

"Was it my fault I got beat up?" she asked.

He felt he needed to make a stand. "Look, Donna. I understand what you're saying," he said. "But I can't make an exception."

"Can I come down and see you? Right now? I just want to talk …"

Her image welled up in his mind. He wanted to see her. He felt clammy, confused. "All right," he said, exasperated with her and himself as well. "Come down."

She was there in fifteen minutes, so disheveled that the receptionist buzzed her in at once. "Look at me!" she cried. "I'm such a mess." She pulled her hair aside to reveal a fresh bruise over her temple. An' look at this." She opened her blouse. "He punched me in the boobs. Here. And here. It's all black and blue." She showed him bruises on the side of her breast. "And here." She pulled up her skirt to show him a mark on her thigh. "You see?"

"I see."

"So can I please get my meds. Just this once. I'm not making trouble for you. He threw everything down the john. I can't go through this anymore, not with my daughter in the house."

What was he supposed to do? She was all banged up. And if she was, then she was a victim, and he had to help. "All right. Just this once. But for only twelve pills each." He wrote out the prescriptions and handed them to her. "But not again. And make sure you report this to the police. If he can do this, he can do worse."

"I will. And I'm staying with my girlfriend. He won't know where I am."

"Okay." All the bruises made him feel unsettled. "And don't forget the ultrasound and your appointment with Doctor Wells. I'll see you at your next appointment."

In his office, later, Bigham tried to put together what was going on. He hadn't gotten the woman's records. He didn't have a diagnosis. And here she was, coming in, showing him her bruises, getting him to refill prescriptions. She seemed so pathetic, but yet ...

Bigham had chosen medicine when he was nineteen, wanting something concrete and useful in life. The world's chaos frightened him. When he'd left his parents' home, the strange streets in Davidson had fascinated him. He'd wandered through them at night, passing home after home, peering into lit windows, his attention drawn by the moving figures, fantasizing about what lay beyond. Unbounded, the world seemed too enticing. He needed more confines, a world as measured as his parents' house with its clearcut values, simple guidelines, and plain expectations. Medicine was a well-paved avenue cutting across the unpredictable swamps, which could conduct him safely from one point to another. It would be a safe, structured way, shepherding him and his family past life's chasms. Medicine was a guarantee.

But now, with this Donna LaGrava, he felt cast into the swamp. He couldn't follow her like a detective to check out her story. But he couldn't wash his hands of her, either, because something in him wanted to see her again. Her helplessness made her vulnerable. He again imagined her swollen breasts, her gaping mouth, her bruised thighs. And, as he sat wondering what to do, the image of her on his examining table welled up in his mind. She was on her back underneath the sheet, naked except for her shoes, her legs spread apart to display her puckered lips, and he was about to insert his gloved fingers ...

Half an hour later the police called. They were at a pharmacy a few blocks away, with Donna LaGrava. The officer said she'd handed the pharmacist a prescription with Bigham's signature for a hundred and twenty Percocet pills, but it looked like it had been altered. The pharmacist had called them.

"What?" Bigham exploded. "I gave the woman a scrip for a dozen pills and told her it was the last one she was going to get."

"Well, it's been changed to read a hundred and twenty now," the officer said. "This patient of yours, LaGrava, we've run across her before. She often tries to pass prescriptions for narcotics, and from all sorts of doctors. You're not the only one. Do you mind if we come by and get a statement?"

They were there in five minutes. Two officers. Bigham showed them into his office. "I think things with her just got out of hand," he said, stammering. He was feeling both outraged and scared. He didn't want the officers to think he prescribed loosely, didn't want to get into trouble. "Look, I usually don't prescribe these drugs, but ..."

One of the cops held up his hand. "Doc, don't worry. We've heard this all before. The fact is, there's a large drug ring here in Chadwick. The mob's got their hands on it. They get these young women, hookers they pick up in the Combat Zone, runaways, whatever. Get them onto drugs, then send them to all the doctors in town. It's like pimping. The women have to bring in a certain amount of drugs every week. They get some for themselves, but the rest goes to the mob."

"She came in here all black and blue!" Bigham said. "She was really in pain."

"Right," the cop said. "When the girls don't bring in enough drugs, these guys'll do anything—cut them up, beat them, throw them down the stairs. It doesn't matter to them. Then they'll send the girls back to the docs, hoping for a scrip they can alter. After all, a Percocet on the street goes for between five and ten bucks. Tylenol with codeine for three to five. People always want Valiums or Xanax. They give each girl a different story, an identity, some kind of gimmick. One'll have belly pain. Another'll have to have Valium or she'll go crazy. Another's had too many operations and can't live without codeine. These guys aren't stupid. They read the medical books. They know just how to prime the girls, tell them what stories to tell. And they always get the most pathetic-looking, pretty kids. For instance, this one, LaGrava. Did she wear sexy clothes the first time you saw her?"

He remembered. "Yes."

"And, excuse me for asking, but did you have to check her tits, do an internal?"

"Yes. In fact, I did."

The cop grinned at his partner, then looked back at Bigham. "That's their specialty," he said. "They love to get you hooked. They'll flash some tit, a little beaver, then ask for drugs." Bigham turned red. "Hey, relax," the cop said. "You're not the only one. This gal's been to five different docs in town. She pulls the same kind of shit on every one of them."

"But if you know all this, why don't you do something! Tell the doctors what's going on?" Bigham said. "Really! If I'd known, I'd have done something different."

"We've been watching the operation," the other cop put in. "We don't want to shake it up yet. We've been onto it six months now, tracking the whole thing. It'd be stupid to haul in just one or two of the girls and not have enough evidence to get the guys behind it, wouldn't it?"

"Right," Bigham said. He felt stupid, humiliated, no matter

what the cop said. "So, I'm just one gullible guy among many," he said weakly.

"Seems like it," the cop said. "They may be amateurs, hookers to begin with, but they soon become pros. What difference does it make if they do a trick with a john or pull their pants down for a doc? It's all the same to them."

"So … are you going to arrest her?"

"We might take her down to the station, fill out a sheet. But we'll make it seem that we think it's just *her* idea. File some charges. Give her a warning. It won't do any good. She'll be at it somewhere else next week."

"It's sad," Bigham said, his throat feeling very dry. "These women are victims. They're being used. And to think they're being beaten up just to get pills. It's sick."

"What can I tell you, doc," the officer said. "That's the way it is." He put his notebook in his pocket. "Anyway, thanks for your help."

"Right." Bigham saw the two of them out, then went back to his office. He sat in his chair for a long time, running over the story again and again in his mind, as if he was trying to get it straight. Recalling his own reactions, he felt embarrassed. He hoped the story wouldn't get around. He kept remembering how Donna LaGrava looked, how she carried herself when she walked, how she had lifted her skirt to show him the bruises on her thighs. Once again, he pictured her helpless face, her breasts, her open, cavernous mouth.

Rooms

Mr. Haggerty is in the same room now that Mrs. Gruenberg was four months ago. West Two, Room 214. I can still remember going there every day for weeks, morning after morning, smiling, trying to be cheerful: "Hello, Mrs. Gruenberg. How are you, Mrs. Gruenberg? Did you eat your breakfast today, Mrs. Gruenberg?" And then a side remark to the nurse, who was standing by the bed with a glass of juice or a spoon of cereal in her hand, poised, hovering in midair, temporarily arrested in its descent towards Mrs. Gruenberg's quivering mouth, and looking at me quizzically, like I was a dummy. "How's she doing? Is she eating?" And then Mrs. Gruenberg would start crying, and she'd cry and cry until my heart was breaking, and I'd want to get away as fast as I could.

Mrs. Gruenberg had suffered a stroke. That was after surgery on both her carotid arteries, which was supposed to increase the circulation to her head and *prevent* a stroke. After her first operation, she had a brief stroke, but she recovered from it. Then there had been a question about "doing the other side." The vascular surgeon strongly advised it. The family was unsure. Finally, her son and his wife said go ahead. She should have "the best possible chance," they said. But after the surgery, Mrs. Gruenberg didn't regain consciousness. Her right side was paralyzed, and she couldn't speak. At first it seemed she could understand but couldn't talk. After a while, though, it didn't seem she could understand anything. Of course, you could never be sure.

She would lie there all morning and cry. She couldn't talk, couldn't move her right side, couldn't nod or smile. I never knew

185

if she felt sad, or if sadness was the only thing she could express, so she expressed it all the time. I didn't know if she was in pain, or if she knew where she was, or who she was, or who I was, or if she recognized her son and his wife, or anything. All my special tricks ("Okay, if you can understand me now, Mrs. Gruenberg, close your eyes.") failed. I faced her morning after morning, bantering with the nurse, trying not to miss the formation of any bed sores, comparing Mrs. Gruenberg's oral and intravenous intake with her urinary output, following her fever, checking that the intravenous line was patent, watching to see if she was moving a finger on her right hand or not. And every few days, I'd get the inevitable call from her son: "So. Doc. How's she doing?"

After waiting more than three months, Mrs. Gruenberg finally got transferred to a nursing home. She lasted about five weeks before she died. The day she moved out another patient moved in, of course. I guess that's where I started. Then that patient moved out, and another came in. And then another. And now there's Mr. Haggerty. Of course, I hadn't been the physician for the others. Just for Mrs. Gruenberg and Mr. Haggerty. So, for me, Mr. Haggerty's room is filled with the spirit of Mrs. Gruenberg.

I sometimes wonder if the rooms are inhabited by the ghosts of patients past. Invisible, they sit against the walls or lie in heaps in the corners, as thin as fish food. Perhaps they glower from the ceilings or huddle in the bathroom, in the crevice behind the john. Inhabitant after inhabitant, patient after patient, year after year. How many would that be? And the beds, there are close to two hundred different beds in the hospital, each with its own history, its own pedigree; each one unique.

"Look at me," one bed might say. "In 1972, it was I who held Henry Klootz, who had six consecutive cardiac arrests. In 1975, I was taken by Mary Washburn, who, recovering from gallbladder surgery, saw each of her five children every day. In 1978, I remember ..."

The beds themselves never change. They are almost always where they were the day before. The rare exception might be when one has to be shoved into the hall because its patient is being obstreperous, shouting and screaming, trying to climb over the side rails all night long, keeping everyone awake. But aside from such special circumstances, they stay in the same place all the time. They might get dirty, their rails might not go down, they may have two pillows or three, but they will be the same, day after day: persistent, enduring.

The same is true of everything else in the hospital rooms. Room 307, for example, on East Three, has a window which always looks out on the small row of houses across the street and on the downward-sloping hill behind it. The bed light stands, silent and ready, above the bedstead, over the pillows, its cord ending in a special button that lies at the patient's right (or left) side. The bed stands flat against the wall, flanked by the brown bedside table, its three drawers a home away from home for the patient's private goods—key ring, Kleenex, address book, and glasses; hearing aid, pen and pencil, writing pad, Get Well cards, and Bible—that bring familiarity to the strangely antiseptic room, and a large imitation leather chair.

Across the room from the bed is the bathroom, its fixtures unchanging and predictable, day after day: the white porcelain sink, the johnny bowl, the roll of toilet paper that the orderly changes every day, the small molded plastic white rack for washcloths and towels, the toothbrush holder, the soap dish and the shelf for toothpaste, razor, and cosmetics, the stand for the plastic cups. Back in the room, there is the bed, the table beside it, and the imitation leather chair, squeezed next to the window, pressed against the radiator. It's usually visitors who take that chair. Sometimes patients do, however, if they can get out of bed, if they have recovered from whatever infirmity brought them there in the first place. They can sit in the morning sun, drinking their breakfast coffee and leafing through the morning paper. Just yesterday, in fact, Mr. Candeloro was enjoying himself like that in Room 117 on West One. He looked so jolly in the bright sunlight, so unlike the previous resident of that room, Mr. Horton, who lay mired in bed for weeks, anchored to intravenous tubing, Foley catheter, heart monitor, restraints ...

Other features are identical in every room: the drapes, lino-
leum floor, ceiling lights, buzzers, intercom, lamps; the curtains
which enclose the bed when necessary. They only change when
the hospital decides to renovate.

Even the disposable objects have a predictable, standard feel.
To be sure, the patients may be different. Mrs. Hodgson may
be short, obese, and elderly; and Miss Appleberry (who took
over her bed) may be tall, slim, and young: but the IV bottles
and tubing, the sheets, wash basins and towels, the respiratory
equipment (masks, sprays, pumps, oxygen tanks, spirometers,
bags, cups, charts, instruction sheets) are the same. The EKG
machine and portable X-ray equipment, the steel trapeze for the
bedridden, the catheters and emesis basins (baby blue plastic for
the latter) never seem to change.

The reality of the hospital lies in its objects. The patients are
transitory, ephemeral. The objects remain and give the hospital
its essence, its identity. The objects endure. Let the ghosts of
past patients haunt the staff in the wee hours of the morning.
Let the memories of cardiac arrests, unearthly shrieks, purulent
odors, linger in the air, unnoticed except by a few old-timers. No
wonder the patients feel they're in another world. They are. They
are in the World of Hospital Things. No wonder the staff scrubs
the walls so religiously, polishes the floors so devotedly, changes
the beds like clockwork. The objects must be maintained. They
endure, while the patients come and go.

The older staff gradually seems to resemble the desks, chart
racks, and counters: stolid and stern, unyielding, enduring; things.
They slowly turn into fixtures, too. Just like the bed in Room 307.
Ever-present, unyielding, secure.

The patients ... Who remembers, after all, the roster of past
souls now hovering in Room 113, East One? What were their
names? When were they born? Where? What were their favorite
desserts? What illnesses did they have? Who visited them?

No one remembers. But ask anyone to hang up 500cc of normal saline and run it in at 60cc an hour, and they'll know what

you mean. The IV team will start it. The nurses will monitor it. The fluids will flow. They'll do what they're supposed to do. Ask someone to make the bed, or get a wheelchair, or bring the white enamel scale with the rollers, or get a basin, or wash the floor: people will know what you're talking about. Who remembers Mrs. Gruenberg?

The objects, the objects alone endure.

Early Autumn

For years they'd rejected the traditions they'd grown up with, but, as they neared forty, Matt and Clara Marks found themselves longing for something familiar. Rootless disbelievers, estranged from their families, they determined to create their own rituals through a series of holidays which would mark the changing seasons. They'd celebrate some of these with their children, but others would be for them alone.

One summer, driving through upstate New Hampshire, they'd passed an inn overlooking a valley so picturesque, they resolved to spend their next Columbus Day weekend there. That stay had been so successful, they repeated it the following year; and when they left, they reserved the room for another year as well. Now that weekend had come.

This was the second marriage for each. Clara, a psychotherapist, had custody of her two teenagers, Gail and Sam. Matt taught physics at the local high school and saw his children every other weekend.

Early Friday morning, they packed carefully, choosing books for light reading and clothes for hiking and dinner. Gail and Sam were staying with friends. Matt's two children were with their mother. To discourage burglars, Matt turned on the kitchen radio, and Clara turned on the bathroom and bedroom lights. Then they loaded up the car, locked the front door, and headed out.

Matt stopped for gas at the corner station, then drove to the liquor store. "Just want to get some brandy," he said, letting the engine idle.

"I hate doing errands before we leave," Clara said. "Why can't we just go?"

"It's no problem. Our time is our own. I'll be right back."

"Okay. Go get your brandy," she said.

They drove north. The suburbs gave way to large, wooded areas, flat stretches of highway lined with trees; fields dotted with small lakes, creeks, and an occasional farm. The leaves were changing. Slashes of crimson cut across the landscape. Bright orange patches emerged amid the green. Yellow whorls dappled the hillsides. Here and there a factory complex rose up along a river, red brick and angular, only to recede quickly into the distance.

Matt turned the radio to soft rock. "Let's enjoy being together," he said. "Just the two of us." He stuck a cigarette in his mouth, pushed the lighter knob on the dashboard. "Away from school. Away from students, phones, the city."

They listened to the radio and marveled at the leaves. Every so often a flaming red tree would appear, or clumps of dazzling orange and yellow.

"What are the innkeepers' names again?" Matt said. "Carl is the man. But what's her name?"

"Let me think. Nettie? Nellie?"

"That doesn't sound right either. Nancy?"

"I don't think so."

"I think it's Nancy."

"It still doesn't sound right." She paused. "Well, we'll find out when we get there."

"I'll feel foolish if we forget."

"I'm sure they'll understand. They meet people all the time."

Above them, the sun pulsed in a cloudless sky.

"Sam seems to be straightening out," Matt said. "He's been calmer at home, getting better grades."

"He's doing better, but I still worry. Sam's always in the back of my mind, just waiting to make me crazy."

"Maybe you should set clearer limits for him."

"That's not the answer. He's marvelous with other people. Everyone who meets him thinks he's an angel. He's just a monster with me."

"Probably because he feels safe with you. He can let his feelings out. Right?"

"Right. I'm the only person in the world he dumps on. And I do more for him than anyone else."

"But it's always like that. Moms."

"That doesn't make it any easier."

He shook his head. "Kids."

They drove on. "That friend of Gail's, Peggy, is a nice girl," Clara said. "Very sincere."

"Very."

"She's over the house a lot these days."

"I'm glad they're friends," Matt said. Then he paused. "You know, other people's kids are part of our lives. Our kids' friends. We've watched them grow up. Like, we knew Peggy when she got her braces, when she had her first crush." Clara nodded. "The sad thing is, we don't know them all that well. I mean, we get a glimpse from time to time. Some movie they saw, a song they like, a fight they're having with their folks. But that's it. We only see them a few moments across a huge expanse of time."

"What are you saying?" she asked.

"That I only know people like Peggy in bits and pieces. I don't really know her. I mean I like her, I'm interested in what happens to her, but ..."

"Do you know our friends any better?" she said. "How many times do we see most of them? Once a month? Every couple of weeks?"

"Well, I guess, except for close friends, like Ben and Peter, you're right."

"We know Peggy the same way we know most folks. We see

her a few times, some of them significant, some not. Isn't that what knowing usually is?"

"But there's more to it than that. Knowing someone more deeply. Like you and me. Don't you think?"

"Of course. But that develops over time, and only with people you really love."

2.

They reached the Inn of Twin Pillars at one-thirty. Carl, the innkeeper, was at the desk. He checked them in and showed them to their room. "Same one you had the other two years," he said, chuckling, opening the door and waving an arm at the bed and dresser. "Hey, Nancy's cooking. But she'll want to say hi as soon as she's done." They put their clothes in the dresser and closet, then sat down on the bed. Matt opened the brandy and poured two glasses.

"Nancy," Clara said. "You were right. That was her name."

He handed her a brandy and they clinked glasses. He took a gulp, then stretched out on the bed and closed his eyes. Clara took a sip, then put her glass on the side table and moved around the room, straightening up and patting things into place. Then she returned and sat down beside him. He put a hand on her shoulder and smiled. She smiled back but twisted away. "Matt, let's take a walk while it's still sunny."

They put on their coats and went downstairs. Nancy was at the front desk now, leafing through the reservation book. She seemed happy to see them and quickly began talking about her dining room renovations and the new menu, but just then the phone rang. When she picked it up, Matt and Clara moved towards the door, waving and shrugging apologetically. As they walked out, Matt bumped into a tall blond girl in her late teens. She glared at them, then slammed the door as she stalked inside.

"Jesus!" Matt said.

"Isn't that their daughter?" Clara asked. "I think I remember her from last year."

194

"Could be. What's she so angry about?"

"Beats me."

The mid-afternoon sun was slipping lower in the western sky, its color deepening. They climbed their favorite hill, admiring the valley to their left. Mountain crests rose above the fields, their tops sheathed in clouds, their sides ablaze with lemon and scarlet. A dairy farm extended down one side of the hill towards the valley. Cows lay in the hilly fields, chewing quietly, staring at them as they approached. Puffballs and goldenrod crammed the roadside; and giant milkweed pods, their green sacks bursting, clung to their stalks, entrusting their silken treasures to the wind.

"This is gorgeous," Clara said. "Let's keep on walking."

Beyond the second turning of the road was another inn, ramshackle, sprawling, and white, the smell of burning wood rising from its chimney. A small lane wound past it and disappeared further along into a grove of trees. They took it, Matt reaching for Clara's hand.

The lane became a dirt path as it entered the woods. Sunlight streamed through the branches. Dust motes trembled in the breeze. Piles of leaves lay underfoot. As the wind stirred, dozens of burnt orange, red, and corn-colored leaves cut loose from their limbs and spun lazily downward, joining the others already by the path's edge.

"What are you thinking about?" she said.

He looked startled. "Nothing."

"Don't keep secrets."

"You really want to know?" He hesitated. "These woods. I swear, the way they look reminds me of the woods when I was first courting Brenda. Don't ask me why. The late afternoon sunlight filtering through the trees. Those colors. The memory just … came. That autumn smell. The light."

When they got back to the inn, neither innkeeper was in sight. They went to their room and had a few more sips of brandy, then lay down again.

"It's so peaceful here," she said. "but I still feel like a spring

195

all coiled up."

"You've been working hard."

"Haven't we both."

He propped a pillow beneath his head. "It's hard to clear your mind."

They lay side by side quietly for a few minutes. Then Matt took a deep breath. "You know, most of my students don't care about physics. They don't want to know why things are the way they are. They just want to get through the year. I'm starting to feel that way, too."

"I know what you mean," she said. "I love my practice, but it wipes me out."

"Why do we keep on?" he said.

"It's our life," she said. "We're not twenty anymore. This is what we trained for. We can't drift around the globe, doing a little of this and a little of that."

"True," he said wistfully. "We have responsibilities."

"You make it sound horrible."

"It's not horrible. It's what it is. But sometimes I feel …" He paused. "Locked in."

Her eyes glistened. "Wow, I'm sorry life with me is such a drag. Maybe you should go wandering in the woods again, with Brenda."

"Clara, that's not what I mean. I'm not unhappy with you."

"Really? If not for me, you could cut loose. You wouldn't have so many 'responsibilities.'"

"That's not it. It's really me I get tired with. I just have to come to terms with it."

"That's what I mean. Maybe you have to 'come to terms' with me, too."

"That's not it at all." He shook his head. "There's nothing I'd rather be doing. And no one else I'd rather be doing it with."

"Good to hear," she said. Then she turned away. "Is it okay if I read for a while?"

"Sure."

She read and he stared at the ceiling, sipping his brandy. It grew darker outside. He sighed loudly.

"What?" she said, looking up from her book.

He put his arm around her waist, his hand reaching up, his fingers teasing her sweater. "I remember when we were courting, too, Clara. Not just Bren. I remember we also started seeing each other in the fall. We took that walk together up Carver Canyon." He grinned. "Maybe everything romantic happens in September or October."

"Then there's always hope for you, isn't there," she said.

He withdrew his hand. An airplane was droning overhead. "Sure," he said, "whatever you say."

3.

They had dinner in the inn. The dining room was decorated with early American prints and craftwork Nancy had made herself: etchings, theorems. Hand-painted wooden cats perched on the mantelpiece beside an authentic player piano. Antique dishes hung on the stenciled walls. The lights were dim. Each table had candlesticks, and a fire was sizzling in the fireplace. Guests sat in twos and fours, the sound of their conversations diffusing through the room.

They studied their menus, then ordered.

"I think you're right," Clara said, sighing. "I have to dissolve sixteen layers of crud just to get down to 'me' again."

"We shouldn't have to go away to relax."

"But it helps. Every once in a while ..."

"Remember that vacation we took near Conway?" he said. "With Peter and Toni. When we were first getting together. You were convinced I loved my kids more than you, and I thought you were going to break things off."

"I almost did."

"That trouble-maker Toni tried to make it worse."

"She didn't. You know, Toni actually stuck up for you. I was the one taking a hard line. Toni liked you. Still does, so far as I know. She thought you'd been badly hurt by your divorce. Said it was good you wanted to be near your kids. She was criticizing me."

"It didn't feel like it then."

"Well. She was."

"I thought she was meddling. And I didn't like how she treated Peter, who was my friend."

"Peter treated her horribly."

"Maybe." He licked his lips. "I don't know."

"I did worry that you loved your kids more," she said. "Maybe because they already had a history with you. I didn't want to be put second."

The waitress came with their salads, and they waited until she left before continuing.

"I said I loved you both," Matt said. "But in different ways."

"That didn't help."

"But it was true. It was true then, and it's still true now. There's a certain kind of love between parents and kids. You have the same thing with Gail and Sammy. They depend on you. You have to take care of them, be there for them." He shook his head. "Love between a man and a woman is different."

"So you still feel the same way."

"Well, in a sense. I mean, don't you?"

"I think there's something between a man and a woman ..."

"Of course, there is. Something special. But ..."

"Let me finish. There's something very tender between parents and kids. I get that. But there's something else between a man and a woman. At least there should be." She looked away. "I don't know. If you don't feel it, then you don't."

"Of course, I feel it. Why do you say I don't?"

"I sometimes wonder. You seem so business-like lately. Scientific, self-possessed."

"Detached, you're saying."

"Well, all right. Detached."

"You know I don't mean to be."

"How do I know what's going on inside your head?"

They had to stop again, as their main course arrived. The waitress picked up their salad plates, then brought over their main dishes. "Everything all right?" she said.

"Fine," they muttered, and smiled as the waitress left.

They tasted their food, and Matt spoke again: "Clara, you know I love you, deep down."

"Yes. I know." She was silent. They ate their dinner. "Maybe we're just different." she finally said.

He looked down. "I don't understand why you'd bring that whole thing up again, about Peter and Toni."

"What?" Her eyes flashed. "I didn't. You did. And you're the one who was talking about Brenda in the woods."

"I don't think you should be so upset."

"But maybe I am." Her voice was quivering. "Maybe I do wonder whether you love me, deep down. And whether, if it came down to it, you'd choose your kids or me."

He grimaced. "That's never been a question."

"But if it was?"

"You mean, if I had to choose …?"

"Yes." She leaned forward. "Which would you choose?"

"But …" He twisted around, his face in a painful expression. "Neither! That's what I'd say. You're creating a false choice! I love you so much. And I love them, too. I couldn't give either of you up."

"Then you won't answer the question."

"But why put it that way? Are my kids competing with you?"

"No. It's just that I needed, then, and I guess I still do now, to know I'm the most important person to you …"

"This is incredible," he said. "When I wanted to get close to you, a few minutes ago, you pushed me away."

"I was tired!" she cried. "When I get into myself, for just a few minutes, you take it personally."

"I don't think sex and closeness are the same thing," he said. "I thought you knew that by now."

"Shh!" she said, looking around.

"Sorry."

Her voice broke. "I just want a little reassurance, which you seem either unable or unwilling to give right now. That's all." Her lips were trembling. "And don't try to make this into some kind of typical second marriage thing."

"I won't," he said.

She breathed deeply, then wiped her eyes with the napkin. They ate more of their dinner in silence. After a few moments, she spoke again. "I'm tired of the kids always being put first. It's the classic woman's role. I can only give for so long, and then I need something back."

"Don't I give you something back?"

"Yes. But those kids are skillful, Matt. Especially after a divorce. They know how to play on your guilt."

"I don't feel that guilty."

"Then why do you argue about every minute you're supposed to have them? If Brenda keeps them ten minutes longer, you get upset. And when they're with us, you drop everything if they have a question. You cut me off in mid-sentence. That's guilt."

"Okay," he said. "You've made your point."

They'd finished their dinner. Their waitress, a woman in her mid-thirties wearing a colonial outfit, cleared their plates, then brought them homemade Indian pudding with vanilla ice cream for dessert, and refilled their coffee cups as well.

Matt looked around the room. "Say," he said. "Isn't that the innkeeper's daughter over there?"

"That's right," the waitress said. "Hannah usually helps out on the big weekends."

He waited until the waitress had left. "Hannah looks as sour now as she did yesterday."

Clara turned her head. The girl was striding out of the room, head held high, a tray balanced on her shoulder with one hand. "Maybe they're making her work, and she doesn't want to."

"She looks so haughty carrying that tray. Almost arrogant, don't you think?"

Clara dried her eyes. "Not necessarily. Maybe her mind is a thousand miles away. On a vacation she'd like to take."

"What's a girl like that think about," Matt said. "Does she worry about college? Does she dream about some movie producer stopping here, being taken by her, whisking her away? Is she just aching to get away from her folks? How old do you think she is, anyway?"

"If you're so preoccupied with her, why don't you go over and ask her? I'm sure she'd be delighted with whatever you have to say," Clara said. She reached into her pocketbook for a cigarette, lit it and blew smoke at him. "She'd be fascinated with all your theories about her."

"Wait a minute."

"She is pretty," Clara said. "I'll grant you that."

"What are you talking about? Are you jealous …?"

"Of course not."

"… of some little girl? She couldn't be more than sixteen, the same age as Gail."

"I know how old Gail is."

"She's just some huffy teenage kid. I mean, Jesus, I was just making conversation, talking about, whatever, local color. You know, like we usually enjoy doing. Speculating about this person and that one …"

"Let's drop it. The girl's working. I'm not interested in her anymore."

"Clara, why are you …? I was just kidding around."

"Maybe because you seem to be thinking about one woman after another. Brenda, the girl. Falling in love when the leaves turn colors."

"You think I'm that fickle?"

"It does seem to be a pattern."

"That's not fair. I'm not interested in any other women. I mean, you left your husband. By that criteria, I should be the anxious one."

"Maybe you should." She said, staring defiantly at the candle.

"Let's just change the subject," he said. "I don't like where this is going."

"Okay." She finished her coffee.

"Do you want to take a walk after dinner?" he said. "I'm really stuffed."

"I'd just as soon go back and read a little more," she said. "Read, relax, get some sleep."

4.

The next morning, sunlight streamed through the windows and made the dust-motes dance. Frost lay outside like a carpet of needles, covering the entire landscape. The windows were iced up, yet the room was warm and smelled of burning wood. Matt and Clara stayed beneath the quilted comforters for a while. Then they got up. Clara showered. Matt got dressed and sat in the armchair. He stared out the window, then browsed some magazines about New England antiques. When Clara was ready, they went down to breakfast.

"I'm still stuffed from last night," he said.

The innkeeper, wearing his kitchen apron, brought a steaming pot of coffee to each table. He poured cupfuls and asked how they had slept.

"Everything is marvelous here," Matt said. "Just perfect. As good as last year, Carl."

"Glad to hear that," Carl said, pouring the coffee with a flourish. "And you can correct me if I'm wrong, but I think you're going to enjoy this breakfast, too."

They had the same waitress as the previous night. She gave them each a dish of bananas and cream and placed a basket of hot rolls in the center of the table. "Home-made," she said. "Now. What would you like for breakfast? We have a choice of shirred or fried eggs with English muffins, waffles, and ham, bacon, or sausage."

They ordered, then began eating their bananas and cream.

"There she is again," Clara said. "Your girlfriend."

"What?"

"The innkeepers' daughter. Over there."

"Clara, I don't want to fight today."

"Just kidding."

"Don't kid any more. It's not funny." He reached for a roll, then glanced at the girl. She was about five foot eight, tall like her father, and wearing a long, checkered apron over a green sweater and jeans. Her hair was drawn into a bun, but wisps of tawny gold pushed forward around her face. She caught him looking at her and looked away. "You think you'd like working in an inn your parents ran?" he said to Clara.

"You know my parents. I wouldn't like spending any time around them. Besides, they're too selfish to run an inn."

"I wouldn't like working in my parents' inn," he said. "Not having any privacy would drive me nuts. Suppose you met someone you liked. You'd always be feeling they were watching you." He looked away. The innkeeper's daughter, bending forward, was serving bananas and cream to the guests at the other table, a bemused expression on her face. "Do they pay her, I wonder?" he said.

"I don't know," she said. "You can ask her."

"Maybe I will."

Their waitress brought their breakfast. "These eggs look fantastic," he said. "You want a taste?"

"No, thanks. I'll stick with my waffles."

They were quiet for a few minutes, eating. Carl came by and refilled their cups.

"Any special plans for today?" he asked.

"No."

"There's a crafts fair down the road, in Bethlehem," he said.

"And some good antiquing. If you're interested, I could give you some addresses."

"We might just take a drive," Matt said. "Stop somewhere and walk."

"Fine. Just let me know if you need any help."

"We will."

"Enjoying yourself?"

"Oh, yes."

After breakfast, they headed back to their room. "Let's take the car," Matt said.

They got their coats and headed for the front door. As they did, the innkeepers' daughter came into the lobby, holding a magazine.

"Oh, hi," she said. "You folks stayed here last year, too. Didn't you?"

"Yes. And the year before," Clara said.

"Wow," she said. "That's neat."

"Are you in school?" Clara said. "I mean, college?"

"No. I'm still too young for that." She laughed. "Next year, I hope. I'm still in high school, junior year."

"Oh," Clara said. "My husband teaches in high school."

"Oh yeah? What subject?"

"Physics," Matt said.

"I love biology," she said. "But it's wicked hard. All those things you have to memorize."

"We've got a teenage daughter, too," Clara said.

"What's her name?"

"Gail."

"Do you have other children, too?"

"We have children from our previous marriages," Matt said.

"Wow. That's neat. Must be interesting. Well, don't let me spoil your day," she said, stepping away.

"It's no bother," Clara said. "It's nice to talk. We saw you helping out, waiting on the tables. My husband was wondering if you enjoyed it."

"It's not bad. Everybody's got to help around here. A couple weeks ago, I was cooking. Which is better than doing the rooms."

"Do you like living here?"

The girl shrugged. "Well. There's not much privacy. But, yeah, I like it. You meet a lot of interesting people."

"Would you run an inn yourself?"

"No way," she said. "I'm learning computers, maybe get a job down in Salem after two years of college."

"You should find something good there. There's a lot of places," Matt said. "Well," he edged towards the door. "We ought to be off."

"Nice talking to you. Where are you going?"

"Driving around. May see some antique stores," Clara said.

"Have a nice day," she said.

They walked outside. There was a smell of burning wood. The mountains in the distance were cloaked in clouds.

"I guess she wasn't so sullen after all," Matt said.

"No. Just a teenage kid, trying to be herself."

"Funny. I thought she looked haughty. But in real life, she's a little shy."

"You never can tell," Clara said. "Actually," she went on, "there is something fetching about her."

"True," Matt said. "Seems like a decent kid."

Clara took a deep breath and stretched her arms over her head. "Right."

They got into the car and he started the engine. "So," he said. "Are you still angry with me? Clara?"

She shook her head. "I don't know. I think we needed to unload some stuff we've been sitting on for a while. Sorry if I've been a little edgy."

"Same here. But this is why we needed to get away. Clear the air. Get back to being ourselves."

"Yes."

"I meant what I said last night. I still love you very much, and I depend on you."

"I know. Me, too."

He turned towards her, and they embraced, then kissed. Then they hugged each other for a long time. "Shall we go?" he said.

They drove on further north. "Matt," she said, "what are those lights in the sky? Are they clouds?"

"Where?"

She pointed to the right. "Like saucers. See?" In a clear space in the eastern sky, two radiant discs glimmered on either side of the morning sun, luminously pink, glowing brightly, with glittering yellow and blue edges. "They're like tiny rainbows. I never saw clouds like that before."

He stopped the car and they both looked out. "I've read about them," he said. "They're not clouds or rainbows. I think they're called sun dogs."

"They're on either side of the sun."

"Right. In ancient times people said they were the two hunting dogs that accompanied Apollo, god of the sun."

"What causes them?"

"The cold air in the atmosphere freezes, and the sun's rays get refracted into all those colors. Beautiful."

"Lovely," she said, staring at the sky. "So beautiful."

"They're special," he said. "Like you."

She gave him a coy look and a smile. "Matt, how corny can you get?"

He smiled back. They climbed back into the car, and Matt continued to drive, glancing upwards from time to time. Clara kept looking at the sun dogs through the window, watching them keep pace with the car, floating, radiant, like sky-borne prisms, arching high in the east, until they disappeared, like ethereal creatures, behind a group of mountains.

Davidoff

It's six-fifteen on a cool September morning. Maple leaves are rustling in the wind, and maple branches are rubbing against the side of Howard Zinman's house. Indoors, Dr. Zinman is dawdling over coffee, not yet ready to begin his daily routine of hospital rounds, office hours, and phone calls. He scans the *Times*, half-listening to the Haydn symphony on the radio. After the front page and international news, he leafs through the business, sports, and food sections. Feeling sluggish, he can't stop fussing with his paper or get up from his seat. He picks up the first section again....

Zinman is a paunchy man in his early forties, with greying temples, horn-rimmed glasses, and thin lips. He's dressed in his "doctor clothes:" a white shirt, striped tie, and dark blue pants, his jacket hanging on the back of his chair. His wife and two children are asleep upstairs.

As he turns to the Obituary Page, a familiar name makes him pause:

Sol Davidoff, 62, Psychiatrist,
Was Director of Beachmont Mental Health Center

There's a photo. Davidoff hasn't changed. It's the same cherubic face, the boyish lock of hair over his right temple, the half-smirking smile, the rhomboid nose jammed unexpectedly between expressive, searching eyes, the sensual lower lip. Zinman suddenly recalls Davidoff as he was when he first saw him, nineteen years ago, when Davidoff was the bright young man in Manhattan Medical School's Department of Psychiatry and Howard a second-year medical student....

Howard had come to Davidoff's initial psychiatry lecture knowing his reputation as the best teacher in the department, and he was looking forward to seeing him. As the hour began, Davidoff entered through a side door, a trim, fit man in a brown suit. He strode briskly to the podium and scanned the class, glancing at each student in turn. Then he nodded and grinned. "Good morning, everybody." The class settled down.

Howard doesn't recall what he said. If you asked him to write down what he remembers of that first lecture, or of any of Davidoff's subsequent ones, he wouldn't be able to repeat five words. But he does recall how Davidoff spoke and how he moved—and that memory is as fresh now as the day it happened. Davidoff's voice was clear and mesmerizing. His eyes continually sought contact. And his hands, resting on the podium, rose now and then to make a point.

At one moment Davidoff's eyes settled on him. Davidoff continued to speak, but his eyes clung tenaciously to Howard's, fixing him with their gaze. Howard felt a rush. It was as if Davidoff, enjoying the tension, was daring him to stay in contact. Howard could hear what Davidoff was saying, but he felt a deeper connection, a sense of being drawn into the man himself, a magnetic attraction. In that instant, Howard, without knowing it, resolved to be a psychiatrist, to study with Davidoff, and to become his friend. Part of him would want to stay forever within that riveting glance.

Howard had never been attracted by anyone's gaze before; and if you'd asked about his response he would have been confused and bothered and tried to shake it off. He would have said he liked Davidoff very much: admired him, respected him, even wanted to be like him. But Davidoff's eyes had stirred him deeply. They had touched a vulnerable spot; and Howard would now do things he didn't fully understand and undertake a course he'd never complete, modeling himself after a shifting phantom he'd never grasp.

During his third year, Howard spent hours rummaging through books and articles in the psychiatry library, compiling a vast bibliography on identity. He hoped to win the third-year psychiatry essay contest by writing a masterful paper on the topic, then ask for a fourth-year psych elective with Davidoff. He wrote and rewrote his piece, and his efforts were rewarded. His essay won the prize, and he received the elective. He fantasized that Davidoff, after getting to know him, would find him the most promising member of his class and encourage him to stay on at Manhattan as a psych resident.

For the elective, Davidoff invited Howard to work on his newest project, a study of first-year college dropouts. What made these kids, most of them outstanding students in high school, collapse so soon after leaving home? He also assigned Howard one of the adolescent in-patients, a young woman who'd broken down during her first college semester. Davidoff would supervise him. But he insisted that Howard say nothing in his sessions except to repeat the last few words the patient said. Otherwise, Howard had to keep quiet and write down what he heard.

"I don't get it," Howard said.

"Watch and listen," Davidoff responded. "Write down what you see and what you hear. We'll go over the transcripts together."

"But why should I act like an *analyst*?"

The Davidoff grin: "Why do you think?"

"I don't know."

"Come on, Howard."

He thought. "Okay," he said. "You want me to be a mirror?"

"And why?"

"I don't know."

Davidoff gestured, palms up. "Howard, I want you to know her so well, you think what she's thinking, feel what she's feeling ..."

Howard nodded. "Okay," he said. "I understand."

"You can't just approach the world with your head. You need your feelings, too."

The following month, Davidoff told Howard he thought he'd make a good psychiatrist and advised him to apply to the Manhattan residency program.

They never finished the project. Howard reviewed dozens of articles about college dropouts, but Davidoff never found time to read his first draft of their results. He'd just been named Director of Manhattan's new Community Unit.

Unlike the elite psych wards for which Manhattan was famous, where the disturbed sons and daughters of New England's upper classes received long-term in-patient treatment, the Community Unit was for people from the surrounding neighborhood: drug addicts and alcoholics, depressed housewives, the disoriented elderly, teens in crisis. Davidoff had gotten a pilot grant for the unit, and he was thrilled.

"Community psychiatry's the coming thing," he raved to Howard. "Psychiatry has to deal with ordinary people. It's the new frontier."

Howard told him he'd applied for the residency. "If I'm accepted, I'll spend my second year on your unit," he said.

"You'll get in," Davidoff said. "People are impressed."

Howard left feeling jubilant.

Howard was a middle-class kid from Cincinnati, the older of two brothers and the apple of his parents' eye. His dad owned a shoe store, his mom stayed home. He'd majored in history at Penn, where he'd met his wife, Peggy, and then went straight into med school. Peggy was working as a secretary in the Dean's office to supplement the support his dad sent. They had no children. They rented a small apartment near the med school, rode the subway to Macy's (to shop) and to the Village (to see movies), and talked a lot about their future. Their love life was innocent and unadorned, and they often spoke baby-talk to one another.

A few weeks before the end of med school, Howard's residency acceptance arrived. He hurried to Davidoff's office to tell him. Davidoff was at the window when he walked in.

"I'm in!" he said.

"Congratulations, Howie," Davidoff replied.

They shook hands. But Howard felt Davidoff was preoccupied. "Is anything wrong?" he asked.

"No. Just thinking."

Howard paused, waiting for him to go on. He wondered if he could call him "Sol" now.

"It's strange," Davidoff began, turning towards the window again, his hands in his pockets. "Once you reach a certain point in this profession, you can work as many hours as you want. There's always someone who wants to be your patient and there's always a new project to take on. The end point comes only when you can't do any more. Ultimately, you find yourself weighing time against money and career. On the one side, you're giving up hours with your family; on the other, you're making money and moving ahead. So, you tell yourself everything you do is really for *them*." He laughed sarcastically. "And you chase the dollars and titles, because when you go home you're not a god anymore … you have to face the kids' squabbling and the wife's complaining, and someone's got to take the garbage out."

Howard thought he knew what Davidoff was talking about. "But everybody needs time for their family, don't they? I mean, unless you need money so badly …"

"It's not a question of money, Howie," Davidoff said. "There's enough money to go around. It's a question of how you spend your time, of who you are. You can spend more and more time at your career, get more and more money, prestige, or …"

"But if you don't spend enough time at home, you'll lose contact with the people you love," Howard said. "I mean, I already find that, with Peggy …"

"Of course. But the other side is so tempting. You don't know it yet, Howie, but you will. And it will be difficult to handle. That delicious intimacy you have with your patients. The thrill of a challenge. Nothing compares to that. You get put on a pedestal, paid for it. You can't do anything wrong. At home, you're just another schmuck."

"I see."

"As you get older, you'll run into more choices. You'll start to think, let the wife wait, she'll keep." He shook his head. "It does a number on you, believe me. Who wants to go home and get nagged when he can make hundreds of bucks an hour and be adored?"

"But," (and he said it) "Sol, are you having problems like that? I mean, with your wife?"

"We all are. It's part of the profession."

"I see," Howard repeated, not daring to push any further. He was pleased that Davidoff confided in him. It meant he saw Howard as a colleague.

After a year interning in one of the city hospitals, Howard returned to Manhattan's Psychiatric Center. The residency was a three-year program: first year, clinics; second year, inpatient; third year, electives. During his first week one of the third-year residents took him aside. "Want some advice, Howie? Don't rock the boat. That's the only principle here. They don't care if you're smart. They don't care if you're creative. All they want is for you to think and act like them. Be predictable, and you'll get lots of referrals when you leave, and maybe even a faculty post."

The advice made Howard angry. Manhattan had a reputation for being stodgy, and he didn't plan on being part of the establishment. He was aiming beyond that: at discovering something different. He was going to work with Sol Davidoff and learn about community psychiatry.

During his first year, though, Howard saw Davidoff very little. They were both busy with their own routines, and their paths rarely crossed. He saw Davidoff in the staff lunchroom, but their meetings were shallow and short. Davidoff was distant. Howard would see him, surrounded by the Community Unit staff, all laughing and gesturing, and he was reluctant to barge in. Nor did Davidoff invite him over. Hurt, Howard rationalized it by saying that since he wasn't yet on the community floor, it wasn't appropriate for him to join their group. Things would be better next year.

His first year was hard. The clinics were exhausting. He felt isolated, unappreciated. Impatient for more contact with Davidoff, Howard impetuously invited him and his family to visit him and Peggy in the Berkshires in March. They had rented a small farmhouse with two other couples, and often spent weekends there together. To his surprise, Davidoff said yes. He said his family loved skiing, they'd missed it, and he'd be scheduling a trip to Catamount soon. When that weekend came up, he'd be sure to drop by.

Howard was thrilled. He imagined Davidoff and his family around his fireplace, sharing wine and cheese with him, Peggy, and their friends. They'd have a chance to spend informal time together. And so, one Saturday afternoon around four, Davidoff, his wife, and their three children appeared at their door. It was awkward at first, but a drink loosened everyone up. Davidoff had a four-year-old son and two daughters, seven and nine. His wife Marcia was quiet, rather joyless. Howard and Peggy gave them a tour of the house, from the top-floor bedrooms to the root cellar they'd built, then handed the kids some drawing paper and crayons. Everyone chatted for a while, but Davidoff declined their invitation for dinner, saying they had to get their kids calmed down and back to the inn. Marcia drank several glasses of sherry and got into a wrangle with Davidoff about babysitters; and before Howard knew what had happened, they'd gathered the kids up and were gone.

At one point, Davidoff was talking to Howard about being a "bright young man" in a stodgy department. "I think you're starting to see how this works," he said. "It's fine to be bright when you're a student. But on a faculty, there are resentments ..."

"I'm not all that competitive," Howard said.

"Really?" Davidoff looked at him quizzically. "Interesting."

After they'd gone, Peggy lit into Howard. "*That* was your famous Davidoff? That egotist!"

"What?"

"Didn't you see how he treated his wife? And the *patronizing* way he treated you? His arrogance …"

"Are you serious?"

"Howie. Didn't you see?"

But he didn't. "I saw Sol Davidoff and his family. Here, in our own place. Charming and witty …"

"Oh, right. Sorry. I forgot, he's your idol."

"Peggy," he pleaded. "Please don't be melodramatic."

"I wouldn't put up with him for a minute. And his 'little woman' there, looking grim while he plays to the house …"

"Peggy," Howard said. "I don't know what's gotten into you. Are you somehow jealous?"

"Should I be?"

"It's not such a mystery," their friend Bess chimed in. "That's just how I saw him, too."

Howard shook his head. "You're wrong. He isn't like that at all."

"And you want to be like him? Go ahead."

"I don't understand. Everybody loves him."

"Not me," Peggy said.

When Howard reached his second year, the Community Unit had changed. What had been one group was now divided into two teams, both run by people Howard regarded as very "conventional;" and Davidoff was absent. Gwendolyn Schachter, Howard's team leader, was a stern, combative stickler who argued with him from the start. Benson Mann, the other team leader, was a tedious pedant who wore three-piece suits, spoke in clichés, and constantly looked at his watch. Neither of them seemed really concerned with "community."

Howard was frantic. Here he was, finally on the service he'd dreamed of, and Davidoff was absent. Rumors circulated that the pilot grant had run out and wouldn't be renewed, and that Davidoff was somehow *persona non grata* with Manhattan's "powers that be" and was trying to salvage his career.

Howard had to find out. He marched up to Davidoff's office. It was a hot day in August, and Davidoff was in his shirtsleeves, shuffling papers on his desk. "Hi, Howie," he said. "How's it going? I'm just getting ready for my vacation."

"Sol, you've been on vacation for weeks as far as I'm concerned," Howard said. "What's going on?"

Davidoff put his papers down and turned. "All right. Sit down, Howie, and I'll tell you." Howard sat. "Here's the story. For a year or more, there have been plans to build a big community mental health center here at Manhattan. Right up the street. My Community Unit was only a pilot project, which was supposed to segue into the new center." He paused.

"So?"

"So, this is the third and last year of the grant. Dr. Behrenson had supported the idea, so far as I could tell, and I thought he was totally behind our transition to the new center. It would be a huge plum for Manhattan, you know?" Howard nodded. "The idea was to get the Community Unit going, then get Federal funds for the new center. Everything was going great until some extremist elements heard about it. Community activists, they call themselves. Troublemakers would be my word. They complained that no one had asked their opinion, and that they were being left out. They didn't like the plans. They wanted input into hiring, staffing, and design." He shook his head. "So now it's become impossible."

"I don't understand. Why can't they have input?" Howard asked.

"Because Behrenson doesn't want them to be part of the discussions. He doesn't have the foggiest idea about how to deal with the community, doesn't want to get his shoes dirty. The idea had been to get everything off the ground first, get the funding tied up and in the bank. But now …" He raised his hands, then dropped them limply. "Now it's finished. Behrenson's so pissed off he simply pulled out. He's got another idea. Turn the Community Unit into a drug treatment center and get money from both the Feds and the drug companies. He says it'll be easier and safer and the community can't touch it. So … back to biomedicine." He turned towards the window.

"What does this mean for you?"

"I was going to be in charge of the center, Howie! Christ! Now I'm dangling in the wind."

Howard's face burned. He was dealing with several feelings at once. "I'm so sorry for you," he stammered.

"Thanks." Davidoff was quiet. Then he leaned forward. His tone changed. "From what I hear, you're not happy this year, either."

"That's an understatement. If you want to know the truth, I hate it."

"Howie …" He sounded sympathetic.

"I hate it. Gwendolyn Schachter has her head up her ass. She doesn't know anything about ordinary folks and she doesn't *want* to know. And Mann is a wimp. To them, it's just another job. Their hearts aren't in it …"

"It's still a good program."

"It's falling apart. You know the only reason I wanted to come back here was to work with you. And now that I'm here, you've pulled out. That's great!"

"Howie," Davidoff said. "I'm sorry. But things don't stand still. Just when you think you've got it figured out …"

"Sol," Howard said. "Please don't lecture me."

Davidoff's grin faded. "I'm sorry, Howie. Really. But you'll just have to make the best of it."

"Right." Howard moved towards the door. "Anyway, thanks for telling me. Have a good vacation. Maybe we can talk when you get back."

"I'd like that."

But they didn't talk when Davidoff came back. Instead, Davidoff pulled even further away. He became inaccessible, lost in his own thoughts. The social workers said he was spending hours in his office by himself—reading, thinking, planning his next move. They said he was a lame duck: he'd have to leave Manhattan. He'd already cut his patient hours. He was growing a beard. They said he was having an affair with one of the nurses, his marriage was falling apart, he'd gone back into analysis.

In the meantime, Howard was struggling. He was wondering if psychiatry was the right field for him. Nothing he said or did could please Schachter. Benson Mann advised him to go into therapy. Rudderless, he was arguing with Peggy, criticizing his fellow residents, and staying up late at night listening to talk shows.

What did he expect, he asked himself. What had he wanted from Sol Davidoff, that he should be thrown so off-stride when he didn't get it. He had to accept the facts. Things had changed, and quickly; and Davidoff had changed, too. Howard couldn't expect him to stand still, to hold back the sun and the moon just so Howard and he could spend a year together. Davidoff was in crisis—his whole career in jeopardy. He didn't have time to worry about Howard, a student he'd worked with, but not an intimate friend.

Towards the end of the year, he went to see the man again. Now, instead of books and papers, there were rolls of blue and white architectural drawings on top of his desk and a large picture of a group of buildings pinned to his wall.

"Sol, what's all this?" he said.

"Hi, Howie." Davidoff gestured at the drawings. "Good to see you. Look at this. It's the plans for a new mental health center in Queens."

"Queens!"

"I'm leaving Manhattan." Howard felt his stomach drop. "After the fiasco with Behrenson, some people from Washington contacted me. They'd been talking to people from Queens, people who are really committed to community mental health and who are planning a new center. They've asked me to head it up. Beachmont, it'll be called."

"Oh." Howard felt stunned.

"It'll be a huge place," Davidoff went on. "Bigger than the one we were planning to build here at Manhattan. Community-based, with a community board. The whole schmear. Done the right way. And people there want it to happen." He paused. "So I've been speaking with them, meeting with the architect, helping design it." He looked happy. "Jesus, Howard, when you start thinking about how to organize actual living space—where to put the johns, the beds, the elevators, the stairways, the eating areas …" He waved at the drawings. "We've finally got a therapeutic milieu that's part of its community."

Howard sat down. "Great, Sol. I'm glad for you." He felt wrenched inside. "But do you have any idea what's going on without you on the ward? It's total chaos. Gwendolyn Schachter is tearing people apart, me included. People know you're leaving. They're seizing the opportunity to dismantle your ideas while you're still here."

"It's not a surprise."

"They're saying the Community Unit's going to disappear next year anyway, and it was a mistake to begin with. They're ridiculing the whole idea!"

"Welcome to Manhattan, Howie. That's why I'm leaving."

"Don't you want to make a fight of it? Now?"

But Davidoff looked at him, his jaw set, his lips pursed. "No, Howie. The cards are stacked. You don't have the experience to understand. There aren't any straight lines in this world, only zigzags and curves. So, you retrace your steps and head somewhere else."

Howard was quiet. His eyes had misted up, and his lips were

trembling. He stood up. "So, I guess you're going."

"I have to move forward. I want to run my own center, and now I have a chance. I know this has been rough on you, too, Howard, and I feel bad about it. But it wasn't my choice."

"Right."

The year moved to an end. Davidoff continued his leave of absence from the Community Unit and stayed in his office, working on plans for Beachmont. Howard muddled through. Schachter and Mann continued as they'd begun. Not knowing what to do or who to trust, Howard drifted further. He stopped listening to his patients, fought more with Peggy. He toyed with the idea of going into therapy, then rejected it.

Just before his third year began, he and Peggy decided to move from Manhattan to a small apartment in Tarrytown. Howard hoped it would sweeten their marriage. Peggy had gotten pregnant, and they'd need more space. The new apartment had a playground and fresher air: shrubs and gardens. For July, though, they'd be stuck between leases. Unexpectedly, he got a phone call from Davidoff. He'd heard about their predicament and wondered if Howard and Peggy would be kind enough to house-sit for him that month, as he and his family would be out of town.

At first, he hadn't wanted to. He felt peeved and didn't want anything to do with Davidoff. But Peggy said they'd be foolish to turn it down. They needed a place, even if it was Davidoff's. So they accepted the offer.

When they arrived, Marcia took them around the house and showed them how everything worked, including the pilot lights for the stove and the heater, and the emergency switches. She left them a list of phone numbers—plumber, electrician, yardman. They all shook hands and Davidoff and his family drove off.

Howard and Peggy tiptoed from room to room. The house was elegant. There was a screened-in back porch. The kitchen had every imaginable device. The rugs were thick and immaculate. Each room had bright modern furniture, chairs with rich fabrics, art objects on sandalwood tables. A long winding staircase connected the floors.

They explored the place like children. Howard browsed through Davidoff's books. Peggy took Marcia's clothes out of the closets. They slept in the Davidoffs' bed, watched their TV, and stayed up watching old movies. They watered the plants and vacuumed the rugs, took in the mail, swept the front walkway.

After a few days, the house began to feel too big. Room after room opened off the hallways, but there was no one to run in and out of them. The children's rooms seemed like tombs, preserved forever with their memorabilia intact: beds forever made, Lego towers eternally fixed, dolls' expressions frozen. The record player, the silverware, the stacks of toys: everything was in place. The house was like a sleeping cat, waiting for its owners to return.

Howard awoke early every morning. He descended to the kitchen and made coffee, then climbed up to Davidoff's study where he sipped his cup, elbows on Davidoff's desk, and looked out through the picture glass window at the sprawling flowered hill behind the house. He tried to imagine what Davidoff thought when he sat there. If the light was right, he could see the surface of the Hudson River, glimmering far off through the trees. Tarrytown would be a comedown after this, but it was more his kind of place.

His last year at Manhattan passed dully. Howard did start therapy but stopped after six months. To pay for it, he had to moonlight in a Jersey clinic, which kept him away from home longer. Peggy had the baby, a boy, but Howard felt out of touch with them both. He began an affair with a social worker from the Center who lived on Third Avenue, but soon broke it off, sensing it had no future. He became infatuated with a patient, a young woman who hung around with artists and poets, but kept it to himself. When his residency was over and it was time to leave Manhattan, he felt confused and angry. He wanted to get away from psychiatry, from his patients, from New York, from everything and everyone he'd known for the past eight years.

Before he left, he went to see Davidoff one last time.

His office was on the fifth floor of the new Beachmont Center in Queens. Howard arrived late in the day, and the lights on the Whitestone Bridge were on, transforming that majestic structure into a sparkling blend of arcs and lines. Davidoff was at the window, looking past the Bridge, far across the Bay.

"Sol," Howard said.

Davidoff turned around. "Howard Zinman."

They shook hands. "I'm leaving town next week," Howard said. "Just wanted to stop in and say good-bye."

"Already?" Davidoff's mouth stretched into his old grin: boyish, seductive. His hair was greying. "We haven't seen much of each other, have we?"

"No. I heard your marriage had broken up. Sorry."

Davidoff gestured. "One of those things. It had been rocky for a long time."

"You moved out?"

He nodded. "Yes. Marcia kept the place."

"It was a nice house."

"I loved it."

They fell silent. Davidoff studied him for a moment, then crossed the floor and pulled a folder out of the bottom drawer of his desk. "Here." He handed it to Howard. It was the first draft of their paper. "I haven't forgotten," Davidoff said.

"Neither have I."

"I was just rereading it in fact. You know, it said some good things. Someday we ought to …"

Howard grunted. "Well, I just wanted to drop by, say hello, so long. I'm heading off and I don't know if or when I'll be back. I'm glad you got what you wanted. The center and all." He held out his hand. "So long, Sol. I wish you the best."

"How are things with you?" Davidoff said. "Things with Peggy? I hear you have a son."

"Yeah. Robbie. He's a sweet kid."

"Where are you off to?"

"The Air Force. Berry Plan. After they defer you, you've got to go in. For two years. After that I don't know." He shuffled his feet.

Davidoff looked uneasy. Did he want to talk longer? "Well, then. Good luck to you, too, Howie." Davidoff extended his hand. "Think about Beachmont when you're done. We'll still be here."

And then Howard was gone. With Peg and Robbie in tow, he left New York and headed west, his mouth on fire from a violent outbreak of herpes. First, they drove to Texas for three weeks of USAF orientation. Then they traveled to a base on the vast Dakota plains. He never saw Davidoff again.

When he finished the Air Force, Howard left psychiatry. He divorced Peggy and spent a year roaming through the Caribbean. Then he drifted back north. He worked in clinics, first-aid centers, and Emergency Rooms, and finally joined a small medical practice in the Bronx. He dated various women and married one, a nurse. They bought a house, had children. He developed a routine.

To Howard, people he's left behind are lost and gone forever, and it sometimes surprises him to discover that they're still alive: writing papers, making money, raising children, growing older. To him, the notion of parallel lives means parallel worlds. He knows that if he wants, of course, he can always pick up the phone and call someone from the past—but he doesn't want to. Deep down, he doesn't believe it's possible to reconnect. What's past is past. You live in the present and forget the rest. He prefers to let memories of people he once knew dry up slowly, like mountain flowers: gradually losing their scent and color, until there's nothing left but the shadow of their form.

But today's paper has brought Davidoff back into his life as powerfully as if he was sitting at the kitchen table, still grinning his grin and drawing Howard's attention to the architectural drawings so suddenly tacked to the wall. Howard can see him across the table, still forty-three—the same age Howard is now—and it's as if the two of them have become colleagues at last, spending their time talking about what moves them, and getting ready to drive in to the hospital together. He basks in the image for a moment, then takes a deep breath and shakes his head. He folds the *Times* first section and slaps it on the rest of the paper. Then he stands up, reaches for his jacket, and puts it on. His pens and phone are in his pockets, his pager on his belt, all in the right place. Already feeling the day's fatigue, he heads out the side door. It's time to go to work.

The Oldest in the Family

Whenever I brought up my Aunt Sophie, people in the family changed the subject. But Sophie was my father's oldest sister, and I was curious about her. I recalled her, vaguely, as being affectionate and warm-hearted, if a bit disheveled. I also remembered she had to be restrained at my grandfather's funeral.

I'd come in from college that day to be with my father, who'd flown in the night before. It was chilly and rainy, in March; and, after a service at a funeral home in Queens, the family had gathered in a sad-looking Jewish cemetery in the Bronx. All my uncles and aunts were there, as well as relatives I had never seen—cousins, great-aunts and -uncles: all Orthodox Jews from around Vilna who lived in different parts of New York.

My Aunt Sophie, a tall, heavy woman in her sixties, was wearing a thick coat and a stained black dress. She was agitated all day and seemed constantly on the verge of fainting. One of my other aunts had to hold onto her all the time. As the mourners gathered at the gravesite, Sophie began to tremble. She pushed to the front of the group, just a few feet from the coffin, and continued swaying and moaning throughout the service. Then, as the coffin was being lowered, she started shouting: "Poppa, let me go with you! Don't leave me alone. Poppa, don't go!"

I was only twenty, and this was the first burial I'd seen, and I was writhing in embarrassment. The attendants continued lowering the coffin, and Sophie became more upset. "No! Poppa! No! I can't go on without you!" My uncles and aunts pressed around her, restraining her, holding her so she wouldn't jump into the grave. "My father went to her, too, consoling her, but all the time she was shouting that she loved her Poppa, and couldn't go on without him, and nobody understood what she felt. Everyone was dealing with their own grief, and her raw emotion made it that much harder to cope.

One day, years after this, I was visiting my parents in Savannah. It was a hot, muggy day. Purplish clouds were gathering overhead, promising the relief of a summer storm. My father and I were sitting on the patio in the rear of the house, overlooking the rose bushes, sweetshrub, and viburnum, chatting together, and I asked him when his parents first came to New York. He said he thought it was in the late 1890s. They came with their two oldest children, Sophie and Jack. All their other children were born in the Bronx. And then I remembered Grandpa's funeral.

"What was the story with Aunt Sophie?" I asked. "Why was she so upset that day? And why didn't the rest of the family ever talk about her?"

"It's difficult," he said.

"You visited her whenever you went to New York, but you wouldn't say much about it."

"Yes. She was living in a small room at the time, and I'd always check in to make sure she was all right."

"So, dad. Tell me."

He took a deep breath. "All right. Since you asked." And he began to talk.

"You see, Sophie was the oldest in the family. She was a bright girl, outgoing, very smart and very attractive. When she was in her twenties, she had a head of flaming red hair, which she wore piled high in a bun, in the fashion of the day. And she was always stylishly dressed.

"In those days, and here I'm talking about the nineteen-teens, my father was struggling, working in a liquor store with his brother Jacob. With seven children in the family, it was very hard. I remember one morning there was only one egg for breakfast.

I'm telling the truth. And we had a big argument about who would get the white and who the yolk. My mother, who didn't work, tried to make the food stretch, and she bought the most inexpensive cuts of meat or fish; but it was still very hard.

"So when Sophie got a job in a dress shop, making $15 a week, it was a big thing. Fifteen dollars was a lot of money in those days. While the rest of us were growing up, she and my father supported the family."

"Were you all living in that apartment we used to visit them in?"

"Yes. In the Bronx, near Van Cortlandt Park."

"With the bakery around the corner, just past the subway stop. I still remember that smell of fresh bread."

"Yes. Anyway, working in a dress shop, and being an attractive woman, Sophie naturally met a lot of interesting, high-living people. She was tall, and with that striking red hair and good figure, and her smile and the fancy clothes she could get from the store, she cut a dazzling picture. She spent her days working hard, but in the evenings, she dated a variety of dashing young men. I believe she was a local favorite at the time. She would go carousing, to the theatre, to nightclubs, to back rooms where they served whisky and gin, to dance halls: in short, she went everywhere people went to have a good time. And she was immensely popular.

"After a while, she became serious about one of her beaux. I believe he was a divorced man, a few years older than herself, in some kind of jewelry business. There was a rumor he was involved in some shady things, but that wasn't important, because many people whom we respected were, too, at that time. This man was serious about Sophie, and one day he asked her to marry him.

"Oh boy," I said. "I can see this would be a problem."

"Right. She was thrown into a panic. On the one hand, she loved this man very much, and she was drawn to the kind of life he could give her: parties, evenings on the town, nice clothes. Everything her disposition favored. But, on the other hand, she was the mainstay of the family. My mother was sick with arthritis. My father was still struggling. And here we were, my brothers and sisters, growing up and in need of clothes, food, school supplies, things like that.

"I believe she asked the man, Ernest, his name was, if he would wait a certain period of time, and then she would feel free to marry him. But he said no. He was an impatient man, Ernest, used to having his way. And he had his plans. He wanted to get married, have a family, buy a home. I think he was interested in leaving New York and settling elsewhere. He had business connections all over the East Coast, you understand, and he felt he couldn't wait.

"He told her she had to marry him immediately or he would stop seeing her. That was the kind of man he was."

"What a choice," I said. "Like it wasn't up for discussion. He was 'the man' and he made the rules." My father nodded. "Was she in love with him?"

"No question about it. Ernest was the love of her life. But what could she do? She was the oldest in the family. She couldn't leave us without any support. And so, she said no. Ernest disappeared. He stopped dating her, he never called, she never saw him again.

"She became very depressed. She tried to cover it up by going out even more, with a great variety of men, and by drinking. She would come home some nights at two, three o'clock in the morning, barely able to stand up, she'd been drinking so much. But she kept her head above water. She'd wake up the next morning, put on her fine clothes, and off she'd go.

"Her job was a good one; and, because she was so capable at it, she'd become the manager of the shop and was making even more money. As my brothers and sisters grew up, we had enough to eat, and we were able to wear decent clothes. My brother Cal went to college, and I did the same.

"But Sophie wasn't the same person. There were rumors in the neighborhood about her behavior. People said she was a boozer and too free with men. They criticized her appearance, which had become more and more flashy, almost cheap. The better elements started avoiding her.

"Like I say, I don't think she ever came as close to another person as she'd been with this fellow Ernest. She held herself back. She'd have a good time, but she wouldn't let herself get involved."

"I can see why she wouldn't," I said. "It would be too dangerous. She didn't want the same thing to happen again."

"Something like that," he said. "As she grew older and the rest of us grew up, there was less and less need for her to support us all. Millie had a good job, and Cal was already working in his store. Still, Sophie kept working in the dress shop, because this had become her life. But, as time wore on, men asked her out less and less. She was less desirable to the better element. So, she stopped going to fancy parties. And she was drinking more. A lot more, I think."

"So she was still depressed. She couldn't put it behind her."

"No. Men wanted to go out with her, but they weren't serious. They just wanted a good time, and she knew it. As she drank more, her appearance grew a little sloppy. She became careless. There were little things I'd notice, like rips in her stockings. Smudges on a blouse or skirt, which she didn't seem to have time to clean. Part of her just seemed not to care."

"She was an alcoholic?"

He nodded. "By this time, yes. She kept up the job, but she no longer spent money on clothes or cosmetics. I think she'd given up. She was giving her whole paycheck to our parents, except for what she spent on the booze. By then she was drinking alone, either in the house or else in some lonely bar down the street.

"Everyone grew up and left. My sisters got married. My brothers went into business and got married. My brother Cal, who'd gone to law school, wound up working for his father-in-law in a men's goods store in Queens. My brother Herb joined the Marines and moved to California. Sophie was the only one left home.

"She grew slovenly. Eventually, after a number of warnings, she lost her job. They didn't want to keep her around anymore. She couldn't even put her make-up on right, she looked a mess. So she was dismissed."

"Talk about a comedown! From the belle of the ball to an unemployed drunk. How did the family react?"

He shook his head. "How do you think? Here they were, with their nice jobs and families, and homes in nice neighborhoods, and Sophie was an embarrassment. They disapproved of what she'd become. They felt ashamed. They didn't want to help because they thought it was her own fault. You know, there's a lot of 'attitude' in our family about shikkers who can't handle their alcohol. Here you had her brothers and sisters, all making decent money, and Sophie was in tatters, drunk much of the time.

"I'd been away from New York for many years by then, and I was out of touch with her. Jack, who had his own store, and Rachel, who was in Jackson Heights with your Uncle Abe, had nothing to do with her. They invited her to dinner once, I think, but she showed up completely drunk, wearing some kind of shmatta, and they were very embarrassed and said they didn't want to see her anymore.

"They were also angry at the way she treated our father." He took a deep breath and continued.

"You see, when my mother died, Sophie stayed in the house with my father; and, according to Rachel, she gave him a lot of aggravation, staying up at night, rambling through the house talking to herself, shouting at him when she was drunk, abusing him. The neighbors were afraid of her. They wouldn't come near the place because of what she might do. And the street kids teased her."

"And nobody tried to help? Get her some kind of treatment?"

"There wasn't really much 'treatment' then. She wouldn't go to AA, if that's what you mean. She'd get angry and nasty with everyone, so they left her alone. They were raising their own kids now. Sophie, they'd just as soon forget about.

"When my father died, she went to pieces You saw her at the funeral. Naturally, everyone felt sorry for her, but the family was ashamed at how she acted. They made her move out, leave the apartment.

"That's when she found a place with a couple, an Italian family in the Bronx. I think he was a welder. There was some kind of agreement with welfare at that time, that families would take people like Sophie into their homes, in exchange for which welfare paid a certain sum of money per month. Well, this is what those people, DiGiorgio I think their name was, did. She had a little room of her own there, and a closet where she kept her things, and they looked after her.

"For some time, I lost track of her, because no one else in the family had anything to do with her. But I finally tracked her down, and I would send her money from time to time, a letter, maybe a dress, some underwear. Whatever I could.

"Then she got sick. I guess it was from all the drinking. Her liver was diseased, the doctors said, and one day she began vomiting blood. The couple didn't know what to do. They put her in the hospital and called me. By the time I got to New York, she was dead. The only ones at the funeral were this couple, the DiGiorgios, and myself.

"You know how it is. Families drift apart. People form resentments and grudges. Sometimes, there's no turning back the clock.

"When I went through her room, I found all the money I had sent her, folded up in little paper bags, along with the letters I had written, and a few photographs of our parents. There was also a letter Ernest had written her many years ago."

He paused, his lower lip quivering. The air was pregnant with moisture. There was a deep rumble of thunder, then a flash of lightning, and another, louder rumble, closer. The wind began to blow, bending the bushes in the back yard and making a whooshing sound which appeared to sweep up from all sides.

The storm was imminent.

"It's funny," he went on, with some difficulty. "The most vivid memory I have of her goes back many years. It must have been just after the War, say around 1918. My mother was sick in the hospital, and all of us were frightened and worried. So Sophie organized us go together to the synagogue and pray, so that our mother would be all right."

He paused. "I can still see us that day, Jack, Millie, Rachel, Cal, Herb, and me. God, I couldn't have been any older than six or seven at the time. We were all walking up the street to the synagogue, holding hands and pressing together, with Sophie leading the way. She was bringing us, and we were following ..."

He paused again and swallowed. And then, as the rains approached with a mighty, heaving sound, sweeping over the back lawn from the west, and then falling heavily, drenching the parched lawn and bending the sweetshrub and rose-bushes with an insistent force, my father stared at the oak far in the back of the yard and began to sob like a child.

Piano Lesson

Music was a sacrament in our family. My mother, who'd grown up poor, received violin lessons from a neighbor when she was sixteen, and she never forgot the magical experience of drawing the bow over her strings. Although she never continued (the neighbor died), she held onto that violin for the rest of her life. When I grew up it was mounted on the wall over the record cabinet in our living room, a mute testament to its place in her heart.

She taught me the piano when I was five, using John Thompson's "Teaching Little Fingers to Play." Eight months later, when she thought I was ready, she brought me to Jeremy Carroll, whom her friends had recommended as the best piano teacher in town. Sitting at his piano, I performed my little pieces, and he agreed to take me on. I studied with Carroll for over eight years, taking lessons once or twice a week.

When I was very young, my mother would drive me to his house and wait until I was finished. But once I was nine, I'd take the trolley bus into Atlanta, leaving right after school (on Wednesdays) or from the end of my street (Saturdays) and walk from the bus stop on Peachtree Road to the Piedmont neighborhood where Mr. Carroll lived. My mother would come at the end of the lesson to pick me up.

Jeremy Carroll was a quiet, dignified man in his mid-sixties. He was short, trim, and spry, with an oval-shaped bald head, blue eyes, and a patrician nose. He reminded me of the Wizard of Oz in the movie. He spoke in what I first thought was an English accent but later realized as the languid tones of a Virginia-born aristocrat. He always wore a formal white shirt and bow tie. I admired him greatly and thought he and his wife Nora were the epitome of civilized folks. Their lives seemed devoted to Good Things—music, his pupils, their garden, and their marriage— and I practiced hard to win his praise.

Carroll and his wife lived in a white house in an old, respectable neighborhood. The house was on a small hill, so I had to climb a stone stairway to reach it, ascending through a profusion of flowering plants, cactuses, herbs, and ferns, some of which were always in bloom. There was a broad wrap-around porch in front, with two wicker chairs, a bench, and a dark green swing with cushions. After I let myself in, I'd be in the living room, where the pupils waited.

I must have spent hundreds of hours in that space. It was always dim and cool, the lamps were never lit, and everything smelled of old books and aging slipcovers. Heavily flowered dark purple wallpaper encircled the room, and an assortment of four- and five-shelf glass-enclosed bookcases stood against the walls. All the furniture was dark wood and gave off a deep reddish glow. Everything was polished: the antique side tables, the brass lamps, the varnished paintings; even the Swiss music boxes.

I'd sit in a plush red and yellow striped armchair with lace doilies, a small table to my right. Further to my right were two darkly lacquered sliding doors, which opened into Mr. Carroll's studio. Across the room, a yellow-curtained glass door led to a dim corridor to the bathroom, kitchen, and rear of the house. To my left was a long couch with a profusion of cushions. And beyond that, against the far wall: two massive bookcases.

I'd sit in my chair, trying to do my homework, but I'd always be distracted by something. Sometimes it was the sounds of the lesson before mine: I'd put my schoolbooks and papers on the floor and listen. Other times, I'd walk over to the bookcases and reach for a book I'd seen behind the glass doors.

Some shelves were crammed with musical books and scores. But others held books on a variety of mystical, esoteric themes.

There were dusty books on Egyptology, the writings of Nostradamus, and Kabbalah; a shelf of Hindu mysticism, Freemasons, and the Gnostics; and, finally, a collection of the Loeb Classical Library.

My parents had books in their living room, but theirs were ordinary, like John Gunther's *Inside the USA*, a biography of Abraham Lincoln, or Modern Library editions of de Maupassant and Dickens. Jeremy Carroll's library was unlike anything I'd ever seen. I was especially drawn to a thin volume of *The Oracles of Nostradamus*, which implied that whatever was going to happen was already foretold in the stars, discerned by seers such as Nostradamus himself. I leafed through this book over and over until I began to attribute its clairvoyance to the Carrolls as well, believing that, since they owned the book, they too must know the secrets of the stars, as well as those of the human soul.

When I was fourteen, the student who took lessons before me was named Karen Alterman. She was thirteen and slim, with an olive complexion and long brown hair. She had a delicate mouth with tiny teeth and a delightful, shy smile, and she'd usually be wearing a pleated skirt and high socks, her bony knees jutting out between them. I liked Karen a lot. I liked her hair which was always neatly brushed. I liked that she was serious. She had a kind, not competitive, disposition, and she clearly loved music. While I waited, I'd listen to her play. Mr. Carroll would often stop her in the middle of a piece, just as he did with me, and point out some error of phrasing; and sometimes he'd riff off one of his cadenzas. But Karen would sometimes just stop playing, and then I'd hear her tinkling voice. She was full of questions.

"Am I supposed to keep my fingers straight here or let them curl?"

"Should this be louder, Mr. Carroll?"

"Can I use the middle pedal, Mr. Carroll, or just the one on the right?"

"Should I play this part slower, Mr. Carroll? It sounds so

much nicer that way."

And I'd hear him answer patiently, in a low, soothing voice, and she'd start playing again. For me, there was a dreamy alternation between the passages of music, her piping questions, and his deeper voice, answering and reassuring her. I'd get hypnotized listening.

The approach of my lesson made me nervous. The clock on the side table would near four, and, knowing I'd have to play soon, I'd worry I hadn't practiced enough, and Mr. Carroll would be upset. I'd listen keenly to what was happening in the studio and marvel at how Mr. Carroll could get Karen to stop playing at exactly the right moment so her lesson would end and mine begin. She'd stop. I'd hear him say what she'd done well and what she needed to practice on. And the clock would chime four. The wooden benches in the studio would scrape, their two voices would murmur, and the wooden doors would slide open and Karen would emerge. She'd look at the floor and then at me, smiling and pressing her music books to her chest.

Sometimes Mr. Carroll would go to the bathroom for a few minutes or walk down the hall to say something to his wife, and Karen and I would chat.

"How's it going?" I might say.

"Okay. I'm working on a new sonata."

"I could hear. It sounds hard."

"It is. I'm playing it slowly now. I did just the left hand for four whole days, and then the right. And now I'm beginning to put them together. What about you?"

"Still on the same piece. And he's got me doing scales and arpeggios again. He says I don't practice enough." I'd shake my head. "There's just too much to do."

"He knows right away if you don't practice."

"I know."

Karen was in the sixth grade and lived out past Buckhead. She liked cotton candy and had a younger brother whom she thought was spoiled. Karen's mother would open the front door at four o'clock, and step into the room just as Karen was coming out. She'd nod to Mr. Carroll and then turn and remind me to say "Hello" to my mother for her.

Every so often, especially during the spring and summer, Mr. Carroll would leave the studio doors open. And then, perched in my striped chair, I could watch Karen play. I knew she didn't mind, and she'd often ask me afterwards how she sounded.

Mr. Carroll had two pianos in his studio. He'd sit at the one closer to the door, and his pupil would sit at the other. If Karen had trouble with a particular passage, Mr. Carroll might spin about on his bench and dash the passage off on his piano, showing how it was supposed to sound; or he might move behind her and put his hands over hers to show her how to play the passage more precisely. When Mr. Carroll played, he played with great virtuosity, and his performance would stir us to try harder the next time and earn his respect.

Mr. Carroll's wife Nora was a more mysterious figure. I rarely saw her, for she usually stayed in the private part of the house. When she did appear, it was with a flash of silken gown, a glimpse of powdered face, and a quickly averted eye. She was tall and severe, with remarkably frizzy brown hair and a taste for deep green dresses. Some people said she'd been an actress; others, that she'd been born rich and never worked a day in her life. But everyone agreed that she'd become infatuated with Jeremy Carroll when she was twenty and he was a dashing young pianist, and had pursued him from city to city, brazen about her affection for him, until he eventually married her. But nobody knew for sure.

One Wednesday in June, I got to Mr. Carroll's house early, about a quarter to four. It had been a rainy, stormy day, and I was drenched. My sweater smelled like a wet dog, my books were soaked, and water was trickling down my face. I hung my dripping coat in the closet, happy to be in a warm, dry place, and sat down on my chair.

Karen was working on a Mozart sonata. "Can I use the pedal here, Mr. Carroll?" she piped.

"No, Karen. No. Just play the legato as it's written."

"But doesn't it sound better with the pedal?"

"Karen, if Mozart had wanted the pedal, he'd have written it that way."

"Okay." A pause. "Do you think Mozart was a happy man, Mr. Carroll?"

"Without a doubt, Karen. Without a doubt."

"Do you think he ever wondered when to use the pedal?"

"I think Mozart always knew when to use the pedal," Mr. Carroll said.

"And he knew what fingers to use all the time, too, didn't he?" Karen said.

Mr. Carroll didn't answer. Karen played some more, and then he stopped her. "No, no. Here, it's staccato," he said. "Tep-tep-tep-tep. Tep-tep-tep-tep. You see?" He played it for her.

She began the piece again. A few minutes later I heard her again. "Mr. Carroll, can I play this with my fourth finger or do I have to use my pinky?"

"Karen, use the fingering we wrote down on your score."

"Okay." Suddenly, the door to the hallway opened and Nora Carroll entered, wearing her dark green frock, her hair frizzed about her face, a glass of lemonade in each hand. She nodded at me without speaking—I was there before the hour, therefore not really "there"—and walked to the studio doors, her shoes clicking on the parquet floor. "Jeremy? Karen?" she called. "Would you like some lemonade?"

The music stopped. The doors opened, and Mr. Carroll looked out. "What? Oh, Nora. That would be lovely." Nora Carroll stepped inside the studio and handed them each a glass and a cork coaster, then took a single step back towards the sliding doors.

I sensed an eerie tension between the man and his wife. It

was like I'd come into a play several minutes past the opening and found the plot already in mid-stream. There was something strained in her voice, something taut, which made me wonder if they'd been fighting. And Nora Carroll was hesitating too long on the threshold. It seemed like she wanted her husband to say something. But he appeared flustered, thrown by her sudden appearance. He sipped his lemonade.

She took another step towards the door, but I sensed she didn't want to leave.

"Norah. Wait," Mr. Carroll said hastily. "How would you like to sit here for a few minutes and listen to Karen play her latest piece? Really. She's been doing remarkably well."

"Oh, she is?" his wife said. She turned towards Karen. "Are you getting the knack of it, Karen?" From where I was sitting, I could only see her from the back, but I suppose she glanced at Karen and smiled: spuriously, I think, for the girl, her hands still on the keys, looked back with a puzzled expression on her face. I could tell she didn't know what to say.

"Umm. Yes," she stammered.

"Well," Nora Carroll said, speaking now more to Carroll than to Karen. "Maybe I *will* join you, then. So long as Karen doesn't mind."

Karen shook her head and licked her lips. She rubbed her hands on her skirt. "It's okay," she said.

Nora arranged her dress and sat behind her husband in a straight-backed rocking chair. "Just pretend I'm not here, Karen. Go on with your piece. Please."

Karen turned to the piano and took a deep breath. "Start from the beginning," Mr. Carroll said. "Just like you played it a few minutes ago."

Oh, God! I thought. Please let Karen do well. She lifted her hands, then placed them on the keys. Mr. Carroll was sitting at his piano, legs crossed, turned to the left so he could see her better. Nora Carroll was sitting behind her husband, rocking slightly back and forth. I could see her face from the side, and

I thought her expression was one of triumph. I didn't think she cared at all about hearing Karen play. She'd gotten what she wanted by remaining in the room.

But Karen didn't know that. She wasn't looking at Nora Carroll, but at the piano. She was trying to remember her piece and play it well. But her body was a lightning rod, absorbing the couple's tension into its small muscles and bones: for her usually precise playing foundered. She made a mistake in the second measure and started over again, then made the same mistake, pushed on past it this time, but stumbled again. She blushed.

"That's all right," Mr. Carroll said, in his kindest voice. "Don't let it bother you. Start again, Karen." He waved his hand. "And-a-one-and-a-two-and-yatta-ti-yatta-ti-yatta …" Karen hesitated. Mr. Carroll turned to his own piano and played the beginning of the piece, the part where Karen had gone astray, to show her how it went. "Yes? Go ahead."

Karen took a deep breath, placed her hands on the keys, and started again. She was leaning forward, her face closer to the keys, trying to keep her poise. I held my breath, not wanting her to be humiliated before Nora.

She approached the same run, attacked the keys more slowly, and got it right, but then stumbled on the next sequence. Tears rushed to her eyes as she stopped and put her hands in her lap. I thought, enough was enough.

"No, no, no," Carroll said. "Take your time, Karen. Don't rush it so. Like this, now. One-and-two-and-three-and …" He played the piece himself again, all the way from the beginning this time, showing the melody's development, bringing out the counterpart. He leaned forward, swayed, shook his head dramatically, then brought his hands up and lowered them for the crescendo. It was a burst of virtuosity, building tension in seconds, then relieving it just as quickly, modulating up, then down, then resolving everything, like a summer squall. "Now you, Karen. Try again."

Karen tried, but her fingers were blocks of wood. And she

was crying. I knew Nora Carroll was making her stumble, her presence shattering Karen's concentration. Still, trying to please Mr. Carroll, Karen plodded ahead. But the more she played, the more confounded she got. She lost her rhythm, slid off the keys, lost her spirit. And the more undone she became, the more torn I felt. I admired her desperately for trying and cursed Nora Carroll for being there. Why, I wondered, had Mr. Carroll let her stay. And why was he letting this torture continue? I wanted him to tell Karen to stop, to help her relax, soothe her, talk gently to her, let her play something else later, maybe, after she'd calmed down, something she knew by heart. I wanted him to tell Nora to leave. I was so distraught, I'd begun to sweat.

But Jeremy Carroll did not intervene. Perhaps he was proving something to his wife. I don't know. He let Karen flounder further and further, sliding deeper into the morass he created until there was no way she could get out. He let her fail; and yet I thought he liked Karen, I thought he knew she worshipped him. Just then I saw Nora Carroll make a sour face and sigh, heaving her bosom with a rustle of silk; and then, so unexpectedly I couldn't believe my eyes, I saw Jeremy Carroll glance at his wife and grimace. Karen, still concentrating on her cloddish fingers, couldn't see him, but I could. I saw him turn towards Nora and, wrinkling his nose as if he'd smelled some stinky cheese, shrug and tip both palms up in a gesture which expressed both his distaste for the girl's playing and his helplessness to change it.

My stomach tightened. How could he do such a thing? Karen idolized him. Didn't he have any sympathy for her? His wife and he had read the wisest books, appreciated the finest music, owned a glorious house. Had such elegant possessions. How could he grimace at Karen's suffering?

And then I had an awakening. This Jeremy Carroll who grimaced at his wife was Jeremy Carroll as he'd been all along, but who'd escaped my knowing. And I realized that whatever I thought people were thinking or feeling, I could be mistaken. I could no longer take kindness for granted. Like Karen, I might be concentrating so intently, I couldn't see what was really going on, and I'd never know if someone wasn't grimacing behind my back.

A few weeks after that, I stopped taking piano lessons. I told my mother that, since I'd be starting the tenth grade soon, I wouldn't have time to practice. It wasn't like I'd been planning to be a concert pianist, anyway. I knew she felt bad about it, but she didn't argue. Not much, anyway.

Now, even though I'm older, I can't forget that moment. I can imagine that Jeremy Carroll's may have been an idle gesture, no more significant than someone's look of annoyance at the ringing of a phone; but I sense it was more than that. Perhaps I shouldn't have been so affected by it; but I was.

I've never been quite the same. Ever watchful, I move through the world on tiptoe, appreciating the music, but wary of the musicians.

good line

Bree

1

Will first met Bree Henley in high school. She was one of the "good-time girls"—cheerful, high-spirited, and eager to be seen. Her wavy, auburn hair spilled over her forehead. Her face was long and expressive, with deep, recessed brown eyes and drooping eyelids that gave a languid cast to her otherwise animated features; and, although she was slim, her figure had already filled out. She'd show up at school in a pleated skirt and tight sweater or a loose skirt and simple blouse. She was always in motion—coquettish, good-humored, and quick to smile. By the middle of ninth grade Will was in love.

The high school was in Atlanta, its students drawn from the families of well-to-do local merchants as well as from poor families who had migrated down from the North Georgia hills, folks who had farmed for generations but who now lived in dusty suburbs, their dads working in the drug stores, banks, department stores, and factories that were expanding outwards to Buckhead and Brookhaven during the great growth of the 1950s. There were Baptists and Methodists, Episcopalians and Presbyterians, a handful of Catholics, and a rare Jew—like Will.

The students were divided a dozen different ways, but they were all Terriers; and every autumn Thursday they crammed into the gym for the pep rally led by Principal Jenkins and Coach Dennison, clapping their hands and chanting "Hit 'em again, hit 'em again, harder, harder!"—and later, that evening, they filled the stands in the stadium, cheering for their team.

The different groups co-existed because each clique had its turf. The college-bound kids from respectable families ran the Student Council, the Honor Society, and the school paper ("The Scribbler"), as well as the French, Spanish, Science, Math, and Drama Clubs. They also made up the bulk of the school's Special Choir, which performed throughout the South and abroad. Another group of upward-mobile kids played sports; they participated in the Key Club, Future Business Leaders, and Young Masons, and organized the school's social events. There were others who smoked and drank, avoided clubs and sports on principle, and sometimes caused a ruckus in the classrooms. The more serious non-college-bound kids studied shop or homemaking; the religious ones bolstered the school's Student Christian Fellowship. Everyone had their group. But the sharpest divide was between the "good-time girls" and the guys their age.

They'd all been going to parties and dating since they were eleven, but by fifteen the guys and girls lived in different worlds. The guys were way behind. For years in their early teens they couldn't drive on dates, but girls their age were going out with guys three and four years older. Going to parties at twelve or thirteen was easy: your parents drove you there and back. But serious dating—something besides hayrides or dancing to records and playing Spin-the-Bottle in someone's rec room—required a car. So the guys would cultivate older friends to double-date with. When they couldn't—well, they'd be stuck going to rec room parties, taking a girl to a movie by bus, or hanging out shooting hoops with their friends.

That's how it was. It was the South. Except for the college-bound girls, more cautious and from stricter families, many of the tenth-grade girls were already partnered up. They expected to be married at twenty-one and saw their high school years as the "best time of their lives," their time to have fun.

Bree Henley and her friends Anne, Mary Lou, Carol, and Bunny were the heart of the good-time girls. They dated the school's top football players and spent weekends at rowdy frat parties at Emory or Georgia Tech. They were, in a word, untouchable to ordinary peons like Will. But for some reason Bree Henley and Will Hartman became friends.

It began when they sat next to each other in ninth-grade World History. One day Bree asked Will what page the teacher was reading from, and the next day she asked him again and they started kidding around, and, before you knew it, they were chatting like old ladies whenever there was a lull in class. Will thought she was daring and exotic. And Bree seemed to admire him. She said he was smart and "going somewhere," and she loved the free-wheeling tone of their chats. Nobody else talked to her about the same things in the same way. To Will, Bree was a gift from the gods. It thrilled him that she'd spend any time with him at all.

As one of the few Jewish kids in school, Will knew he was marginal. Sure, he was a good student, he'd taken piano lessons and sang in the chorus, and he had a friendly attitude; but he didn't go to church, and some kids said his soul would burn in hell forever. Students were always tapping him on the shoulder in study hall to remind him, "Will, we're prayin' for your soul," and it bothered him. He knew the rules: Jewish guys didn't date Christian girls, and vice versa. Protestants dated one another (but not Catholics), and Jews dated people from their temple or synagogue. But that didn't matter to Will: he was obsessed with Bree.

In tenth grade Bree asked Will to help her with math during third period study hall. Every day he'd sit next to her, inhaling the fragrance of her musky powder and sweet perfume, feeling the soft fuzz of her sweater as she leaned towards him, while he showed her how to solve quadratic equations or find square roots. She'd be so close, strands of her hair would tickle his face.

Of course, Bree didn't stick to math. She chattered away about everything, from the parties she was going to, to the movies she saw, her favorite dance music, and the most recent guy she was dating. She seemed as naïve and star-struck by these older men as Will was by her. And, because she apparently saw him as non-threatening—somewhere between a brother and a pet rock—she'd often ask his opinion of this or that person, or his advice on how she should handle some situation. For forty minutes, every third period, he felt included in a world whose level of sexual intimacy exceeded anything he'd imagined before.

True, he'd dated Carol Jacobson and Eleanor Schrader. He'd been on hayrides and felt Barbara Kahn's firm little breasts through her sweater. He'd danced with girls at parties in Lanna Braun's basement. But none of this had stirred him a thousandth as much as Bree Henley's hair against his cheek.

That year he and Bree were a pair. They were in several classes together, joked about their English teacher's accent. and shared ideas on Big Issues like Sex and Drinking. But then they drifted apart. She simply moved beyond him. In junior year, they had no classes in common and only saw each other in passing. She and her friends seemed involved in their social lives. In the meantime, Will was in the college-bound crowd, heading up the Science Club, acting in plays, learning French. Still, they smiled when they passed each other in the halls. And sometimes, at lunch, they stood together, leaning against the wall, chatting. And sometimes, in the morning, he'd stop by her locker to ask how she was doing.

"You still dating that guy, what's his name, Kenny?"

"Kenny? Oh, no! He's history."

"Too bad for Kenny."

"Yeah. I'm going out with Wade now."

"Wade?"

"You know Wade! He's a handsome devil."

"Really?"

"Our quarterback!"

"Oh. Right."

"I'll tell you more about him later."

Early in their senior year, Bree got pregnant and dropped out of school. She would not graduate with their class. Rumor had it she'd been going out with a man in his twenties who drank, but who she was crazy about. Her mother, an unhappy divorcee who worked at Rexall's, was furious. Bree was her younger daughter, the one who was supposed to do well, now that the older one had moved up to Memphis with her musician husband and their two kids. Bree's charm and looks were supposed to bring her a respectable match. Now everything was ruined. Some people said she'd gotten an abortion. And then even her friends stopped talking about her.

Will thought about her but couldn't bring himself to call her. He wasn't in her circle. And now she'd landed in a mess in a world he didn't know. In truth, he was too shy to seek her out, but he told himself he didn't want to get her into trouble with her mother by phoning her. And, after she'd been through, what could he say to her? Who was he to her, really, now that her life had taken such a turn?

But that summer, in the weeks before leaving for college, he couldn't stop thinking about her. What had happened? Did she have the baby? Did she marry? What would she do now? A few days before he was slated to head north, having worked himself into a state, he dialed her number from the student handbook. He didn't know if she was still there. But maybe someone, her mother, could tell him where she was.

The phone rang, but there was no answer. Impulsively, he took the keys to the family car, drove straight to Bree's house in Garden Hills, and rang the bell. But no one came to the door. As he was driving away, he saw a car in his rear-view mirror, turning into her driveway. When he got home, he called again and her mom answered. She seemed cordial, once he introduced himself, and said that Bree would be home at 5:30.

She answered on the second ring. Somehow, he found the courage to ask how she was, and could he see her before he left town. She said, sure, he could come over the following afternoon.

It struck him how dark her house was. The blinds were down, the drapes shut, and only one or two lamps were lit. It was August and hot and stuffy inside. Bree opened the door slowly. She was wearing a white blouse and a simple skirt that rustled as she moved. Her mother was there, too. She shook Will's hand; and then he and Bree sat on the living room sofa and Bree's mother brought them some iced tea and then disappeared upstairs. Looking at her beside him, Will saw that the circles under Bree's eyes had grown deeper, and he noticed she kept looking at her hands in her lap.

Sitting next to her thrilled him. He'd never known a woman who'd gotten pregnant without being married. Her humiliation made her both vulnerable and intriguing. Will was drawn to actresses who looked bruised by life, like Lizbeth Scott, and he saw Bree in much the same light. The distance between them, he felt, might not be so great now.

He suddenly looked around, puzzled. She sensed right away what it was. "I gave the baby up," she said. "I couldn't raise it."

He swallowed. What should he say? "Was that hard to do?"

"Well," she said. "Well, yes." She lifted a hand and let it fall with a slap against her thigh. He remembered that sound for a long time. "I just wasn't ready."

He nodded as if he understood and sipped some tea.

"Mamma doesn't want me going outside much," she said. "She thinks I'm a fallen woman." She gave a little smile. "I guess I am."

"That's ridiculous," he protested. "It wasn't …"

"Wasn't my fault?"

"Well …"

"Oh, yes it was. Whose else?" she said.

"But you can't let that hold you back."

She paused. "No. I guess. But …"

There was a clock ticking somewhere; a dog outside, barking. "So, your mom is keeping you in the house?"

"Mostly, she is."

"Until when?"

She shook her head. "Until she feels I've learned my lesson,

I guess."

He swallowed. "So, what will you do?"

"When?"

"When she's done keeping you shut up."

"I don't know." She took a deep breath and looked away. Will glanced at her figure. The living room was stifling. A wave of longing rose inside him, and he suddenly imagined taking her away, making her his own, taking care of her. She needed someone like him, someone who really cared for her and wouldn't use her. Someone she'd love with all her heart in return.

The barking started up again outside, and there was the sound of someone shouting, and a car driving down the road.

"I'm going to college in four days," he announced.

"That's wonderful, Will. I'm glad for you. You know, I'm sure you're going to be great at everything you do."

Which wasn't what he wanted to hear, of course. "I can write, if you like. You can let me know how you are."

"That would be nice," she said.

On the train going north, he met a young woman going to Swarthmore. They talked about how exciting it was to leave their families and all the things they were going to do in life. They ate dinner in the dining car, and later, as the night deepened and the lights in their car switched off, they kept talking. While the other passengers slept, they cuddled together side by side under a blanket, and he kissed her. Will took it as an omen of good things to come.

And then he was in college. Atlanta seemed far away. Providence, with its old brick buildings and Yankee style, ushered him into an old, yet contemporary, cultural wonderland, and Brown's lush urban campus, with its colonial halls and wide lawns, made his spirit soar. He met his new roommate, began his courses, and explored the campus. Some evenings he clambered up one of the smaller trees in the College Green, where he perched, happily looking down on the other students. He rented a piano practice room and played his favorite Rachmaninoff concerto as loud as he could at one o'clock in the morning, singing accompaniment at the top of his lungs.

He joined the school theatre group, studied art history, and read Greek philosophy. At eighteen, Will was elated at the thought that he'd escaped the small-minded drudgery of Atlanta and had gotten away from his parents. The more he threw his energies into his new life, the easier it was to let Bree Henley, as part of the old, fall out of his thoughts.

He wrote her one letter, in November, on his new creamy beige stationery (with the embossed college seal at the top, and his name and school address printed in raised Gothic letters), gushing about how wonderful it was to be out of the South. Bree answered in a few paragraphs. She'd gotten a job at Woolworth's and was taking evening classes for her GED. "I'm going to college, too," she wrote. "To Wesleyan, if they'll take me." It was a women's college in Macon. There was a final sentence in her letter that he never forgot: "But it will be some time before I feel the desire to date," she said.

Almost two years went by. Will was absorbed in his classes and enthusiastic about his friends, many of whom were fledgling writers or active in Sock and Buskin, Brown's theatre group. In his freshman year, he had a minor role in the winter play. In the spring, he assisted the highly regarded junior Amberly Goolde in directing "Love's Labor's Lost," an imaginative production in which the actors painted their faces and wore masks. Inspired, he began writing one-act plays. That summer he worked on campus and continued to write. In his sophomore year, he decided to major in French and signed up to spend his junior year in Paris. A math major named Randall, who lived in his dorm, was also going, and the two of them could be buddies. In the months before he sailed, he worked as stage manager for a local summer stock repertory group.

In all this time, he'd written Bree only two letters, but on his way to Atlanta for a quick visit with his parents, he thought of her again, and realized she'd been lurking in his mind.

Atlanta was hot and muggy. Many of Will's old friends were gone, and he wasn't interested in seeing those who'd remained. On the second day he phoned Bree's house, but she was out of town, working in Macon. Her mom gave him her number, and he called that evening. When she answered, she seemed distracted. He told himself she probably felt odd, hearing from him out of the blue, but she seemed so distant he wondered if she really wanted to talk.

"Oh, Will," she said, singing his name slowly. "I'm afraid you've caught me at a bad time."

"Sorry," he said. "But look … I'm back in town for a few days. How are you doing?"

"I'm still alive," she said. "Still very unattached. I'm having a rather boring summer working in the school library."

He told her he was heading off to Paris for a year.

"Will, that's wonderful," she said. "I guess you'll have all kinds of adventures."

"I don't know," he said, then paused. "I hope so."

"Will you write me?"

"If you write me back."

"I'll try."

Then she said she had to go. He was willing to stop talking. What else did he have to say? He'd always felt uneasy on the phone, without visual cues. He put the phone back on its receiver and stretched out on top of his bed, staring at the ceiling.

Like many first-born Jewish sons of his class, Will idealized himself. In the realm of the actual and the possible, he saw himself as all potential, with his future spread out in front of him like a plate of fruit. Reading French literature in college had made him only more romantic; and so—turning from thoughts of Bree Henley in Macon, Georgia—he imagined arriving in Paris and falling into the arms of a Madame Arnoux, the heroine in Flaubert's *Sentimental Education*. She'd be the first of his many conquests. And he'd soon have a coterie of fascinating literary friends and become a great playwright. In fact, though, he was love-starved and longing for sex. The best he'd been able to manage in the latter arena so far was a few encounters with Lisa, a chunky, promiscuous Temple teenager who was willing to put out for college boys in their cars.

Beneath the idealization had always lain a core of self-doubt. His summer of repertory theatre had only worsened his feeling of inadequacy, both as a writer and as a person. To start with, he knew he had no acting talent. Worse, he'd had trouble writing in the little spare time he'd had. The older members of the company—professional actors from New York—had continually teased him about his pretensions, and even the sixteen-year-old intern Sally Mosely rebuffed his invitations to go out. His romantic veneer was a protective skin, but he wasn't aware of it at the time. All hope and bluster, he set sail for France in August with Randall by his side.

The France he arrived in was poor and still recovering from World War II, but to him it was a thrill to be there. He was in Paris, free to wander wherever he wanted. Defying the rules of his Sweetbriar program, he insisted on finding his own lodging. This resulted in his renting a tiny room in a Latin Quarter apartment owned by a cranky elderly Hungarian refugee with a daughter. Randall found his own lodging, too, all the way at the other end of the métro. All the other students lived with carefully chosen pro-American families, and their lives were tightly supervised.

Will reveled in living around the corner from the Café Les Deux Magots, where Sartre and de Beauvoir had hung out after World War II. He'd go there some mornings and stand at the bar beside the burly workmen smoking Gauloises and drinking vin rouge. He'd order a café au lait and a tartine, a sliced half-loaf of French bread smeared with butter, and listen to the talk around him.

On sunny mornings, he'd wander the Jardin de Luxembourg, glancing at people on the benches with their books and newspapers, the young Parisian mothers with their carriages, the children shouting. Later he'd amble through narrow streets filled with odors of beer, cheese, and garbage—the butcher stalls and bars, green-grocers, creameries, and fruit stands. He and Randall often ate dinner at a University restaurant, filled with steam and the smell of damp clothes and the noise of students talking loudly. He bought cheap tickets to the Opéra and Comédie Francaise and saw the performances alone.

Of course, he didn't meet Madame Arnoux. But he did fall in love with a dark-haired, pouty girl from Barnard named Ruby, who had always wanted to be French. Ruby dressed in black turtleneck sweaters and knew Paris like the back of her hand. She took Will on a three-hour walking tour of the city the night after they landed: past Notre Dame, the Latin Quarter, the Place de la Concorde. He was besotted with her, and she seemed to like him, too. But he was self-conscious, timid, and afraid to show his affection. Several times he took her out, only to feel paralyzed by the end of the evening. Initially, he realized, Ruby may have thought he was a Francophile like her, and she admired his wanting to be a writer. But once she saw how American, Jewish, shy, and conventional he was, she lost interest. After a few weeks, Will realized that Ruby had her own agenda, and he wasn't on it. She soon hooked up with a group of young Parisians and began sleeping with a waiter, the first of her many *amours*. Will barely saw her the rest of the year, except at a Music Appreciation course, which she stopped attending after two months.

The pain of having loved and lost so quickly haunted Will. He blamed his own passivity. He roamed the streets late at night with Randall, wailing "Ru-beee!" at the top of his lungs; and for months, whenever they'd hunch together over a couple of beers, he'd bemoan his failure to have acted more decisively. It made him resolve never to remain passive again.

Although his romance had collapsed, it left him a wealth of angst which he eagerly mined in his journals and plays. Ultimately, he said to himself, he didn't mind, because his day would come. Now he was in his apprenticeship, gathering grist for the mill, preparing. As he and Randall travelled around Europe, he took meticulous notes that recorded his experiences, and he annotated his readings, dreams, and feelings.

He discovered Ionesco and Beckett in tiny left-bank theatres and imitated them in plays of his own, feeling he was on the cutting edge of contemporary drama. Wait until he got back to Providence, he thought! He was thrilled when Sock and Buskin, back at Brown, chose one of his plays for its spring festival.

And then he wrote Bree. As his yearning for Ruby became more tragic, and his chances to win her impossible, he began fantasizing about other women. Bree seemed a combination of old friend and old flame, and he sent her a stream of postcards, notes, and letters, describing the places he'd seen and the things he was doing, pouring out his hopes for being a New Light of the American theatre:

Dear Bree,

You will wonder why I'm writing now, in December and in Paris, months and continents away from each other. I doubt there's a conscious answer. Perhaps it's the mood, the bleakness of a lonely afternoon. But I'm in France and you're back at school. I'd love to describe everything I've seen and have you breathe the atmosphere of "high exotic adventure," but my adventure has not been all that exotic. In fact, Bree, its most distressing result so far has been to smash the brittle ideas I had of Europe. It's not a dream world, but an old, tired, and suffering continent. It's not a haven for artists, but an earthly place where ordinary people are trying to face, or escape from, life. Lesson number one.

As for me, I'm trying to see as much as I can, but I have yet to make any French friends, which I suppose is my fault. More of that unwelcome timidity which sticks to me like a disease. and which I have yet to cure. But at least I'm on my own, independent. I can do what I want.

I've got a one-act play in my drawer and another in my head, waiting to crystallize and be set down on paper. And I'm even attempting some poetry, though I am far from being published yet. I think things are moving in the right direction. Maybe I'm unjustified, but there it is.

Life here is so different from college. Have you ever seen old men in raggedy black coats lie down on the street, cover themselves with papers and go to sleep on a cold December night? Or be walking along an apparently ordinary city street in the fog and suddenly see, looming up in front of you, outlined vaguely against the haze, a huge church built centuries ago? It's insane. I feel as if I'm really living, heading to whatever awaits me. I'm optimistic even if I have no reason to be.

But let me to ask about you. What's been happening. Are you still without a boyfriend? What do you think about when it's night and the only thing you can hear is the wind scraping outside your window?

Beautiful, simple things are everywhere: not only the chateaux of the Loire, the cathedral of Notre Dame, and the grand ornate buildings ... but also the river, the trees in the autumn, the smell of the seasons, a girl cautiously peering up and down the street before she crosses, the smell of cooking, the sounds of eating and singing and living. These too make the day worthwhile, and even an old grouch like me can get lyrical.

Do drop me a line and let me know about that fairyland of opportunity across the Atlantic. The French say it must be heaven.

Yours, Will

She responded fitfully. Her letters had the same tone, and they saddened him. On the one hand, they mirrored and validated the exaggerated view he had of himself, repeating that he had a great talent and would be a success. But then she gracefully stepped aside. She took herself out of the picture, as it were.

In her neat, careful hand—her letters were written on pale blue Wesleyan stationery, with a school seal at the top but no address in raised Gothic letters—she presented herself as a girl like many others, high-spirited but low-brow, unimpressive and (unfortunately) sullied. She was struggling for average grades at an average school and had modest ambitions. She was sure *he* was going to distinguish himself, and she wished him luck. But, as for herself, she'd be happy just to graduate and find a responsible guy. In fact, she was already dating one now.

It was maddening! On the one hand, she bought into Will's self-inflation; but, on the other, she backed away by saying he'd gone far beyond her. She asked to be an admiring friend, who was, alas, too insignificant to be a partner:

Dear William,

I feel as though I should call you William now, for you don't seem to be the Will I knew before. You seem to have matured a great deal, and probably even more since I last heard from you. Tell me. After these months in gay, exciting Paris, is your poetry still naïve? I would like to read some, but if you don't want anyone to see it yet, I would understand of course.

Do you remember the girl I spoke of when you called last summer? The crazy poetess? When I read your last letter, I realized that, as much as I love and enjoy receiving your letters, I could never really get up to your level. Well, Polly would be able to, and really, she seems so terribly lonely. Her full name is Polly Broderick, and if you don't want to write her, okay. But I think both of you would enjoy it very much. I remembered your mentioning that you liked to write letters, so here's your chance to correspond with a brilliant girl who would love to hear from you. You can just write her at Wesleyan. Of course, if you stop writing me I shall never forgive you. I realize that I'm terrible about keeping in touch. I'm sure I'm very dull and always too slow. But I so enjoy hearing from you, I hope you'll put up with me.

Yes, I'm still without a boyfriend, but things have improved. I've at least found someone I'm interested in. He's very good-looking, extremely charming, 23, and is on his way to becoming a doctor. We have a wonderful time together, see each other whenever it's convenient for both, but yet we have an unspoken understanding that neither of us will fall in love. It's really very strange, but it's a comfortable feeling. I know that someone is there, someone to think about, someone to look forward to seeing, and at the same time, there are no strong ties, no worry about the future.

Classes are calling. Write if you have a minute—I love hearing from you. Most Important, stay optimistic. You have a wonderful mind, and someday, I know, you will have the things you are searching for now.

Yours always, Bree.

She was right about one thing. He *was* becoming different from the Will she'd known. He was being exposed to a level of culture his parents had never experienced—history, languages, Gothic churches, Italy, the Paris opera. He had no idea what it would ultimately mean for him to acquire this "education" they'd worked so hard for and encouraged him to have, and he had little sense of what it was he was supposed to be acquiring; yet he believed they were right in wanting him to have it. He was a third-generation American, and, after his grandfather's rise from poverty and his father's plodding career in merchandising, it was his mission to break into the professions. Medicine or law would be fine with them.

For the year, then, he remained on his own, nineteen and doleful, in the City of Lights. His landlady, Madame Kamenska, took no interest in him; he came and went as he chose. She didn't even give him breakfast. Her main concern was that he shouldn't talk to (or even see) her twenty-three-year-old daughter, even though that scrawny young woman slept across the hall from him every night, their heads on their pillows a mere six feet apart, and would regularly utter sighs, small sniffles, and moans that he could hear through his wall. For that matter, he could hear her pad about her room, open and shut the drawers of her dresser, even slip off her nightgown in the morning—or so he believed. His fantasies would have been fulfilled if he'd found Clementine an eager soul, a kind consoling heart, and a kindred spirit, and had a romance with her, thereby thwarting her mother's protective impulse; but Clementine was a thin, skittish young thing whose interests he never discovered. She'd dash into her room whenever he appeared, and—except for a quick "Bonjour" or "Bonsoir"—was never in the same place at the same time long enough with him to start the tiniest of chats.

For a while, he partied heavily at night. He and Randall had been accepted into a rowdy band of Ivy League kids who liked frequenting bars in Montmartre, getting drunk, and picking fights. Invariably, halfway through the evening, Clay, a fair-haired Classics major from Yale, would approach some hapless Frenchman sipping wine at the bar and sneer, "What are *you* looking at?" And then there would be a scuffle. Clay, Eddie, and Julio (from a wealthy family in Cuba) enjoyed this kind of life—they believed it was what young Americans in Paris should do—but after a while Will and Randall tired of the drinking and the fighting. The allure faded dramatically after they were all arrested one night when Clay destroyed one of the bars' glass doors with a chair.

And so it went. Will and Randall studied, explored Paris, and travelled. They sent papers to Providence and diligently mailed cards and letters to their friends and parents. Will wrote plays and poems and scribbled in his diary. Much of his time, though, he and Randall wandered the streets. They talked endlessly about finding a woman. Will wanted a soulmate, not just a mistress; Randall said he'd be happy with any warm and fuzzy body. Evaluating the women in the Sweetbriar group, they pronounced them all lacking and talked instead about the women of their dreams.

As Will abandoned his obsession with Ruby, Bree became his main fantasy. He talked to Randall about her and determined to court her when he returned to Atlanta.

"What's so great about this woman?" Randall said one day, as they were gazing at the Mediterranean on a trip to Nice. "Remind me."

"Besides being gorgeous, brooding, dark and sexy …"

"Yes, she's a southern flower. And ...?"

"She believes in me," Will said solemnly. "She believes I can make it."

"And what do you know about *her?*" Randall said, grinning like a monkey.

"It doesn't matter," said Will.

By year's end he couldn't wait to get home and see her. This time, he'd decided not to take "no" for an answer. He wouldn't be put off by nonsense about their being on "different levels." He'd tell her they belonged together, and she wouldn't resist. As he saw it, her past humiliation had ennobled her, and the fact that he had now suffered, too, drew them closer: for now, he believed, they would have the power to heal one another.

Will returned to the States in mid-August and headed to Atlanta. His house didn't have air conditioning, and all the rooms were hot, except for the screened-in back porch, whose fans were going non-stop. His parents were delighted to have him back. They praised his appearance ("much more mature") and begged him for stories. Even his sister, a gangly thirteen-year-old who would have spent the day with her friends at the Standard Club, the playground for Northside well-off Jewish families, stayed home to talk. Will begged off, saying that he was jet-lagged (which he was), but they wanted to hear "all about" his year anyway.

The second day, his mom cooked him eggs and bacon; and after his dad had gone off to work, she refilled her coffee from the percolator, sat down at the kitchen table, and leaned her chin on her palm, staring at him and asking questions until he felt like a bug in a collection. He especially didn't want to talk about whether he'd met any girls in Paris and whether he was "sweet" on somebody he should tell her about.

It wasn't his home any more. His room was small and full of kids' things. His desk had a drawer crammed full of travel pamphlets he'd collected in the fifth grade. His bed seemed cramped, and the radio nestled in its headboard, on which he'd listened to Atlanta Crackers' night baseball games for years, no longer worked. The house seemed filled with his parents' tedium—letters, bills, clothes, records, dishes, food, furniture—and his sister's teenage stuff. He felt changed in ways he couldn't describe, but in any case, he didn't want to talk to his parents about it.

He was impatient to move on. For starters, he had exams as soon as he got back to school, and he needed to study. He also wanted to see his friends at Sock and Buskin and find out what position he'd have this coming year. And he had to talk to his advisor about a thesis. There were people he wanted to see in Atlanta as well—an old high school teacher, his best friend from the twelfth grade who'd enrolled at the Naval Academy, and the theatre director he'd worked with the summer before college.

He also wanted at least one night out with Lisa. Maybe at a motel. If nothing else, that would boost his self-esteem. And of course, he was going to see Bree.

His third day back he phoned Bree to see if she was free. He imagined taking her somewhere quiet—maybe a drive out Dunwoody way where they could park. She answered the phone and sounded delighted to hear from him. She "couldn't wait" to see him. But she was working a part-time job in the evenings and was only free some afternoons. Maybe the day after next.

He thought about it nonstop, hating the idea of seeing her in the afternoon. The afternoon was all wrong. And where would they go? He didn't even *know* Atlanta anymore. Where could they be alone? The last thing he wanted was to be stuck in some small coffee shop, staring at her across a formica table. It would be like sitting down with his mom.

Then he thought about the woods near Peachtree Creek. They'd probably be the mildest outdoor place in the afternoon. He and Bree could find a shady spot, walk by the water. Anyway, he didn't know anywhere else they could go.

He was already sweating when he got into his car. It felt like ninety-five degrees. He told himself again it wasn't the right time of day, it wasn't the right temperature for a romantic meeting. Still …

He drove to her house. Some pale blue hydrangea bushes were in front, and little pink and yellow flowers stood in rows along the walkway. Someone must have been watering them, because the air smelled moist and earthy. Standing at the door, he remembered being there three years earlier, before he'd left for college. Since then, they'd written and talked on the phone, but he hadn't seen Bree in person.

He rang the bell. There were sounds of footsteps, and voices. Then the door opened and there she was, in a summer dress with a pattern of flowers.

"Shall we find a place for a walk?" he said. They drove for about five minutes, across Peachtree and over to the wooded area he'd chosen. When they stopped, she had a funny look on her face.

"Is this okay?" he said.

She hesitated a moment. "It's all right."

"We can take a walk and chat."

She nodded.

The sun glared fiercely through the gaps in the trees. Will's light shirt was already wet, and the backs of his pants were sticking to his legs. There wasn't a bird in sight. Bree's eyes were deep and lustrous, just as he'd remembered, sunk into the dark circles above her cheeks. Beads of sweat had formed on the tiny hairs on her upper lip, and he felt aroused.

They set off on a path. It was dusty, the bushes on either side brown, straggly, and dry. Their arms brushed against each other as they walked. He couldn't believe they were really together.

"So. Don't you look grown up," she said, tilting her head back. A flood of memories hit him, and he was back in the ninth grade.

"Do I? You look just the same."

"I can't believe that. I'm a college girl now. Studying hard, working to pay my bills …"

"It's so good to see you." He took a breath. "It's been a long time."

"Yes. I think we've each been on our journey." She paused. "So you have to tell me all about yours."

He didn't want to. "I've thought about you a lot …" he began.

"I loved your letters. They made me feel like I was right there with you. In Paris."

"And you were here in Georgia. Getting yourself an education, too."

They stopped on the bank of the creek. It had dried to a trickle. The riverbed was filled with stones and rubble, dried branches, cardboard, and broken bottles.

"Well. Probably not that much of an education. Not by your standards …"

She was so close, his head was about to burst. He wanted to take her in his arms and kiss her.

"But you like it. Wesleyan, I mean," he stammered.

"I do. I really do."

She was wearing a perfume that smelled like freesia.

"And what happened with the guy who wants to be a doctor …?"

"Oh that." She bit her lower lip and made a face. "That's already over, I'm afraid. It didn't last very long."

"There must be a lot of guys who want to take you out."

"Not so many." She laughed. "Remember, it's a girls' school."

He'd thought there would be some shade, but there wasn't a cool spot anywhere. A brackish smell rose from the creek. His forehead was wet with perspiration. He wiped his face and tried to concentrate.

"So how about you?" she continued. "You must have seen so much."

He took a deep breath. "I told you in my letters," he said.

Then he couldn't talk any more. She stood looking at the creek, a wistful expression on her face. "Bree ... I ..."

He leaned forward, took her shoulders in his hands and kissed her. She let him do it, but she didn't kiss him back. When he tried to kiss her again, she twisted her head to one side. They were both sweating. "Will, don't."

"But I'm just ... I've been thinking about you this whole year ..."

"I've been thinking about you, too."

"But?"

"You're a good friend, Will. But I don't want to ..." She looked away, then down. Then she pulled a small white handkerchief from the pocket of her dress and wiped her face.

"What?"

She shook her head, then put the handkerchief back in her pocket and smiled oddly, as if she was having a conversation with herself. "You know," she said. "I mean, how could you know?" She paused. "I used to come here with ..." Her hand fluttered, and tears sprang to her eyes. "With the man I was dating when I had to leave school."

"The one who ...?"

"Yes. Billy."

"I didn't know."

"How could you know?" she said.

That was the last time he saw Bree for forty-seven years.

2.

When he got back to Brown, Will found his colleagues had blocked him out of any major role at Sock and Buskin; and, although he wrote another play or two and planned to write more, his career as a playwright quickly trailed off. He pulled back from the drama crowd, denouncing them as false friends, and decided to pursue an academic career in French.

In the spring of his senior year, he met the woman who

would become his wife. Connie was innocent and dreamy, from a farming family in Iowa. She had long blond hair, sang and played the guitar, and wanted to travel. She dressed in jeans and tee shirts; and when she was happy, she whirled about, singing, arms encircling her head. They took walks in the woods and spent a weekend in a Newport motel. Their romance blossomed, and by the time Will had graduated, they were a couple. Randall, who had fallen in love with a tawny-haired British teenager on the Riviera just before leaving France, joked that they'd each finally found what they wanted and were now beyond adolescence.

The Fulton Country Draft Board had rejected Will because of a cardiac murmur, so he was free to do what he wanted. He studied French at graduate school in Boston; Connie finished up at Smith and joined him the following year. They got married. Connie got an M.A. in History. They had one child, then another. After Will got his doctorate they moved to Cleveland, where he filled a one-year opening; then, suddenly, they were a family living in Syracuse. Connie stayed home with the kids; Will taught at the University. He published his thesis on Flaubert and *L'Éducation Sentimentale*.

He corresponded off and on with Randall, who'd forsaken his romance to become a psychiatrist, and then they fell out of touch. After three years he and Connie moved to Lawrence, Kansas. He taught, she got into the American History grad program, and they made friends with other academic couples.

He felt himself drifting, thought he was bored, thought he'd never dealt with his adolescent feelings. He and Connie bickered. She complained he was no help in the house or with the kids. She became evasive, inconsistent in her affections. They couldn't find a way of talking about conflict, so they avoided it and simply tried to be kind. He poured energy into his teaching and started writing his second book. She joined a consciousness-raising group. They went to therapy for a few sessions, but then stopped.

They focused on raising their children and on being good friends to their friends. Will felt the marriage was "good enough" and had no interest in threatening it. Even though some coeds in his classes flirted with him when he was lecturing, he refused to get involved. He felt himself hunkering down. There was some kind of hole inside him, he felt, some unfulfilled space, and he let his spirit curl and shrink down to fill it.

Connie, too, seemed content to soldier on, so long as he didn't criticize her. She had her friends and interests and said she might want to go to work when the kids were older. They bickered less. Eventually they moved to Madison, where he found a home in the French Department, and she worked for the University Press.

3.

The notice of his high school's fiftieth reunion came with a big packet of papers, as if the organizers assumed he'd be attending. There was information about hotels and housing, a sheet with information on Atlanta's museums, a maroon-colored pamphlet listing the weekend's planned activities, and a map to help navigate the city Atlanta had become. Another sheet asked for an updated autobiography. Will hadn't gone to any of his previous reunions, but his old friend Dickie Mason phoned and asked if he was planning to come.

Will and Dickie had been pals since the sixth grade. Dickie had been a serious Boy Scout, always heading off to summer camps in places like Flagstaff, Arizona—and, later, with other explorers, to Antarctica, Peru, and Bhutan. Now he was widowed and retired from his research job at Corning.

Dickie and Will had enjoyed astronomy together. They'd spent many evenings at a nearby golf course, staring at the stars and shining a flashlight on a book on the constellations, and they'd even attended some meetings of the Emory astronomy club. They'd also teamed up on science projects, as well as recurring humorous announcements on the morning P.A. system that plugged forthcoming high school events. Dickie was excited about going to the reunion.

Will talked to Connie. Usually, it wasn't the kind of thing she liked to do, but she'd gone to a reunion of her own class a few years back and surprised herself by having a great time. Maybe, he thought, it was time for him to settle some of the "old business" he felt about Atlanta. Both his parents were dead, his sister was in Massachusetts, and he hadn't thought about the city for years. Bree suddenly appeared in his mind like an apparition, and he realized how much she'd meant to him.

"Why not?" said Connie. "You might learn something new about those people."

"Will you come, too?"

"Sure," she said. "I've never been to Atlanta."

Bree had been part of the class until senior year, but then she'd left. Had she been asked to the reunion, he wondered. There was a phone number for Mary Lou McClusky, the class Secretary, on the letter. Will phoned and asked if Bree would be coming.

"I certainly hope so," said Mary Lou. "We all of us want her to be there."

"She's still in Atlanta?"

"No, she's been living down Macon way for years. You and she were friends back then, as I recall."

"We were."

"It such a shame what's happened to her," Mary Lou's voice suddenly honeyed with pity.

"What do you mean?"

"Why, didn't you know?" she said. "She has cancer."

He felt his head expanding, helplessly.

"She's not doing well, poor thing. But I know she so much wants to come up to see everyone, if only for a day. Oh, Will, she'd be so happy if she could see you, too. We all knew she cared a lot for you."

"I didn't realize ..." he stammered.

"Yes. She's been sick for a while now. It's her colon? And I do believe it's spread."

He listened as the woman kept talking. His head felt like a balloon, and her voice was zooming exponentially away.

"The girls have stayed real close with her. Carol and Anne, especially. And Claire Hendon. They talk all the time on the phone. And Carol's gone down a number of times to see her."

"Do you have her phone number or address?"

"Why, sure, Will. Just a minute." She gave them to him, and then he hung up. He'd been ready for the news that Bree was dead, or that she'd moved away. But not for cancer.

If she was sick he didn't want to intrude, he didn't want to bother her by phoning, so he sent a short note instead: he was sorry to hear she was ill, he and Connie would be down for the reunion, and he hoped she'd be there too. She replied with a short note saying she hoped to be well enough to attend. If her husband Mack didn't take her to the reunion, then Carol Clark said she'd drive down from Atlanta and bring her up herself.

When he and Connie checked into their motel, Will found that not only was Dickie Mason staying there, but so were some other classmates as well. After resting for an hour, he and Connie descended to the reception area, preparing to head out to the day's first event, an outdoor picnic lunch. Bobby Kaufman immediately grabbed him by the sleeve, introduced him and Connie to his wife Gwen, and offered to drive them. As they walked to the car, Will saw that arthritis had so riddled Bobby's body that he needed a cane.

Will had used to double date with Bobby because Bobby was a year older and had a car. Now he was back in Bobby's rear seat again, driving through the dogwood-lined streets. From behind he saw that Bobby's close-cropped curly hair had gone completely white. Gwen talked nonstop all the way. Will didn't want to be stuck with the Kaufmans for the whole weekend and sensed that if they were a foursome now, they'd still be one two days later; so, after Bobby parked, Will waved at him and Gwen, then pulled Connie quickly ahead.

Fifty yards away he saw people in their late sixties, hand in hand, clomping over the wooden boardwalk to the recreation center. Large flowing banners with the school's name and colors (brown and gold) hung over the entrance. "Terriers" flags decked the walls. Elderly women welcomed them at tables strewn with nametags, markers, and information packets. Old fifties music blared from two loudspeakers, and the odor of popcorn and barbecue sauce filled the air. Behind the tables there were ice tubs filled with soft drinks, wine, and beer. On the side were counters with platters of fried chicken, hamburgers, raw veggies, and dips. Inside the center were linen-covered tables of eight. A squadron of ceiling fans were busily spinning.

People lingered by the walls or drifted over to the tables, looking for familiar faces. Classmates who'd stayed in Atlanta were standing in groups, talking and laughing. Every few minutes another woman with grey hair would shriek someone's name and there'd be a lot of jumping and hugging.

A short red-faced woman was suddenly at Will's side. "Will? It's Mary Lou. Remember me?" She bobbed her head from side to side. "And who's this lovely woman?"

Will introduced her to Connie, and a husband appeared beside her. "You remember Gene."

"Yes. Gene." He'd been the halfback on the football team and a baritone in the Special Choir. He was still wiry, but with a paunch.

Gene squeezed his hand. "Good to see you again."

Mary Lou leaned in closer. "Will," she whispered. "Bree Henley did say she'd be here. I know she'll be glad since you've come all the way from Wisconsin."

Will nodded. Other people came up. Hank Mayberry and his wife Claire were down from Virginia. Hank had worked for newspapers. George Davis and his wife Ethel had moved to Memphis, where they'd been very active in their church. George and Will had been on the debating team together. Ethel told Will the class math genius, Sam Willis, had just died. And he'd been gay, as it turned out. He'd stayed in Atlanta and started two software companies, but he'd just had a heart attack and died. Eddie Polk, who'd been the class cut-up, was carrying an oxygen tank. Will remembered that Eddie could imitate anybody's speech and posture. Now he was hunched over and shaky. "I guess I indulged a bit too much in the good stuff while I could," Eddie said, grinning sheepishly.

Then there was some loud shrieking near the welcoming tables. A woman had come in, walking slowly, leaning on the arm of a big man with a cane. It was Bree. The good-time girls all rushed around her and jumped up and down, squealing. Will led Connie towards the hubbub, then hung back. "Yes, that's her," he whispered.

Bree looked frail in her pale-yellow dress. Her hair had turned gray. Her head was bent and her shoulders a bit hunched. She still had her smile, but it was wistful and tenuous—a memory playing all too lightly on strained features. The circles under her eyes were still dark, but her cheeks had hollowed. Her abdomen seemed puffy. The man whose arm she leaned on seemed older. He had a big barrel chest, a thick neck, and short-cropped white hair. He was using a cane, and his hips swung from side to side when he moved.

After a moment, Bree saw him. "Will Hartman," she said, stretching out her hand. "How *are* you?"

He took the hand and stepped forward. "Fine, Bree. I'm glad you could make it." For a moment, looking at her, it was like seeing the seventeen-year-old girl and sixty-nine-year-old woman both. "I want you to meet my wife," he said.

Bree gingerly shook hands with Connie, then tilted her head towards the big man beside her. "And this is Mack." She pulled him by the arm. "Mack, this is Will Hartman." Mack looked puzzled. "*Will*, who I've told you so much about."

"Ah, yes." Mack reached out and crushed his hand. "Good to

meet you, Will."

A throbbing din arose from all directions. People were moving to and fro, waving and shouting out greetings. The good-time girls were bobbing and weaving around Bree. New people were thronging to the front tables, pushing everyone else into the hall. Everyone seemed to be talking at once, and it was suddenly so noisy Will could barely hear the people beside him. He didn't know whether to keep standing there, with Bree and Mack, or to suggest that all four of them move to a table. But just then Betty Sue Dilbeck leaned forward and whispered something to Bree. Bree turned to Will.

"Will … Oh my goodness, you'll have to excuse me. I have *got* to talk with Betty Sue," she said, her voice breathy. "Something about tonight's program. And I've got to sit down."

She was being pulled away. "Of course. We'll talk later," Will said, but she had gone.

The reunion was chaos. As it turned out, there was no program for this first get-together. There was simply a horde of people talking to whomever they could before someone else came over, interrupted, and started asking *their* questions. At one point, the Class President shushed the crowd to welcome everyone and say how happy he was that so many people had turned out and remind them about the grand banquet that night. Then it was mayhem again.

Will was worried that Connie might be feeling overwhelmed, and he didn't want to leave her alone, but just then Bobby and Gwen came over and glommed on to them, just like Bobby used to glom on to Will before. They dragged him and Connie to one of the tables and said how much they had to catch up on (fifty years, during which, Will realized, he'd never once thought about Bobby Kaufman), and then Dickie Mason came over with Wade Clinton and his wife and started talking about the old Boy Scout days. So, on one side they had Dickie Mason talking about how the Scouts had once been lost in this huge underground cave in Tennessee for fifteen hours and no one knew how to get out, and on the other side Gwen talking nonstop about her and Bobby's two kids and their spouses and grandchildren and neighbors.

Will's back was hurting. He told Connie he needed to stretch. Standing up, he moved cautiously around the edge of the room. Bree and Mack were at a table of good-time girls and their husbands. There weren't any open seats, and the group seemed very involved. He decided he'd talk to Bree later, at the banquet.

Moving back to his table he bumped into Scooter Craig, a scrawny kid who'd lived in his neighborhood. Just over five feet tall, with his short crew-cut, tee shirt and jeans, Scooter used to dart around the neighborhood doing wheelies on his bike. Now he was a slim minister with a beard who worked in a half-way house for people with drug problems. Scooter had been in therapy, and he talked to Will about twelve-step groups, "acceptance," and "coming to grips with one's own limitations."

After a few minutes Will felt exhausted. The reunion was worse than a Modern Language convention —and at least *there* he had professional connections to draw on. Now his hip was aching, too. He reflected that he and Connie had just had a long plane trip. And he couldn't stand on his feet for long these days. He wanted to be back at the motel. When he returned to his table, Gwen and Bobby said they were feeling overwhelmed, too, and wanted to leave. The four of them drove back to the motel, and Will and Connie took a nap.

That night everyone was dressed up, the men in dark suits and ties and the women in satiny gowns. The function room of the North Piedmont Hilton was cavernous and didn't feel crowded. A band was booming loud Fifties music. After cocktails, people were invited to sit down at tables of eight. Will noticed that people were sitting down with the same people they'd hung around with fifty years ago. The Catholics and their spouses were together. The Episcopalians as well. And he and Connie had squared up with Bobby and Gwen, Dickie Mason, Wade Clinton and his wife, and Billie Jean Fickling, whose husband had died.

After dinner, there was a slide show with photos of the class back then, the black and white pictures fading in and out to sounds of "Earth Angel" and "The Great Pretender." Everyone groaned and cheered. It amazed Will how young and fresh people looked. The good-time girls looked innocently provocative in their tight sweaters, mugging and posing for the camera. After the slide show the Class President said how wonderful a class they were, how so many people had accomplished so many things, and how even, yes, though there had been illness and losses and disappointments in everyone's life, as a group they were a testament to the school and its always-to-be-remembered teachers. Then he read a list of the people who had passed, and the group grew still.

After the President's speech, the band picked up again. Will was determined to speak to Bree before the evening got out of hand. Connie, who was talking to Gwen, wished him luck.

Mack was on Bree's right, so Will pulled an empty chair over to her left and sat down. "Hi," he said. She looked up distractedly. "It's so hard to find a minute to talk." He leaned forward. It was hard to talk above the din. "I was so sorry to hear about your being ill," he said. "How are you?"

She looked dismayed. "Oh, Will. I don't know ..." She waved a hand, indicating all the people at the table. "Is it all right if we don't talk about that right now? Not here."

"Sure. That's fine."

"Your wife Connie looks very nice," she said. "You must be glad you found her."

"I am."

"And what does she do?"

"She works at our University Press."

"That must be very interesting."

"Yes."

"And you?"

He told her he was still teaching French, and it struck him that she might be so ill, she couldn't process information well. Maybe she'd wanted to attend the reunion, but simply couldn't interact much. The thought upset him. Then he realized she was looking at him in a vague, disembodied way, as if she were floating. "Bree, how are you really doing?" he said.

"As well as I can," she said, smiling with effort. "It's not easy." He realized she was short of breath. "Mack is a wonderful man, and I don't know what I'd do without him. But ..." She paused. "And the girls have been wonderful, while I've been sick." She looked down, took her napkin in one hand, and began to twist it. "You know, I so loved the letters you sent me from France, Will. I keep them in a special envelope and read them whenever I feel blue, and they cheer me up."

"Ah."

"I want you to have them back. I'm sure your grandchildren would want to read them. They could learn about all the wonderful experiences their grandpa had as a young man."

"You don't need to do that," he said. "My grandchildren aren't interested in what I did when I was young. Besides, those letters were meant for you. You keep them."

"Well," she demurred. "We'll see."

There was a loud blast from the band, announcing that dancing was about to start.

"So you wound up a teacher. Of *French*."

"I did."

"That's wonderful."

She looked spent. He felt like they were ghosts talking, their words passing through one another like smoke and drifting into space. There were many things he wanted to say. Here, at last, they were together, but they couldn't get started. He realized it had been foolish to try to talk in the middle of two hundred people, in a ballroom, with loud music playing, and people constantly interrupting.

And then he had another thought. Maybe Bree was avoiding

him. Maybe she didn't want to be, or simply couldn't be, with him. Maybe she was embarrassed about her illness, because of how she looked. Or maybe it was just too hard for her to leap over fifty years and pick up all over again. In any case, the scene was wrong. And now, the music started up, loud and incessant, playing "Shake, Rattle and Roll."

Bree looked up at him helplessly. "You should dance with your wife," she said. He studied her face for a moment, searching for a clue. But there wasn't any, unless it was that she seemed utterly spent. He excused himself and returned to his table.

The next day, Mack and Bree had gone back to Macon. There were more reunion events, mainly in small groups, like going to a museum or walking at the Chattahoochee nature preserve; but the reunion as such seemed suddenly over. Connie and Will sat with a small group in the motel after breakfast, drinking coffee and chatting. Then it was time for them to pack.

"You know, I hadn't expected it," Connie said, "but some of the women in your class turned out pretty gutsy."

"Surprises me too," he said.

A week after they returned to Madison, Mary Lou McClusky called. "Will," she said. "I just got off the phone with Bree. I feel so bad … her doctor said she doesn't have but a few months?" She paused. "You know, Will, Bree thinks the world of you, and I know she'd appreciate you giving her a call. But don't you go saying I told you!"

He thought about it, then picked up the phone. Bree sounded surprised. "Oh, Will! I guess that Mary Lou has been talking. But I *am* glad to hear from you." She had the same low voice, the same drawl, mocking herself slightly. "I hope you won't mind, but I'm in my bed right now, enjoying some afternoon rest."

"Tell me the truth, Bree," he said. "Please. How are you?"

"Oh, my goodness," she said. "Aren't you brave to call an old lady with cancer? I think that must be hard for a lot of people."

"I know it's serious."

"Yes, it is. And I thank you for calling, I do appreciate it. But we don't have to talk about all the details."

"I really want to know," he said. "How are you doing?"

There was a pause, and he could hear the rustle of bedclothes as she shifted her position. "Well, if the truth be told, Will," she said, "I'm not very well. I've been in bed pretty much since the reunion, except to go see the doctor. Not as peppy as I once was. I'm afraid it took a lot out of me to go up to Atlanta."

"I'm glad you came. I know everyone else was, too."

"I so much wanted to see everyone together ..."

She stopped talking, and he realized she was crying. "But you enjoyed it?"

"I did. I did, very much."

There was a pause. He'd called and she'd answered and now here he was. Back where he'd always been.

"So. How are you spending your days?"

"Sometimes I can get myself dressed and walk around the house. Before the reunion I could go for a drive with Mack or even do some shopping. And if I'm lucky one of the girls will drive down and spend some time with me."

"Are you tired?"

"I do sleep a lot."

"Are you in much pain?"

"Sometimes it's pretty bad. But they've given me some pretty strong medicines, in case I need it."

There was a pause. "I know we didn't have much of a chance to talk at the reunion," he said.

"No. I'm sorry. I guess it wasn't the time ... or the place ..."

He grunted in agreement. "True." He took a deep breath. "But, tell me. I'm curious to know what happened to you ... in your life ... since the last time I saw you. You were still at Wesleyan ..."

"When was that? That summer?"

"I'd just gotten back from France. You had another few years to go."

She was silent, then sighed. "Well. Yes. I finished up. I think you may have known, I majored in library science and loved it. In my senior year, I met Mack. We got married soon after I graduated."

"Tell me about Mack."

"You saw him. He's eight years older than me. Handsome. Mack's your traditional southern man. He likes to hunt and fish and work with his hands. He was heading up his own construction company even back then, and I knew I could depend on him. He comes from a broken home. He wanted a family ..."

Will listened while she told him of a life he'd known nothing of. While he'd gone on to marry Connie and become a French teacher, Bree had quickly had three kids. Mack had worked to support the family.

"Did you work, too?" he asked.

"You know, I wanted to. I wanted to continue on with my library science. But Mack didn't want me to, and I didn't want to challenge him on that. So I stayed at home and raised my children. They're the light of my life, and I'm so proud of them, all three. Claire, my oldest, is a nurse at Grady. She's married and has two kids of her own. My son Ben is in Virginia and owns a string of restaurants. And my little girl, Annie, is a teacher just like you, at the University of Texas. I'm so proud of her. She teaches history."

"So you've been with Mack all these years."

"I have. We've become good friends."

"It must feel good to have someone close by, someone you can talk with about how you're feeling ..."

"Oh, no. That's not Mack at all, talking. No. I think he's scared by what's happening to me. He can't deal with it very well."

"So ...?"

"If it wasn't for the good-time girls, Will," she said, "I wouldn't have anyone to talk to. Mack's almost eighty. He's been a good husband, but he has his own health issues now. He thought I'd be around to take care of him when he got old and needed me. And then I got the cancer ... so this is very hard for him ..."

"I see."

"I think he even resents it that I'm sick, because he has to take care of me, and he doesn't know how to do that. And he's afraid of being alone." She stopped. "I don't know why I'm telling you all this."

"Because I want to hear it," he said. "It's fine."

"Well, that's how it is. He's been loyal and a wonderful family man. But right now, he's in a lot of pain himself. And he does drink some."

"You're not sorry you married him ...?"

"I could never be sorry," she said. "Not when I have three wonderful children, not when he's worked and provided and given me the best of whatever he could. But he is who he is. We all have our limitations, I think." She laughed. "I know I have mine. I think we have to be kind and accepting of the people who love us."

"Yes," he said. "I think we do."

"There was one time," she said, "when he and I simply did not agree. This was maybe fifteen years into the marriage. The children were growing up, and I was thinking about myself for the first time in many years. I had heard about a master's program in library science up at North Carolina University in Chapel Hill. And they were accepting people who had been out of school for some time. I mean, it was a perfect program for someone like me, who would be returning after raising their children. They even had scholarship aid. So I called someone in the program and talked to them, and I was ready to apply. It was just a one-year program, but if I finished it, I would have upgraded my skills, so I could have gotten a job at a public library, maybe even a college library. I was very excited about it."

"So what happened?"

"Mack didn't like it. He said that my first duty was to him

and our children and he couldn't manage by himself. We argued. I tried to work out some kind of compromise. But he wouldn't change his mind. He said he'd end the marriage if I went away. I couldn't do that."

"So you stayed."

"So I stayed." He heard the bedclothes slide as she shifted her position, and she grunted. "I know it was a time when people's attitudes were changing, even in the South, but that wasn't who Mack was, and he couldn't change his ideas. I had to take him as he was. A good person who was different from me in some ways. So I gave up those plans."

"I'm sorry," he said.

"Don't be," she said. "We all make compromises. Tell me about yourself, your wife. I loved her smile and spirit ..."

Will talked about his life for a while, and then Bree apologized and said she was tired and needed to stop talking. But she asked him to call again, and he did.

He phoned her several more times over the next few weeks. Sometimes she'd answer herself, and sometimes Mack would pick up the phone, utter a throaty "Hey, Will," and quickly pass him to her. She told him it relieved Mack when he called, because then he didn't feel guilty about not talking to her himself. They talked about how she was doing, what the doctors said, the dreams she had the night before, and events from their past. They shared stories about their children and said how the country had changed since they were young. He talked about his parents and told her how he and Connie had been in the movement to end the Vietnam War. She told him stories of her own. In the give and take of those days, he felt he'd finally come to know her as she was.

At times, they talked about their days in the ninth grade. Will said they were both "innocents" back then, but Bree insisted they weren't as naïve as all that. "Each of us already had our characters," she said. "We were the people we'd be the rest of our lives."

"But didn't we change?" he said. "Through all the things that happened over the years. Didn't we somehow become different?"

"Different, but still the same," she said.

"But how can that be?"

"It just is."

"I remember when we took that walk by Peachtree Creek," he said. "That hot summer day. I was so taken with you ..."

"I knew you were. But I knew I wasn't the right girl for you. You thought I was someone other than I was."

"You moved away."

"It wouldn't have worked out."

"No," he said. "Perhaps not."

Not long afterwards he phoned Bree several times in a row, but only got her answering machine. He assumed she was doing worse. Then he got a phone call from Mary Lou, saying Bree had passed.

He took a long walk in the woods, remembering. He felt sad that she was gone, but he knew she'd been having pain every day and hadn't wanted to go on. Something in him felt released.

He sent a condolence note to Mack. About two weeks later he received a large brown envelope. Inside were the letters he'd written Bree during his year in France, bound together with a little red ribbon. And there was a note:

Dear William,

I know Bree wanted you to have these letters back. They're for your grandchildren to read. You know she got a lot of joy from them. She kept them in a special place and read them a lot, especially after she got sick. I'm sending them for you to do as you want. She was a wonderful woman, and you and I both loved her.

Mack

The letter from that wounded hulk of a man touched his

heart. Had Mack recognized something in Bree he hadn't seen for himself? All his life, he'd told himself he'd had a youthful infatuation for Bree—and then, finally, he'd generated enough compassion to act like a friend. But Mack had written about love.

Will had long believed that, as we go through life, we build up selves like a tree builds up rings. Or, more precisely, like an actor builds up his repertory of parts. The more skilful we get, the more we can step up and play the right part when it's called for. But it takes a long time. As a young man, he knew, his repertoire was painfully thin, and he saw everything in terms of himself. He'd enlisted other people to meet his needs, projected his longings and desires onto them, and made them into a cast of characters in the play he called his life. He didn't see people as they were, but as who he needed them to be. How many opportunities had he wasted, he wondered. What kind of person had he been?

Connie said you needed to be present and not be afraid to open your heart. But Will wasn't sure what that meant, "to open his heart." After Bree died, he sat for long hours by his kitchen window and wrestled with it. Who had he loved, if anyone; and how had he loved them? Suddenly, he had a lot to think about.

Acknowledgments

I've been writing all my life, and people have helped me at every point. For starters, I want to thank my parents, Joseph Sidney Glenn and (especially) Pauline Reisman Glenn for encouraging my early interest in writing. My mother's interest in literature and the arts deeply influenced me when I was young.

I'm grateful to Professor Claudio Guillén, my advisor at Princeton. He encouraged my work and writing, and steered me to graduate school in Comparative Literature. I'm also appreciative to Frank Wittow, the founder and Director of Atlanta's Academy Theater, for his encouragement and support.

I want to thank Richard Kostelanetz, who has been a loyal friend to me and to many writers of my generation. I also owe a shout-out to Julie Fallowfield, an agent from McIntosh and Otis, who worked diligently for several years to circulate my work among various periodicals and publishers.

Paul Elitzik was a friend and fellow radical in the 1970s. Not only did he publish *Trouble on the Hill*, my first book of nine stories, in 1979, but he also took a strong interest in my manuscript *Confessions of a Family Doctor*. I also owe thanks to the Cambridge writer and popular writing teacher Mameve Medwed.

I would like to thank Patricia Crotty, my editor and publisher at Gray Dove Press, for helping me pull this book of stories together. Her suggestions, close reading, and technical help have been invaluable.

Additionally, I'm grateful to my stepson and talented graphic designer Dylan Jhirad for the time and creative energy he put into designing the book's cover.

Finally, I owe my first wife, the late Sara Snow (Glenn), thanks for her patience while I struggled to write in my spare time during the 1960s. But I owe my deepest appreciation to Susan Jhirad, my current wife and partner of more than fifty years, a talented writer and teacher in her own right. Our loving, supportive relationship has been my bedrock all this time, and I owe her more than I can say.

Michael Writing
Susan Jhirad, 1973

Made in the USA
Middletown, DE
03 October 2023

39617181R00179